STEPPING OUT OF MY GRAVE

David Berardelli

STEPPING OUT OF MY GRAVE

GRAVESTONE PRESS

PART 1
THE JOURNEY

Chapter 1

When I opened my eyes, I found that I was standing on the lid of a casket in an open grave.

Not a pleasant experience, to say the least. I would have preferred just about any other setting—except, maybe, standing on the ledge of a thirty-story building. Or crawling on a wing of a plane in flight.

But this was bad enough. I was standing in a cemetery and it was late in the day. Anyone could tell it was a cemetery—the gravestones were dead giveaways, please excuse the pun.

A giant swell of heat rushed up my back.

Casket. Grave. Cemetery.

Definitely not a good omen.

Possibly the worst omen one can think of.

I closed my eyes again and held them shut. When I opened them again, I was convinced I'd find myself in my own bed, awakening from some strange dream. I have strange dreams all the time. Some involve misshapen creatures running around, making weird noises, others a beautiful leather-clad woman whispering sexy things in my ear. Most are nonsensical, pointless vignettes, usually starring members of my software company.

But I knew that when I opened my eyes again, everything would be all right. I might even find myself in a dream with Leather Babe this time.

I opened them. My heart sank.

I was still standing on top of that damned casket. No Leather Babe, no creatures. No one from the office.

Was this *real?*

It couldn't be. For one thing, it made no sense. I didn't even know how the hell I even *got* here.

Only moments ago, I was crossing the road outside my apartment, heading for the mailboxes.

What the hell happened?

I was a logical sort of guy. I had to be, given my profession as one of the heads of a software company. My career depended on solving problems. One important thing I'd learned long ago was that to solve a problem, going back to its source was the best way of figuring it out. You did it calmly and carefully and if you didn't panic or lose your train of thought, you'd eventually find your answer.

I could solve this. I knew I could. All I had to do was go back and take it step by step.

Last thing I remembered, I was leaving my apartment. I was alone, had finished breakfast and just made a fresh pot of coffee. Then I went outside to get my mail.

I live by myself in a two-bedroom garden apartment in Winter Park. My place sits in one of those newer developments they've stuck in the middle of a cleared field that was once someone's farm in the old days, before Disney and Universal Studios and everyone else turned the quiet little town of Orlando into the mega-mess it is today. By the time the apartments were finished, the once-peaceful area was surrounded by a shopping plaza,

6

two strip malls, a mega theater, a foreign car dealership and half a dozen filling stations. Everything is within walking distance.

Our mailboxes stand in metal clusters across the street at each corner. A mere fifty feet away from my front porch. The posted speed limit is 15, making the process of grabbing your bills and newspaper convenient, safe and much less traumatic than crossing a main road or major highway.

I crossed the street as I normally do. I remember listening to the agitated squawking of the sea gulls one hears regularly in Central Florida. I also remember thinking that if I closed my eyes and forced myself to drown out the heavy wash of traffic noise, I might well imagine myself on the beach, watching the bikinis parading by.

When I was about three-quarters of the way to the boxes, the roar of someone's tricked-out muscle car or pickup tore into the warm breeze somewhere on my right, shattering my beach vision. I didn't think too much of it at the time. About a quarter of a mile from our entrance, Semoran Boulevard constantly roars with heavy traffic. When the wind is just right, it sounds like the flow is directly outside the door. In Florida, peace and quiet quickly become fond memories. The longer you live here, the less the commotion fazes you.

Although my mind hinted that a freight train was quickly coming up behind me, I knew that didn't make sense. The closest station was miles away. Even if it was closer, a freight train wouldn't be allowed to enter the complex.

7

My mind had played tricks on me countless times before.

What was different now?

The noise was loud. Hell, it was deafening.

An instant before I could turn around to determine its source, something huge and solid slammed into my side. The next thing I knew, I was flying through the air.

Such a sensation can be strangely pleasant. In my own case, I wasn't able to properly enjoy my sudden catapult. An intense pain exploded from my side, branching outward. A heavy gushing of severe heat poured down my legs and up my back. An avalanche of bright new pain spread throughout my body when I landed.

I lay on my back, unable to feel the hard pavement beneath me. As I lay there, the screeching of brakes reverberated behind me. A piercing scream bounced off the buildings on my right. It sounded female, but you just can't be too sure about such things any more. More screeching of brakes resonated farther down. The constant groan of distant traffic filled my head. The shrill cackle of the gulls seemed even more agitated than moments before.

The pain in my back ebbed.

The sounds diminished.

A warm, heavy blanket of blackness consumed me...

When the blackness finally lifted, I was standing in a rectangular hole in the ground in the middle of a graveyard.

Standing there, wondering what the hell happened.

And most of all, wondering what I was doing in a *graveyard*…

I closed my eyes again. Back to the source.

What happened next? The ambulance ride? A hospital bed? Visitors? A wheelchair? A kindly orderly pushing me outside? *Thanks for your business, Mr. Mild…take care…hope we don't see you again…*

Think. Remember. Retrieve any images floating around that make this predicament more logical.

I remembered only the front porch outside my door, the smooth pavement separating my building from the curb, and the mailboxes at the corner. Traffic sounds, a scream or two, the screeching of brakes…and, of course, the deafening roar slamming into me.

Nothing else.

About a hundred feet away, three figures—two middle-aged men and an elderly woman, probably in her seventies—wandered down the grassy slope, toward the highway at the foot of the hill. All were sloppy-dressed and looked like they'd just come from a soup kitchen. I yelled at them. They glanced my way but didn't lose a step on their way down the hill.

The sight of someone standing in an open grave, I imagined, wasn't something the average person wants to see close-up.

9

I scanned the graveyard, then turned back to where the threesome had gone. There was no sign of them.

Strange.

An old man appeared from behind a cluster of scrub oaks about thirty yards to my right. He was smoking a curved briar pipe and shaving a small block of wood with a penknife.

"Hello." I tried a smile, but my mood prevented me from giving it all I had. He'd just have to settle for my half-assed attempt.

He stared at me for a few moments, then sauntered over.

His pipe smoke, tangy and thick, grew stronger as he drew closer. "Hey, sonny," he said in a high-pitched voice. "Ya new here?"

"What gave me away?"

"Haven't seen ya before. Young, ain'tcha?"

"Thirty-six."

He shook his head and clucked.

"How'd I get here?"

He shrugged. "How d'ya think?"

My first thought immediately went to the idiot in the truck.

But I didn't want to go there. I chose humor instead. With humor, you can overcome a lot of unpleasantness.

"Well, it's been a while since I've had such a wild dream. I had a pastrami sandwich the other night before bed. I have this issue with gas. It does weird things when I'm trying to sleep. Pastrami always—"

"You're dead."

"What?"

"Ya hard of hearing? You're *dead*."

"Dead?"

His grin lit up his tiny gray eyes. "*There* ya go."

It slammed into me. I trembled.

"You...sure?"

"Yup."

"Positive?"

"Yup."

Dead. I was dead. Gone. A spirit.

Nothing left but darkness. For eternity.

No more apartment. Or company. Or women. Or sex.

Don't panic.

Logical. Be logical. It's what you do best.

"I *can't* be dead." I knew how ridiculous that sounded, but I just couldn't grasp the reality of the situation.

"Everyone dies, sport."

"I'm too young. I've...I've got...stuff to do." I didn't have anything specific in mind. My car needed a tune-up, and I had to do something with my underwear drawer. I kept tossing my socks in there. No big thing, of course. But every once in a while I ended up a sock short, and it was beginning to bug me.

I felt I had to justify my existence...somehow...

But it sounded lame the moment it left my lips.

He pushed a heavy wad of gnarled gray smoke toward me. It dissipated almost immediately in the warm breeze. When it vanished, I saw his seamed

11

face more clearly. I could almost see the darkness directly behind him.

"Guess what?" he said.

I was afraid to ask. "What?"

"Ya just ran outa time." He turned and walked away.

"Where are you going?"

He shrugged. "Don't matter none, does it?"

I didn't want to be left alone. The realization of being dead rocked through me. I wondered how I could stay on my feet.

Maybe if I could get him to talk to me, I could find out more about…about all this… "What are you making?"

"That don't matter none, neither."

"Then why do it?"

"Why not?"

"Are you *sure* I'm dead?"

A nod.

"How do you know? I mean, really *know*?"

He shook his head the same way my parents and teachers did when I said something really stupid. "How d'ya think?"

It registered coldly. "You, too?"

"There ya go." He left, chuckling.

Dead. I was actually dead.

Here I was, Jason Mild, co-founder and vice president of MilCo SoftSystems, Inc., standing in spiritual form in a hole in the ground. Killed by an idiot who didn't let speed bumps—or wandering residents—slow him down.

This was it? The?

Dead? At thirty-six?

12

I turned to say something else.

Like the other three I'd just seen, he'd disappeared.

I was alone. And dead.

Talk about being down and out . . .

No one tells you about weird stuff like this—possibly because no one actually knows. No one alive, that is.

All we know is what we see.

We see the funeral guys dumping the corpse into a heavy-duty black sack. They take the corpse to a place where a gaggle of rich professionals stand eagerly over it like a flock of sweet-smelling vultures. What they actually do, they won't say. But what we gather is this: they remove the corpse's clothing and then perform some really disgusting procedures to the body. They take out what is no longer needed and pump in formaldehyde. Then they apply powder, makeup, glue and thread, turning the corpse into a well-dressed clown. They arrange the clown carefully—like some fancy window decoration—in an expensive, polished box.

For the next couple of days, a crowd of people stands over the box and talks about how important they were to the deceased and how much the deceased loved them. The box is then closed, wheeled outside and shoved into the back of a sparkling black limousine. At the cemetery, some empty words are said and an incomprehensible line or two from the Bible is quoted. The box is lowered into the ground and later covered with dirt.

Kind of pointless, when you think about it. Especially the dressing-up part and the lying-in-the-box part.

I don't remember any of that. But I'd seen what those high-priced, sociopathic ghouls did to my parents a few years ago. I'm glad I wasn't awake to see whatever was done to me. I was obviously zoned out at the time. Maybe flying around somewhere, waiting to touch down—I don't know. I don't remember much of anything after being smeared.

What mattered was that I was dead.

And that I didn't want to stay here.

I decided to climb out.

Standing here was bumming me out. If I was indeed dead, I didn't have to spend eternity standing in my own freshly-dug hole, did I? The old man didn't. Neither did the other three I'd seen a few minutes ago.

If they didn't, why should I?

The old man even had things to do. He had a pipe to smoke, a block of wood to whittle. Mind you, those things were a tad insignificant for a guy like me, who used to wheel and deal daily in the software business. But right now, little tasks like that seemed just as important as the business proposals, bank transactions and problems with ex-wives and ex-girlfriends I'd dealt with during the last ten years.

Amazing how things changed so quickly.

But rather than stay here and analyze everything, I decided to see what all this mystery was about.

I immediately discovered I didn't have to climb out. I merely *thought* of climbing out and found myself rising—as if the air beneath me had actually pushed me out of the hole—until I was standing on the grass a foot or so from the hole itself.

Good deal. Apparently death, like most everything else, had a perk or two up its sleeve.

Hopefully there would be others.

The roar of heavy traffic rushed up from the foot of the hill. Just beyond the skyline, the coppery moon glinted in jagged shards behind the distant pines.

Last I remembered, it was around noon—which is when I usually pick up my mail. But now it was obviously well past six in the evening, and traffic was very heavy. Rush hour. In Central Florida, rush hour usually lasted three hours.

It hit me again.

I'm dead.

Truly dead.

Could my day get any worse?

***

Traffic roared by at the foot of the hill, making me feel even more isolated.

I didn't know why that bothered me now. When I was alive, I enjoyed my solitude. I often took long weekends to wander around the apartment complex and just meditate. I even canceled important dates with women, blaming the flu or exhaustion. I liked being by myself. When I wasn't working or engaging in other activities, I spent my time watching movies, enjoying the complex pool or

15

listening to music from my extensive jazz CD collection.

So why was I suddenly having so much trouble with isolation?

Maybe it was the death thing. Or that I feared isolation would be a constant state from now on.

Whatever the reason, I shouldn't feel sorry for myself. Instead, I decided to keep my mind—or whatever it was called now—busy.

I thought about where I could go. What I could do. Why I wasn't somewhere already. Why I wasn't rising toward the pearly gates of Heaven or drifting down to the dark, gloomy depths of Hell.

That's what I was taught as a child. Heaven for the good guys, Hell for the bad boys. Purgatory to cleanse your soul, Limbo for the unbaptized.

I was baptized, so Limbo was out. Since my soul obviously needed cleansing, Purgatory could be up for grabs. I was considered an asshole by many and not too much of a "good guy" by my friends.

Not exactly great epitaph stuff, when you looked upon it objectively.

Even so, the explanations required a belief I hadn't accepted since I was a child. Each of those places suggested a higher power. A Supreme Being. I'd seen no sign of such a power when I was alive. I definitely saw no sign of one now. Only a few older people walked around. They weren't having their souls cleansed. They weren't rising toward the pearly gates, or getting ready for the final plunge. They looked more like they were out for a quiet evening stroll.

If I didn't know better, I'd swear I was trapped in some weird retirement home in a bad section in town.

The figure of a woman appeared straight ahead. She was slender, about thirty and dressed in a business suit. She knelt in front of a marker.

"Hi," I said.

She didn't respond.

I spoke again. She turned and stared at me. I caught a definite blankness in her eyes a moment before she disappeared.

"Was it something I said?" I asked the empty air. "Something I did?"

Silence.

I started walking. At least, I *thought* I was walking. When you can't feel the ground under your feet, it's difficult to determine what you're doing.

I looked down and saw the frayed blue tee shirt, jeans and tennies I had on when I was smeared outside my apartment. My "assing-around-the-apartment" costume.

Why did my form look so indistinct? So blurry?

Was it because my physical essence was gone? That my entrance into the spirit world had made it much less clear?

The old man I'd talked to appeared the same way. Now I understood why I could see the darkness behind him. Why he resembled an over-exposed negative when he turned a certain way.

Was this how I'd be from now on? Dim? Shadowy?

Consumed by darkness?

Seen only by other dead souls?

17

Was there *any* way I could make myself clearer? More real?

If only I could—

A sudden flash.

I looked down. I appeared almost…well, *alive*.

A moment later I faded, turning shadowy again. What was going on?

That ectoplasm thingy, no doubt.

I'd read articles about that sort of stuff. Many TV shows dealt with the subject. The essence of a spirit revealed visually by a sudden dispersal of energy—either its own or something leeched from a physical being to enable it to materialize. Spirits needed this boost to show themselves. To move things. Make things happen. Scare people. Cause mayhem.

Otherwise, there would be no need for Ghostbusters.

I willed myself to appear clearer again, concentrating harder this time to hold it a little longer. Five seconds. Ten. Fifteen--

It dimmed again.

Making yourself visible after death, like anything else, required skill and practice.

One more time. This time I tried to make it last a minute.

I moved down a long row of stones, glancing at them but not paying much attention. Some had flowers, most did not. I wondered what mine would look like once the hole was covered and the stone fitted over it.

Nothing special, I suspected. My parents were dead. So were my two older brothers. I hadn't seen any of my relatives in years. And I'm sure Larry and my other partners and employees wouldn't volunteer to chip in for a fancy mausoleum in my honor. Larry would salute me with a drink, then try and pick up the waitress to celebrate later on.

I reached the crest of the hill and found myself growing tired.

What was the problem? I was in good shape when I kicked off. I'd only been thirty-six, for Christ's sake. Watched what I ate most of the time, kept the booze consumption manageable and never smoked more than a pack a day. I was even choosy about the women I went to bed with most of the time.

But none of that mattered anymore.

Death tends to change your life around.

The ectoplasm thing had a definite limit. That could explain why these guys appeared only for brief periods.

I let myself go dim again. The dizziness gradually evaporated. The energy returned.

Now all I had to do was figure out some sort of plan to get out of here.

Cemeteries were depressing.

Chapter 2

On the other side of the hill, across the dirt road leading to the chapel, a small metal building sat half-hidden in bushes.

A short, emaciated black man leaned against the door, raising a small bottle. Dressed in gray work clothes, he wore a smudged red baseball cap. A long-handled shovel rested against the wall beside him.

I drew closer. His dark shirt sported some sort of emblem or logo stitched over the pocket. The name *ERNEST,* stamped in white lettering, appeared above the emblem. He was obviously an employee.

It was getting dark. The evening breeze whispered through the pines. It sounded like the howling of an animal.

A cemetery is much creepier at night. For centuries horror stories have been written about these places.

A graveyard isn't the ideal place to conduct an in-depth interview—especially with someone who is drinking.

I just wanted to find out a few things. If I was smart, I could forget the conversation and simply wait for Ernest to finish his work, then follow him to his vehicle and bum a ride into town.

But I didn't feel very bright or subtle at the moment. I needed answers to some important questions. I wasn't the most patient person in the world and wasn't comfortable in uncertain situations. I didn't want to spend eternity wandering around in a graveyard like the others. It was too depressing. Right out of *Night of the Living Dead*.

I decided to make my appearance as gently and as tactfully as I could. I'd have to rely on the same finesse I'd used in my mortal days when dealing with certain individuals running rival companies. The same finesse, pleasant smile and uplifting tone.

Ernest had another swallow of whiskey. The bottle was half-empty; I didn't know how long he'd been at it. Grave-digging is obviously not the most pleasant or rewarding job in the world. It most likely causes severe depression and other related maladies. Burying people would appeal only to sociopaths or serial killers.

Ernest tucked the bottle carefully into his back pocket and reached for the shovel.

When I was just a few feet away, I made myself visible. Hopefully I could keep the ectoplasmic illusion going until I'd finished asking my questions. Otherwise, this wouldn't go well at all.

I walked up to him and smiled pleasantly. I'd always had a disarming smile that took the edge off most situations. I assumed that since I was wearing the same clothes, I'd have the same physical form. And the same face—as well as the same disarming smile.

"Evening," I said.

"What the—" He spun around and gawked at me. His eyes filled the sockets. His body shook. He nearly let go of the shovel.

So much for my pleasant, disarming smile.

"Sorry. Didn't mean to scare you."

21

Ernest pulled off his cap and rubbed his shaved scalp. "Ya sure did *that*, by glory..." He stuck the cap back on, a little cockeyed this time. The bill pointed upward. His eyes darted in both directions. "Didn't hear ya walk up."

"I was just taking a walk."

"In a *graveyard*?"

"It's peaceful. Nobody'll bother you."

He snickered nervously. The whiskey on his breath drifted over in a heavy haze. "Right 'bout *that*."

"You're the digger here, right?"

He jabbed a thumb at his shovel. "You done figured me out, Mister."

"You're about to do some digging?"

He chuckled. "Nothin' else they payin' me for. May's well do my job, yeah?"

"Whose hole are you covering up?"

"They don't tell me no names, Mister. Just the plot number. Got three to fill."

A tall, gangly kid around seventeen appeared behind Ernest, grinning stupidly. He winked at me, then blew in Ernest's ear.

Scowling, Ernest stuck his index finger in his ear and rubbed briskly. "Damn skeeters..." He swatted the air near his ear.

The kid snickered, covering his mouth. He reached out with his free hand and touched the back of Ernest's neck with a pinkie. Shivering, Ernest reached up and swatted his neck. He glanced behind him.

I frowned at the intruder. I was trying to find out a few things and this boy was being an asshole.

22

Kids were a pain in the ass even when they were dead.

A little disappointed, the kid quickly vanished into the darkness.

"You okay?" I asked.

"Yeah, Sure. I be fine. Just fine. Damn skeeters." He pulled out his bottle, uncapped it and had another healthy swig.

"So…three tonight?"

"One's right on down that there hill." He gestured toward his left, in the general direction from where I'd just come.

"So maybe you can tell me something about—"

"*Whoa, Momma!*" He jumped backward, nearly tripping on the blade of his shovel.

"What's wrong?"

"Nothin', mister. Didn't see a *dang* thing. Not a *dang* thing…"

I looked down. My body had already blended into the darkness. My legs looked like a photo negative that came out slightly underexposed.

Damn I was going to have to work harder on this ectoplasm thing. I wouldn't get anywhere asking people questions if parts of me disappeared in the middle of the conversation.

I gave myself another blast and fought down the waves of dizziness. I looked down. My lower body came back much brighter. Good deal.

I turned back to Ernest. "Listen. All I need to know is—"

"*Whoa*! *Jesus*! Glory halle*lu*jah!" Trembling, he gawked at my left arm.

I glanced at it. It was gone.

The shovel flew in the air. It landed on the dirt path a few yards away.

Ernest had already disappeared in the bushes.

***

I drifted down the long, bumpy slope.

The sign on the other side of the main highway said:

← *St. Cloud*
Kissimmee →

My instincts proved right: this wasn't Winter Park.

I could tell by the sloping countryside. And by the road sign that said 192.

After a little memory-searching, I knew why they'd brought me to St. Cloud. I'd bought two plots in this area while I was married to Rosa, my first wife. Rosa had family and friends spread out all over St. Cloud and Kissimmee. Her family plot was filled when we married but I was able to buy two adjoining plots fairly close. I'd simply forgotten about them. Since I hadn't sold them during our divorce, I assumed my attorneys went ahead with the original instructions of my will and used one of the plots.

I wanted to get back to Winter Park and look for the scatterbrained jerk that ran me over. I didn't know what I could do if I found him, but the idea fired me up, nonetheless.

And while I was there, I could see what was happening at my apartment. Since I had no heirs, the jackals would quickly come out of hiding to see what they could find. Most of my wealth was invested in my company, but I did manage to save quite a bit of money for myself as well.

Jenna would waste no time organizing her own treasure hunt.

Jenna was a selfish, high-maintenance narcissist. In the three years we were together, she'd amassed an impressive wardrobe and jewelry collection long before I noticed the rapid deterioration of my bank account. Sensing financial ruin, I pulled my assets, transferring them to a new account in a different bank before Jenna could drain me dry. I did it so subtly, she didn't notice until her checks bounced. When she confronted me, I told her what I'd done.

She didn't take the news well. Jenna was a genius at selecting the best of high fashion and good taste but couldn't make ends meet on her allowance of five hundred a week I'd provided once I'd adjusted my accounts.

Our divorce three months ago hadn't been pleasant. When she realized she wasn't entitled to anything other than what was specified in our prenuptial agreement, she tried seducing one of my company's attorneys. When that didn't work, she called me at my office the day before the divorce settlement to tell me she wouldn't contest anything. Knowing her as I did, I suspected she was up to something. In Jenna's world, it didn't matter if she was legally entitled to anything. She'd bide her time.

Jenna wasn't the type to fade quietly into the sunset.

I had no idea what I could do if I found her in my apartment. I couldn't very well reason with her—or anyone else—in my present condition.

Jenna was a stripper when I met her and would be the epitome of superficial the entire time I knew her. Her state of mind depended primarily on her appearance. If everything wasn't perfect, she'd self-destruct. She spent most of her time shopping or at the salon. Every aspect of her look had to be dazzling. I was forced to schedule our sex sessions around her daily appointments because she wouldn't let me touch her after she'd just spent several hundred dollars of my money on her hair.

The same woman who went nuclear finding a blemish, wrinkle or facial hair would be incapable of maintaining self-control when suddenly confronted by the ectoplasmic image of her dead ex-husband.

Such a meeting was inevitable. The fact that I was dead didn't really change anything. She was still my ex-wife and not entitled to anything more than what our divorce decree had awarded her. I would not stand idly by and watch her pick through what I would've preferred leaving to St. Jude or the ASPCA if I'd had more time itemizing my will.

I promised myself I'd have a plan in the works by the time I got back to the apartment. In the software field, working out difficult, complicated problems under duress separates the men from the boys. *Not* working them out often becomes the kiss of death.

Traffic, by this time, had dwindled. The copper moon had dimmed a notch or two in its brilliance from its hiding place behind the tall pines. Even without a watch I could tell it was well past suppertime.

The slender, long-haired figure walking along the road immediately caught my eye.

27

Chapter 3

The girl was probably fifteen or sixteen.

She shuffled along, her head down, the clots of warm air made by the passing traffic slapping her hair across her shoulders. In the darkness, using only random beams of light from the streaming headlights, I couldn't accurately determine her hair color. It was either brown or dirty blonde.

She wore a tee shirt and jeans. Her tennis shoes were well-worn. She either did a lot of walking or didn't have the money to buy new shoes.

The traffic roared past, an occasional catcall piercing the night wind. The girl didn't notice. Isolated in her own little world, she acted like she didn't care where her journey took her.

The way she moved brought back a torrent of childhood memories.

One Saturday afternoon more than thirty years ago, my father hauled me, my older brothers and two neighbor kids over to the local field for Little League tryouts. Except for my father, I was the only one in the car without a glove. Since there were only two gloves in the house, I didn't properly evaluate the situation beforehand. I was too busy thinking about the prospects of hitting the ball…and running…and sliding into third base, like the pros I'd seen on TV.

Anyway, I was six. How much in-depth thinking can anyone do at that age?

Screaming kids filled the diamond, everyone frantically throwing, catching, hitting and chasing grounders.

28

Disoriented from all the commotion and not knowing what to do, I did what I usually did in similar situations—I followed my brothers.

We went out onto the field, where everyone hunkered in staggered rows, waiting to retrieve liners from the grownup swinging a bat in the batter's box. As I crossed the first base line, a potbellied middle-aged beast standing behind the tall, gawky pitcher turned in my direction.

"*Hey!*" barked the beast. "You without the glove! Get the hell off the field!"

I wanted to ask him where I was supposed to go, but another beast standing behind the first baseman yelled, "Get off the field *now!* Before you get *hurt!*"

"Wh-What am I supposed to do?" I stammered.

"Get the hell off the *field!*" he explained.

Frustrated and angry, I retreated to the bleachers, where a small group of other gloveless kids watched the activity. A kid about my age crouched behind the chain-link fence, crying into his hands. Two guys in their early teens angrily plotted to get back at the "old asshole" on the pitcher's mound for keeping them off the field. One of the boys pulled a slingshot out of his back pocket while his friend searched the ground for pebbles.

I went back to the parking lot. Dad had already left. Rather than watch everyone else having fun for the next hour or so—a very long time for a little kid—I began the two-mile walk back home.

I couldn't believe how unfair life was. If I'd had a glove, I could be catching and running after balls just like the other kids. My brothers had

29

destroyed my life—as well as my baseball career—by grabbing the only gloves in the house. They hadn't even told me I'd need one. I'd never forgive them for that. One day I'd buy my own glove and show them the error of their ways. I'd practice and practice until I became the best. I'd humiliate them, make them ashamed to show their faces in the neighborhood.

I wouldn't know that in just a few years, I would no longer care about baseball or getting back at my brothers. College would change many things. College and girls. And instead of busting my butt to become the best player baseball had ever seen, I chose a career that required me to spend my time sitting in front of a computer screen.

This girl moved the same way I did on that sad, lonely Saturday afternoon—shuffling along, shoulders hunched, oblivious of everything but her own private little world. She alone knew where she was coming from and where she was going.

To the casual observer, neither place appeared bright or promising.

I crossed the road. Two tricked-out pickups and a muscle car tore through me from both directions. I felt only two violent pockets of cold wind slamming through me. Another perk with being dead you didn't have to look both ways before crossing the road.

Ironic, since this was how I died in the first place.

I kept back about ten feet behind her. The soft-hearted slob in me wanted to show myself and ask her what had depressed her so much. My more

30

practical side knew that would be a mistake. I'd already frightened off Ernest the gravedigger. Why would I want to do the same to this poor girl, who obviously had something very wrong going on in her life?

Just then, she stopped walking and twisted around.

Startled, I stopped dead in my tracks—so to speak. She couldn't possibly see me, but I remained motionless anyway. I wanted to laugh at myself for being so foolish. But laughing at that particular moment was the farthest thing from my mind.

There was nothing remotely humorous about her left eye. It was swollen and discolored. And the dark swelling at the corner of her lower lip had distorted the symmetry—and innocence—of her mouth.

The rage gripping me, I hastened my clip. My quest to return to Winter Park had suddenly taken a back seat to this unforeseen urgency. For a moment I'd completely forgotten why I wanted to go back there in the first place. After some thought, I remembered. I'd wanted to find the asshole who'd run me down. And also return to my place to see if Jenna was going through my belongings.

But that didn't matter right now. I wanted to make sure this little girl arrived safely at her destination.

I'd never wanted kids but always had a soft spot for someone in trouble. It didn't matter how old or how young the person in trouble was. My shyness and sensitivity as a child made it easy for me to spot similar types.

I'd brought home so many stray dogs that my parents instantly grew nervous whenever I left the house after dinner.

My sympathy for people in trouble triggered my romance with Jenna.

I first saw her at an Orlando strip club nearly three and a half years ago. A gorgeous redhead with a lean, drop-dead body, Jenna was the featured pole dancer for the evening's entertainment. She knew how to move...how to make her long, thick tresses dance across her shoulders and in front of her breasts...how to hypnotize you with a single blink of those heavy dark lashes.

I quickly found that I couldn't take my eyes off her.

When I left the club later on, I saw her just three cars down from mine in the rear lot, being manhandled by a customer. Using my body as a shield, I stepped in and separated them. The man didn't appreciate my interference and decided to teach me a manly lesson. In his drunkenness, his aim was way off. His fist slammed into the brick wall of the building more than a foot away from my face. As he sat on the hard ground, whimpering and cradling his broken hand, I escorted Jenna safely back to her car.

Our romance began that same night.

In retrospect, had I known how quickly the romance would die, I probably wouldn't have bothered to separate her from her attacker.

This case was different. This girl was young. And innocent. And very vulnerable out here, only a couple of feet separating her from the roaring traffic.

I searched my spiritual brain, trying to figure out a way to intervene. I couldn't use my ectoplasm to catch up to her and start up a conversation. That wouldn't be the smartest thing to do. She'd freak and run out into traffic. Then she'd be in the same predicament I was.

I had to do something and I had to do it just right. Otherwise, I'd make a colossal blunder of the situation. She obviously had enough problems. The last thing she needed was to stumble across someone who'd probably fade away into the atmosphere in the middle of the conversation.

I had to come up with some other tactic. I didn't know what it was, of course. I only knew how easily it would be to screw everything up. I tried putting myself in her shoes, imagining myself walking along the highway alone and suddenly hearing someone behind me who wasn't there a moment ago.

My reaction would be horrific.

But I had to step in *some*how…

She was much too young to be out on her own at night. And she shouldn't be walking so close to the traffic.

Most of all, that delicate, innocent face should never be mistaken for a punching bag.

Maybe if I fell back a few yards, then gradually made myself appear…

I could cough. Or stumble on the gravel. That would alert her of someone coming up behind her. That way, she wouldn't be so surprised.

Then I could say I'd just been dropped off a ways back—

A screeching of brakes close behind us made me stop cold.

An older model TransAm pulled over and eased to a stop on the gravel, rocking on its springs.

***

The passenger stuck his head through the open window and yelled, "*Hey!*" over the roar of passing traffic.

The girl kept walking.

She obviously didn't hear him, wasn't paying attention or didn't want to be bothered.

The gentlemen in the TransAm should have taken the hint. But instead of leaving, they continued to sit there.

"Wanna ride or not?"

The girl shuffled down the sloped path.

The TransAm didn't move.

Sensing a potentially tense situation developing, I kept the same short distance between us and prepared to let my ectoplasm fly. I knew how guys acted when they hung around together. Acting dignified wasn't on their list of activities. Testosterone could be damaging if it wasn't kept in check. Once it reached the boiling point, anything was possible. And if drugs or booze entered the picture, males acted even stupider. And since this carload appeared to be in the teen range, I could see all sorts of frightening things happening.

Crunching gravel, the TransAm crept toward her.

34

My gut—or whatever remained in that general area—tightened. My initial instincts rang true—this might not end well.

"Hey, baby! Wanna party?"

The car stopped. The passenger door squealed open.

The girl continued walking.

The boy was about eighteen, six-one and probably didn't weigh much more than one-fifty. He wore a buzz cut. Peach fuzz covered his gaunt cheeks. Dressed in a long-sleeve checked shirt not buttoned or tucked in and baggy sweats pulled down six inches too far, he looked like today's average punk trying his best to exude the image of the hardcore badass. Bad vibes oozed heavily from this boy. He probably didn't appreciate being turned down in front of his buds.

"Want a ride or not?"

She ignored him.

He rushed toward her, tearing right through me. I caught a whiff of B.O., whiskey and more bad vibes. My sense of dread heightened.

He reached out and grabbed her upper arm.

She wrenched it free and spun around. "Lemme go!"

Up close she appeared even younger than fifteen or sixteen. But the spark of anger in her large gleaming eyes told me she was in no mood to be manhandled.

She pushed her hair roughly over her shoulder and walked away.

The way she'd disengaged herself had stunned me. She'd done it so effortlessly, I guessed she'd become an expert by doing it many times before. Someone her tender age should not have to worry about being groped.

Slick obviously didn't have much experience handling rejection. He watched her walking away as if he had no idea what just happened.

At his age, I'd already been turned down a dozen times. Since I'd always been the sort who learned from experience, I decided that being turned down was part of the game. It most likely happened to every guy in existence, and I'd better get used to it.

But that happened in another world. Kids nowadays were the products of broken homes and clueless parents and entertained a warped perspective of the world and what it had to offer.

"We'll take ya where ya wanna go."

She kept walking.

"C'mon, Pekoe!" The driver pulled up beside him and jerked to a stop. "Don't got all night!"

"I wanna get laid," whined a high-pitched voice from the back seat.

My sense of dread jumped another notch.

"That's the Sierra kid," the driver said. "Works for the Mex. Maybe she's got some stuff."

"*On* her?"

The driver shrugged. "One way to find out."

Pekoe straightened and turned. "You're Sierra, ain'tcha?"

The girl stopped. She turned around.

"We seen ya around. Your daddy's the Mex— yeah?"

36

"*Step*daddy!" It came out sharply—a high-pitched rifle shot. "*You* know him?"

"Everyone knows the Mex. Headed home?"

"Dunno." She stared at the passing traffic as if noticing it for the first time. "Dunno," she repeated, almost to herself.

"C'mon." Pekoe gestured to the TransAm. "Take ya wherever ya want."

She squinted as if trying to place him. "You...go to St. Cloud?"

"Graduate in June. Call me Pekoe."

She glanced at the car. "Who's that?"

"Wild Man."

She tilted her head. Her hair slid over one shoulder. "*Wild* Man?"

"Quarterback for the varsity team. Where *you* been?"

"I don't...I don't go...all the time."

"Doin' jobs for the Mex?"

She shrugged a shoulder.

"C'mon. We'll take ya—"

"Don't know *where*...I wanna go..."

"We'll get ya closer while ya figure it out. Yeah?"

She let him guide her to the open door of the TransAm.

I followed her in just before Pekoe slammed the passenger door.

Chapter 4

The punk in the back seat, obviously several years older than Pekoe and Wild Man, reeked of marijuana. He had long, greasy black hair and a full beard. He wore a filthy white tee shirt, black leather vest, jeans and boots. They called him Smoke. His glossy eyes stayed fixed on Sierra as she climbed in beside him.

I situated myself in the small two-foot gap between them. I could feel her nervousness even before Wild Man slammed it in gear and forced the TransAm back into the fast-moving storm of traffic.

The tension from Smoke's pudgy body oozed heavily, like warm molasses. My sense of dread hovered just below the panic mode. I didn't know what I could do if the situation demanded urgent action. But I couldn't let these spaced-out idiots harm this girl.

"So you're the Mex's kid," Smoke said.

"He...moved in," she said, looking straight ahead. "You can drop me off in town."

"What's your hurry?" Smoke moved closer. He pulled a fresh joint from his vest pocket. "Let's fly."

"Don't wanna."

"Sure ya do." Wild Man grinned stupidly behind the wheel. "Loosen ya up."

"Said no."

"Why not?" Pekoe asked.

"Smells funky." She wrinkled her nose.

"What?" Pekoe asked. "The weed? Or Smoke?"

"You two are assholes," Smoke said.

Pekoe and Wild Man chuckled.

"Where'd ya get the eye and the lip?" Smoke fired up his joint. "Your Mex?" He pulled in a thick lungful.

She cringed. "*Not* my Mex."

Smoke let it back out in one long, loud hiss, coughing wetly toward the end. "What didja do?"

She waved the smoke away from her face. "Didn't do nothin'. Came home weird like he always does."

"And whacked ya?"

"Something like that."

"Musta done *some*thin'," Wild Man said.

She mashed herself against the side of the car. "Drop me off at the strip mall past the shopping center."

"Mex musta pissed off The Man," Pekoe said.

"Yeah." Wild Man nodded. "Hear he's always pissin' off somebody. Mex's a butthole, ain't he?"

She didn't reply but I could feel the heat coming from her.

"Move stuff for him?" Smoke asked.

"When he makes me."

"Got any on ya?"

She shook her head and peered out the side window. "Why ain'tcha slowing down? Said drop me off—"

"Wanna *party*!" Smoke pulled in more weed.

"Damn straight." Pekoe held up a half-empty bottle of Jack Daniel's. "Par-*ty!*"

She took a deep breath and opened her mouth to scream.

Smoke slapped his right hand over her mouth. "Heat 'em up, baby." He moved in close, his scraggly beard mashed against her chin. "Get 'em all nice'n hot."

I shifted around behind him.

She struggled in his arms but he handled her easily, pulling her toward him as though she was nothing more than a small bag of groceries.

Remembering the mischievous dead kid at the cemetery, I focused on my index finger, applying it to Smoke's earlobe. He merely swatted his ear with his free hand and pulled her closer.

I knew right then that the situation needed more drastic measures.

Gasping, she reached down and poked his crotch.

"*Fuck!*" Smoke released her and doubled over. "Bitch. Fucking bitch!"

"Bummer, man." Pekoe shook his head and clucked, then raised the bottle to his lips.

"Can't party if your Johnson's all fucked up and junk." Wild Man slowed and turned off the main drag. He coasted the TransAm into a half-vacant parking lot and stopped next to an oak tree behind a small brick building marked with a sign that said *Ida's Eatery*. He put it in park and reached for the bottle. "Might have to get a little rough, Peek," he said softly, having a slug.

"Hear ya."

Cradling his crotch with his left hand, Smoke hauled off to backhand her in the face.

"I wouldn't do that," I whispered close to his face.

40

"What the *fuck*?" Smoke froze. He twisted his head around so sharply, I could hear two vertebrae crack in his neck. "Wild Man? Say somethin'?"

Wild Man lowered the bottle and belched. "Somethin'."

"Asshole. I meant before."

"Can't say much when you're chuggin' Jack's." Pekoe yanked the bottle from Wild Man.

"Heard it, didn'tcha?" Smoke said.

"Whazzat?"

"Some dude, says I wouldn't do that if I were you."

"Some dude?"

"You heard me. Some fucking *dude's* back here."

"Back *there*?"

"Ya fuckin' deaf? Said some fucking *dude's* back here!"

"Sure that ain't your Johnson talking to ya?"

"Just three of us, man," Pekoe said. "What, you goin' all funny now?"

He raised the bottle. "Don't tell me your Johnson's making ya stupid already."

Wild Man took back the bottle. "Three dudes, one babe. I'm fucked up but I can still count to three. Didn't catch Z's in *all* my classes. And I wouldn't listen to your Johnson. He's all fucked up right now. Doesn't know if he wants pussy or meds."

Smoke bent over and checked under the seats. "Didn't sound like none of us. Sounded like...sounded different..."

41

Pekoe belched whiskey. "You that wasted, dude?"

"Sure it wasn't *her*?" Wild Man jabbed a thumb at the girl.

She turned back to the side window.

Smoke straightened in his seat. "That you, bitch? Pullin' a number?"

"Lemme out!" She groped for the door. "Want out *now*!"

"Let her split, Peek." Smoke sat bunched up against the far side of the seat, his bloodshot eyes enormous in the darkness. "Bitch is freakin' me."

"Wanna party," Pekoe said sourly.

"Lemme out!"

"All right, all *right*." Pekoe opened the door and pulled the seat forward.

She lunged outside, tripping and scraping her knee, but didn't lose a beat scrambling to get away.

"Tell the Mex we all said hey!" Pekoe yelled, chuckling.

She ran down the street. Behind us, the TransAm squealed out of its spot and peeled rubber back onto the main drag.

Sighing deeply, she slowed down her pace.

A little while later, she began to sob.

***

I kept behind her as she trudged down the street.

She almost stopped walking entirely, swaying a little as she stared at the pavement at her feet.

I was afraid she might do something drastic, but she just wiped her tears. Then, after some awkward moments, she collected herself. Oblivious of the

42

night breeze pushing her hair in her face, she straightened and shuffled down the block.

I followed but entertained no further intention of showing myself. My brief interference in the TransAm had helped her out of that volatile situation. She'd obviously had enough torment for one day and didn't need to see a dead guy following her on a lonely street at night.

But I couldn't stop thinking about that black eye. Or the swollen lip. If she was headed home, she was returning to a place where a drug dealer with a violent temper lived with her and her mother. Judging from what I'd heard in the TransAm, this Hispanic forced her to work for him. He also slapped her around and kept her from attending school.

These powerful images kept me from turning around and walking away.

How could I possibly change such a bleak situation? Even if I were still alive, I couldn't fix this. Trying to improve such complications as a spirit would be absurd.

Anyway, I had troubles of my own. I was dead, thirty miles away from my apartment, and no way of getting back there. I probably wouldn't be able to return before my ex-wife had picked the place clean. And even if I could get back in time, what could I do to stop her?

I felt very sorry for this girl, but as much as the good guy inside me wanted to jump in and help, I had to face my limitations.

Once she got home safely, I had to find some way of hitching a ride to Winter Park. I needed to focus on my own situation and let this girl get on with her life. I wasn't responsible for her dilemma. There was no reason why I should feel obligated to help her.

The modern world was nasty, difficult and merciless. People experienced more problems and more complications than ever before. Families weren't like they were when I was growing up. Blended families outnumbered conventional ones. Divorces outnumbered marriages. Things no longer made sense.

Did I think I could improve things by becoming a troubled teen girl's guardian angel?

Halfway down the block, a menacing growl erupted behind someone's front bushes.

Sierra froze.

Rustling in the bushes.

I stopped moving. A figure grew visible in the streetlight.

It emerged from the darkness and became a giant Rottweiler.

Sierra trembled.

Its head lowered, the Rottweiler crept toward her. Its powerful neck muscles quivered like nervous snakes encircling its huge round head.

Sierra probably didn't weigh much more than eighty pounds, soaking wet. The Rottweiler probably weighed in at probably a hundred, all of it solid muscle, bone and sinew.

Not very good odds.

I moved closer. The ectoplasm thing proved the only sensible solution. I could appear just long enough to startle the dog out of its attack mode. If I stood behind Sierra, she wouldn't see what was happening. Then she wouldn't be unnecessarily traumatized.

Just as I set about gathering up my ectoplasm, the dog stopped growling and stood very still.

I looked down at myself. I was still invisible.

However, the dog had obviously seen something.

I'd read somewhere that animals could sense spirits. I'd always considered that a myth. You don't pay much attention to stuff like that when you're alive. You don't pay much attention to a lot of things when you're alive—which is probably why so many people remain stupid all their lives and keep doing the same senseless things.

I approached the Rottweiler. Remaining stock-still, it sniffed the air and watched me cautiously.

Frantic footsteps slapped the pavement behind me.

Sierra's tiny, slender form darted down the street.

"Good dog," I whispered.

The clipped ears rose. The dog's head also rose. It uttered a soft, high-pitched squeal, then twisted around and bolted back into the bushes.

***

I found Sierra standing beside a dented black mailbox in front of a one-story brick home similar to the others in the neighborhood. The front yard was neglected and overgrown, the grass a foot high. Many of the shingles on its roof had loosened, exposing gaping sections of tarpaper.

A battered Ford pickup, a late-model Camaro and a beat-up tan Jeep Cherokee sat in front of the two-car garage. Except for the Lexus, dirt covered the vehicles.

The rooms of the house blazed with light. Movement inside the living room window caught my attention. A dark-skinned man around forty sat in a chair, watching TV. He had thick curly black hair and a full beard. He was shirtless, his belly a hairy brown watermelon filling his lap. He held a beer in his left hand, a smoldering cigarette in his right.

A tall, slender woman with thick platinum hair passed in front of his chair. She was about the same age as the man and wore a black brassiere, black laced panties and silver slippers. A cigarette bobbed from her lips.

Chewing a fingernail, Sierra nervously watched the activity. Her eyes had grown again, the glint of rage bright in the darkness. I didn't know if the rage was directed at the Hispanic, the woman, or both. But it didn't matter. Something had obviously infuriated her.

Finally she trudged through the tall grass in the front yard, making her way toward the side of the house.

The backyard was just as messy and cluttered. The tall grass partially hid a small garden shed and an overturned lawn table. A rusty push mower sat half-hidden in the weeds a few feet from the back door.

An oak tree sprawled in front of the privacy fence separating the properties. A crude tree house made from scrap plywood sat wedged in one of its forks about twelve feet from the ground. A ladder made from two-by-four strips ran down the trunk of the tree.

Sierra climbed it.

When I was very small, my older brothers built their tree house in a large oak tree at the foot of the sloping hill behind our house. Since they'd finished their project three or four years before my traumatic experience at the local Little League field, I was too young to remember the day they'd built it. By the time I was old enough to climb it, they'd already moved on, choosing cars and girls over "Fort Destiny," the impregnable fortress designed to repel all enemy troops and spies posing as neighborhood kids.

A rope ladder hung from a thick branch running across the open roof. Once you climbed the rope and entered the small five-by-eight-foot room through the trap door, you could pull up the rope and slam the door shut, sealing yourself off from the enemy.

I'd spent many an afternoon in the fort, keeping an eye out for traitors or possible invaders. And when my brothers bullied me, I retreated to the fort, barricading myself within its solid plywood walls and staying there until I was certain it was safe to re-enter the outside world.

Sierra obviously came here to *escape* the outside world.

She climbed the ladder quickly, crawling inside as soon as she'd reached the plywood floor.

In my present state, climbing took no effort. I merely propelled myself upward in much the same manner as I'd stepped out of my grave. I then hovered a foot or so beyond the open doorway and watched her.

The room was triangular-shaped, about eight feet from the doorway to the tip and about five feet at its widest. Some blankets were tossed in a pile toward the center. A plastic container half-filled with a clear liquid and a small stack of three or four paperback books sat off to the side.

She apparently spent a lot of time up here.

Sierra fluffed up a blanket in the corner of the tiny room, fashioning it into a bed. She used another blanket to cover herself, then grabbed a lumpy, ratty-looking teddy bear lying off to the side. Once she squirmed into a comfortable position, she kept the bear pressed snugly against her tiny chest and closed her eyes.

Sleep didn't come right off.

A few minutes of quiet sobbing preceded it.

Chapter 5

The morning came quickly.

I didn't know if it was because time itself had changed or because I'd drifted off myself. I didn't remember doing so; my mind was too busy for rest or sleep. I suspected that my perception of time had changed when I left the physical world. Everything seemed to move much faster in the afterlife.

For Sierra, sleep hadn't been easy. She tossed and turned, waking frequently, then drifting off again.

In many ways, her situation was worse than my own. My problems had died with me. Sierra's problems were terrifyingly real. She actually preferred sleeping on the hard wooden floor of a ramshackle tree house than in her own bedroom. The rage emanating from her while she stood by the mailbox the night before, watching the activity in the living room window, appeared far too intense for one so young.

Her home had become cold, forbidden. A place she preferred looking at from a safe distance. A drug dealer lived there. He manhandled her, forced her to do things for him. And her mother apparently permitted it.

Child Services would love to know what was going on in that house.

This situation might have resulted from her parents splitting up. Her mother, wanting security and stability, drifted from one man to the next until she found someone who didn't mind hooking up with a middle-aged woman and her teen daughter.

The mother was pushing forty; she could no longer attract the cream of the crop. She had to settle. Living with a drug dealer, in her eyes, was preferable to living alone.

Growing up under the tutelage of two loving parents had made my own childhood stable and carefree. Aside from being bullied and tormented by my brothers, I'd grown up basically normal and uncomplicated. I went to school, then college. I made friends, acquaintances, business partners. My life had never encountered much torment.

Sierra was much more vulnerable, angry and frightened than most of the kids I'd grown up with. She had no choice—life had dealt her a lousy hand. From what I'd seen in the last few hours, people preyed on her. She'd learned early on to fight them off. Turning inward was also a sure way of keeping them from getting too close.

She should be lying in her own bed, sleeping peacefully. She shouldn't be wandering along a busy highway, accepting rides from potheads. She should be in school. Having friends over on weekends. Spending hours on the phone, talking about cute guys. Taking care of her pet puppy. Feeding her goldfish. Laughing. Being happy. Enjoying her youth.

She should be learning to be a child. She shouldn't spend what was left of her childhood running errands for a drug dealer.

Her home life was horribly destructive. She felt no love, no tenderness, no connection. She didn't experience getting ready for school in the morning, joining the kids waiting for the bus, participating in school activities, learning camaraderie, friendship and a sense of belonging.

Only isolation existed in her world. And sadness. And torment.

But despite her problems, she was determined to make it on her own. She had fire in her, stamina. She was a fighter—I'd seen that clearly when she faced the three spaced-out idiots in the TransAm. She was defiant. Her situation might have taken away her childhood, but it had definitely made her stronger.

I had to turn away and focus on what I could and couldn't do. Maybe I'd even realize that she was better off without my help.

If her mother obviously felt comfortable with the status quo, who was I to think otherwise?

I was no one. I'd become part of the atmosphere. A cluster of energy floating around in the warm breeze. A dead guy caught up in a sad little girl's torment.

The reasoning sounded good. It was the only explanation that made sense.

I took one last look at the tiny bundle lying beneath the blanket on the dirty plywood floor and prepared myself to pull away from her life and problems.

"Sierra!"

The high-pitched, crackly voice rushing up from the ground tore through me.

Down below, a shock of platinum-blond hair swayed a couple of yards from the base of the tree. A whiff of strong coffee and cigarette smoke floated upward. The woman wore a light-blue housecoat fully opened to reveal her black bra and laced panties. When she looked up, her pale, creased face displayed both irritation and worry. She might have been pretty once, but that day had long passed.

"See? You up there?"

The small bundle stirred.

"C'mon, now. Get your ass up."

A sigh. The blanket pushed down.

Sierra sat up and rubbed her eyes. Her dirty blond hair covered her face and shoulders in clumps and knots. In the slender beam of the morning sun filtering in through the uneven gaps in the wood, tiny sparkles danced on her head. She pushed her hair away, showing me her face.

Her black eye colored much of her cheekbone. Her swollen lower lip had split almost in the middle. Dried blood spotted her chin.

A fresh wave of heat flowed through me.

"See? You'd *better* not make me come up there!"

"Coming..." Sierra pushed the blanket away.

I turned back toward the ground below. The woman busily puffed on her cigarette, scattering gray smoke everywhere.

Sierra crawled toward me and through me. She pivoted around, lowered herself over the edge and carefully climbed down the makeshift steps.

"Where the hell *were* ya last night?" the woman demanded.

"Went for a walk." She jumped off the bottom step.

"Where?"

A shrug.

"Told ya 'bout that before, dammit. Don'tcha know there's pervos out there?"

Another shrug.

"You were s'posed to do an errand for Miguel." She pushed Sierra's hair back and examined her eye and lip. She didn't say anything, just shook her head. "Don'tcha remember?"

"Uh-huh."

"How come ya skipped?"

Another shrug.

"'Cause he belted ya?"

No answer.

The woman took the cigarette out of her mouth and pushed a thick gray cloud outward. She tried touching Sierra's cheek but the girl pulled away. "Ya know how he gets. They're all hot-blooded and crazy. But sometimes he makes sense. He loses a shipment, we're *all* fucked. Get it?"

A nod.

"Quit being a ditz, 'kay?" She reached out to smooth out Sierra's hair. Sierra jerked away again. The woman laughed—a short, piercing cackle. "Ain't gonna *hurt* ya none, silly-nilly." She swatted Sierra's shoulder. "C'mon. Let's have breakfast."

"What about my schoolwork? I thought we were gonna—"

"We'll do some later this afternoon. Miguel's got something he wants ya to do for him first."

"But I have to take that test—"

The woman grabbed Sierra by her arm and pulled her close. I couldn't hear what she whispered. By the time I floated down to their level, the woman had already finished delivering her

53

message. She released Sierra, then nudged her toward the house.

This was incredible. I had to force myself to stay invisible. To keep my mouth shut and my ectoplasm in check. All I could think about at that moment was strangling the mother. Could I do it? Was I actually capable of doing such a thing? Was my ectoplasm potent enough to cause such a violent act?

One thing was certain: if I *was* able to do it, I wouldn't have to worry about being punished. When you're dead, you don't waste any time worrying about prison, lethal injection or anything else from the mortal world.

But that was a moot point. I'd never been the violent type—not even with Jenna, who was a certified expert at bringing out the beast in *any* man. If Jenna couldn't turn me into a murderer, no one could.

This woman actually deserved a quick death. She was the worst excuse for a mother I'd seen in a long time. She didn't even want to home-school Sierra until the poor girl did a drug errand for her boyfriend.

I knew right then that I couldn't possibly leave right now.

I followed close behind them, fighting down the urge to trip the mother and watch her land in a thick clump of stickers. It would make me feel good but would serve no useful purpose. Seeing how she acted, I suspected she'd take out her wrath on Sierra.

I forced myself to behave and followed them up the overgrown walk.

***

The kitchen reeked of cigarette smoke, coffee, burnt toast and Old Spice cologne.

Miguel sat at the kitchen table, the Orlando *Sentinel* opened in front of him. A cigarette smoldered between his lips. He wore a stained white tank top and loose jeans. His thick black hair, slicked straight back, gleamed in the overheard lighting.

He didn't acknowledge the women when they came in. He sucked on his cigarette, put it in the ashtray, picked up his coffee cup and slurped noisily. He put the cup back in its saucer and picked up his cigarette. "Where'd she go last night?" he asked, staring at the paper.

"She…went for a walk, baby," the woman said uneasily.

The paper lowered. He stared at the woman, then at Sierra. "A walk? All night?"

"She slept in the tree house again."

"You didn't come back to the house? When I mighta needed you to do a job?"

Sierra reluctantly sat down at the table, facing him. She crossed her arms and watched him closely. Fear and anger developed in her large green eyes. "Forgot," she whispered.

The paper collapsed onto the table. "*What*?"

Sierra crouched down in her seat. "Needed air."

"You couldn't find no fucking air here? Not even your bedroom?"

55

She shrugged a shoulder. "Needed *fresh* air . . ."

He glared at the woman. "She pissed I swatted her?"

She brought her cigarette to her mouth with a shaky hand and said nothing.

Miguel turned back to Sierra. His small black eyes grew. "Zat why you disappeared? 'Cause I gave you that fat lip?"

Sierra didn't reply. The anger flickered brightly in her eyes.

"Sometimes you *need* a fat lip, girl."

Sierra shifted uneasily in her chair.

"Listen here, Missy…you don't run off when you gotta job to do." He stood, bent over the table and backhanded her. She pulled back in time but he managed to grab some of her hair. A high-pitched squeal ripped free of her lips. "You know who we be dealin' with, don'tcha?"

She stayed well back in her seat, her hand on her head, gingerly touching her scalp.

"Asked you a fuckin' question."

A nod.

He moved closer. The mother stood off to the side, her back pressed to the stove, the cigarette in her trembling hand scattering smoke.

"These boys, they don't fuck around. You know that. They get pissed, you end up missin' a finger, maybe two. They get *real* pissed, you end up missin' your fuckin' head."

Sierra kept silent, quivering in her chair.

"Good thing they called last night, say they need us this afternoon instead."

She still didn't reply.

"Know what they woulda done, they went for a drop and nobody's there?"

Still shaking, she sat watching him,.

"I *said*, know what they woulda done, you stupid little bitch?" He reached out and swatted at her.

She cringed, pulling away.

"Miguel..." The woman trembled even more than Sierra. "I think she knows—"

"Stupid little bitch don't know nothin'," he growled.

"She's a bright girl."

"The hell she is."

"Miguel, she makes A's and B's whenever—"

"A's and B's don't cut it. Not in the real world. Nothin' cuts it but doin' your job. These boys, they'll have us all for lunch, we don't show when they say we gotta show." He brought his hand back again.

I couldn't stand any more of this. A jolt of ectoplasm would be more effective than making a sudden appearance and scaring the living shit out of all three.

Focusing on his coffee cup, I visualized it shaking and tipping over.

My anger must have triggered the event, making my ectoplasm more potent at that particular moment.

The cup shifted in its saucer.

Miguel turned toward the sound. His oversized gut bumped the table, causing the edge of the cup to lower half an inch. The hot liquid gushed from the

57

tilted cup, splashing his bare foot, knocking him off-balance and sending him to the floor.

On his way down, he reached out for something to grab. The table cloth was closest. Three plates, a platter of scrambled eggs, the *Sentinel*, four wedges of buttered toast, the ashtray, a burning cigarette and several forks and spoons slid toward the edge of the table and toppled down on him.

The woman shrieked. Miguel gasped. A loud flurry of red-hot Spanish exploded from his throat while he floundered on the tile floor.

The mother rushed over to help. Miguel grabbed her wrists and she helped him to his feet. When he was standing again, he looked down at the mess on the floor and on his clothes. Then he yelled more Spanish and slapped the mother's face.

Sierra had already rushed out of the room.

Chapter 6

The door at the end of the hall was closed.

I peered through it.

It was nice, no longer having to worry about opening doors, unlocking them or bumping into them. Yet another perk of being dead.

The small room was done in light-blue, but the paint had faded, peeling in many places. Boxes were stacked against the wall on the right and on top of a writing desk. A window in the center of the wall straight ahead permitted some morning sun to drift in. Other than the bed, a beat-up dresser, the unusable desk and a small chair serving as a night table, the room had no other furniture. There were no posters on the walls. No mirrors. No stuffed animals.

It didn't look like a young girl's bedroom.

Sierra sat on the bed, staring at me. She was actually staring at the door, but the sensation unnerved me, nonetheless. Her legs were pulled up, her arms wrapped around them. She was obviously terrified.

The chaos in the kitchen reached new heights.

Miguel's rapid-fire Spanish became an explosive roar. The walls vibrated.

Sierra's mother screamed obscenities. Miguel responded with another piercing barrage of agitated Spanish. The crashing of dishes erupted down the hall. More shouting followed. Something smashed to the kitchen floor.

I drifted into the bedroom. I wanted to console Sierra, tell her things would be all right...

But my appearing right now would send her over the edge. Even if she did accept my bizarre intrusion, she'd know that anything I said would be a lie. She'd know it as well as I would. Nothing about this household would be all right as long as those two fighting in the kitchen remained here.

Harsh footsteps stomping down the hall grew louder.

Pounding on the door.

"Lemme in!" Miguel barked.

Sierra dove to the floor and crawled underneath the bed.

Her swift, well-coordinated movements told me she'd had lots of practice doing that.

"Lemme in, you little bitch!"

More pounding.

Her mother's frantic, high-pitched voice: "Leave her alone! She's scared!"

The sound of a slap.

A gasp.

"I'll give her a reason to be scared!"

I drifted back out into the hall. Miguel pounded on the door with both fists. Sierra's mother stood a few feet behind him, one hand covering her mouth, the other holding her cigarette. Terror filled her eyes.

It was time to bring this insanity to a grinding halt. Otherwise, someone would end up dead or in the hospital.

The kitchen was a mess. Dishes, scraps of food and silverware covered the floor, counter and table. The newspaper had soaked up much of the coffee spill.

The phone on the counter caught my eye.

I wondered what I could accomplish with a little concentration.

I focused. It was difficult. All that banging and shouting down the hall made it impossible to hear myself think. But I concentrated on filtering out everything but the image of the phone and what I wanted it to do.

About ten seconds later, it rang.

The thumping down the hall immediately stopped.

Five seconds of heavy silence.

I made it ring a second time.

The rush of footsteps instantly grew louder.

Miguel charged in, scooped up the phone and put it against his ear. "This is Miguel," he whispered uneasily.

Silence.

"Miguel speaking."

Nothing.

"Anyone there?"

Silence.

Sierra's mother trembled in the doorway, puffing busily on her cigarette.

Miguel sighed. "This you, Ray?"

"That Ray?" she asked softly.

He shook his head.

"Ray?" He waited a few seconds before lowering the receiver. He stared at it, then hung up. He even stared at it after he'd put it down.

"N-No one?" she asked.

He shook his head again.

"Maybe he…maybe he had to hang up. He's a businessman, he's got Call Waiting on his phone. I bet he'll call back when—"

"Shut up." He slipped past an overturned chair. "Gotta think. That wasn't Ray, then I gotta figure out what the fuck's goin' on—"

"Who else would call and—"

"How the fuck should *I* know?"

"He doesn't know…about…about that last shipment, does he?" she whispered. "The one you—"

"I said shut *up*, woman!" He shuffled into the living room.

She followed him. "You told me—"

"I know what I fuckin' told you." He fell into the armchair, brought his hands together and cracked his knuckles.

"You know I *hate* that." She turned away.

"You don't like it? Then don't listen."

"Hard not to when you're sitting right there, cracking—"

"Fuck you."

"You said…you said they wouldn't miss it." She puffed frantically, scattering smoke. "You said there was…more than enough there. You said—"

"Shut up, woman. You're gonna make me *loco* again." He pushed both hands through his hair. "Got to think. Got to fuckin' think."

"Maybe that wasn't Ray at all."

"Who the fuck *else* would call, then hang up?"

"Kids?"

"Fuckin' assholes, don't have anything better to do, botherin' people."

"I think it was just kids, Miguel. Wasn't Ray at all. Just some stupid kids with nothing else to do."

"Was Ray. I got this feeling..."

"W-Why would he *do* that?"

"To scare the shit outa me. Lemme know I'm a dead man. *Muerto*."

With a shaky hand, she flicked ash at the glass ashtray on the end table. It dropped onto the carpet, but she didn't notice or care.

"I'm a dead man. A fuckin' dead man." Miguel rubbed his eyes and shuddered.

The mother paced. "If it wasn't kids, it was a wrong number. We get 'em all the time. These people around here are all stupid. They dial wrong numbers all the time—"

"It was Ray, goddammit. Fucker knows. Don't know *how* he knows, he just fuckin' knows."

"What about that run this afternoon? He wants See to do it. If he's gonna do us, why would he want See—"

"He wants her to do it 'cause she's a fuckin' kid."

"What's *that* have to do with—"

"Listen here. Pay attention for once. No one thinks a fuckin' kid would make a drug run. Especially a golden-haired white female kid. That's the only reason why he uses us."

"Then we're valuable to him. To them."

"Bullshit. He's using her for one more run. He needs her this one last time. Then that's it. *Muerto*."

"Why?"

"He knows what we did, dammit."

63

"Well, then...what do we do? We can't send her out there when he might be planning to...to do something to us..."

"Why the fuck not?"

"She's my daughter. *That's* why the fuck not. Don't want her going out there by herself when—"

"Fuck your daughter. We got no choice."

"We have a choice. We keep her here. With us."

"You want her here when they come to waste us?"

The mother shivered. "They're not g-going to...waste us..."

"What if I'm right? What if...what if they *do* come?"

She turned to the window. She didn't speak for the longest time. She seemed to be staring at nothing. "I...I want her here. With me."

"Listen to me, woman. She already fucked up. She left the house when she shoulda been doin' a pickup. That's a no-no."

"But you said they cancelled at the last minute."

"What makes you think they cancelled?"

"They said so. *You* said they did. Didn't they?"

"They say a lotta things, Flo. They're mainliners. They work directly with the cartel, for Chrissakes. They lie all the time. They're like politicians, only they don't smile at you while they're doin' you. They only tell you what they want you to know. Tellin' the wrong asshole what you're plannin' gets you killed."

"Why wouldn't they have already come here and done us, then?"

"How should I know? You see a fuckin' book of instructions stapled to my ass?"

"I don't know," she snapped. "You're sitting down right now."

He lowered his voice. "Maybe they called off wastin' us last night."

"Why would they do that?"

"Maybe their hitter was drunk. Or outa town. Or in the can. Maybe they couldn't get him till today. He mighta been—whaddya call it?—all booked up. Maybe they were busy with their hookers and didn't wanna be bothered. Or their horoscope said wait till today. They mighta been watchin' Dr. Phil. How should I know what they were doin'?"

"Why'd they call, then?"

"Make sure we're home—why else? You're gonna do someone, you wanna make sure he's home first. You don't wanna pay three hitters five grand apiece to go somewhere for a hit and find out nobody's home."

"I think you're being paranoid."

"Woman, you work for mainliners, paranoid's the name of the fuckin' game."

She picked up a pack of cigarettes from the end table and lit a fresh one from the hot end of the first one, then mashed the old one in the ashtray. "I think that was a wrong number." She nodded. "Yeah. We get 'em all the time."

"What the fuck do *you* know? You spread your legs and fix food. Sometimes you get on your knees

65

and do what you're really s'posed to do. Other than that?" He shrugged. "Miguel's bimbo. His *puta*. *That's* what you know."

"Thanks *so* much for reminding me of my place." She snorted smoke in his direction.

"Hey, facts is facts."

"I've given you a nice place here."

He jabbed a thumb at the kitchen doorway. "Yeah. Looks real nice. Go in there. Take a picture. Send it to *Home & Gardens*. It'll make the June cover."

"You're the one made it like that."

"Your little bitch made me do it."

"Didn't have to hit her again. Hit her bad enough yesterday. Did you see that eye? That lip?"

"Had it coming."

"Don'tcha know that if the right person sees her like that, they'll come here? They'll come after *me*. Ever hear of Child Services?"

"Fuck Child Services."

"You wouldn't say that if they showed up in the driveway."

"I'd tell 'em fuck you right to their faces, then slam the door."

"Wasn't right, hitting her."

"She's lucky I didn't *really* haul off."

"Don'tcha know that every time you hit her, she leaves and doesn't come back till late, when she thinks you're asleep?"

"Bitch better not leave again."

"You're not gonna hurt my baby again, dammit."

"You gonna stop me?"

"If I...if I have to..."

He made a backhand gesture as if he was going to hit her. She pulled back, gritting her teeth. He chuckled, then reached for the cigarettes on the table. "Your baby. Sick and tired of hearin' about your fuckin' baby."

"She's my kid, Miguel. And I don't want you hitting her no more."

"She does what I say? No need to hit her. She don't?" He shrugged.

"Who'll do these runs if you scare her off?"

"I'll get some stupid punk kid off the street, pay him off with blow."

"I thought you said we'll be dead."

"Might be."

"Then it won't matter, will it?"

"I'll tell ya what matters. That little bitch is gonna do her job today. Maybe that's what Ray's waiting for. He sees we're okay? We don't show him no more surprises? Then maybe he won't wanna do us."

"So you don't think they know what we did with that last shipment?"

He shrugged. "Maybe, maybe not. We didn't take much—just like those other times. These guys, they weigh their money. Two or three bills lost here and there? No problem. They're swimming in the shit. Ray spends a couple grand on his fuckin' sunglasses. Fucker's got two dozen pairs. But like I said, that little bitch does her job? Ray might wanna keep us on the payroll."

"You've got her so scared right now, she won't even unlock her door."

67

He grunted out of the chair. "Go get her."

"Not while you're here."

"What am I s'posed to do? Lock myself in the shitter while Baby decides to come outa her bedroom?"

"Drive down to the 7-Eleven and get us some beer and cigarettes. I only got one pack left. That won't last me till supper."

"Then what?"

"I'll talk to her."

"You'd better."

"And get some milk. She likes milk."

"Little bitch." He shook his head and whispered more heated Spanish. Before he left the room he stopped and stuck his index finger very close to her face. "Talk to her good. She fucks this up, we're all worm-food. I dunno if Ray was lyin' about that run being cancelled last night. Mighta got someone else, for all we know. Mighta got someone that likes doing that sorta thing. If he did, the three of us are toast. Can't have us runnin' around when we know his route. Those boys, they don't like loose ends. But if the run's on for this afternoon, we just might squeeze outa this okay. Either way, that little bitch can't fuck up again. You hear?"

***

Sierra's mother tapped on the bedroom door.

"It's me, baby."

I slipped back into Sierra's bedroom and peeked beneath the bed.

Still there, lying on her side in fetal position. I half-expected to see her sucking her thumb. Her left

68

hand covered her mouth. Her right one played with her hair. Her eyes were red and wet.

"Can I come in, baby?"

Sierra sighed.

"I really need to talk to you, See. Don't worry. Miguel left. He went to the 7-Eleven to get you some milk."

Sierra didn't budge.

"C'mon, baby. I promise I won't let him hit you again."

With a deep sigh, Sierra crawled out from under the bed. She stared at the door, no doubt trying to decide if she should open it.

Another tap. "C'mon, baby. Open up."

Sierra stopped about two feet from the door. She took a deep breath, then stepped closer. She cautiously pressed an ear to the door. "He's...not there?" she whispered.

"No, baby. He's gone. Probably for half an hour, at least."

"You're not...messing with me?"

"Course not."

"Cross your heart?"

"Of course."

She unlocked the door and pulled it open a crack. After peering through the slim opening, she opened it all the way.

Her mother came in. She put her arm around Sierra and took her over to the bed. They sat side by side, Sierra's mother stroking her hair.

I moved to within two feet of the woman's face, examining every line, every crease. She was probably in her mid-thirties but looked older, no doubt from the heavy smoking and drinking. And the abusive relationship she was involved in. She wore a lot of makeup—especially for so early in the morning—and smelled strongly of cheap perfume.

"I hate him," Sierra said softly, looking down at her lap.

"I know, baby."

"I wish you'd never let him move in."

"I keep telling you—"

"I know, I know. Like, you were at the end of your rope. We needed someone to take care of us."

"Yes."

"But why *him*? He's weird, all messed up and stuff. A total creep."

"It's the people he deals with. They're messed up, too. And I wish you wouldn't talk like that. I wish you'd learn to...well, just make the best of things for a while."

"He keeps hitting me. I hate that. It hurts."

"I know it does, baby. I hate it, too."

"He hits you, too."

Her mother got up and went over to the window. She smoked her cigarette and sighed. "Sometimes I deserve it," she said, almost to herself. "It was the same with your father. Only your father never hit me, just wandered off to his workshop to make cabinets and shelves. I've...I've got this mouth I can't keep shut. I always open it at the wrong time and—"

"Still not right, hitting us."

"Maybe it ain't. But that's the way it is right now. Miguel's taking care of us. We gotta put up with...with whatever he does."

70

"This sucks."

"Stop talking like that, now." Her mother put her hand on Sierra's shoulder. "And do as he says. He's got a job for you when he comes back and you'd better do it—for *all* our sakes."

"Don't wanna."

"I don't care what you don't want, baby, just do it."

"It's wrong."

"It's what's paying the bills right now, honey."

"It's still wrong."

"You do as he says or we'll all have to pay. Get it?"

Sierra just sighed.

Her mother shook her. "I said, *get* it?"

Sierra nodded.

"It won't be so bad. You've done it a dozen times before and nothing happened, right? Just do whatever he tells you and everything'll be okay."

"What about my schoolwork? You're s'posed to be home-schooling me."

"I will, baby. Promise."

"Last time was, like, last month. I can't even remember what it was."

"History. Or social studies. I don't remember either, but we'll have a lesson or two tomorrow. Maybe the day after."

"I...don't wanna work for him anymore."

"Just do this one more time, baby."

"Then what?"

Momma pulled in some cigarette smoke and shrugged.

71

"Just one more time?" Sierra asked in a soft, hopeful voice.

The mother nodded. Then she got up and left the room.

Sierra got up, closed the door and locked it. She lay back down on her bed and stared at the ceiling. "This so totally sucks. Big-time." Her voice, a choked whisper, ended with a sob.

She turned on her side and closed her eyes.

Chapter 7

Sierra slept no better than she had in the tree house—tossing and turning, moaning, gasping awake. She propped herself up at frequent intervals and stared at the door, listening. She only lay back down when she was certain no one was lurking out in the hall.

About half an hour later, the front door slammed open.

Sierra forced herself to sit up.

Someone stomped into the kitchen, where Sierra's mother was cleaning up. A loud thump—probably Miguel dropping his purchases onto the table. Words were exchanged. Another thump followed, then more harsh words.

Heavy footsteps shook the walls, quickly increasing in volume.

Loud banging on Sierra's door.

Miguel's voice: "Open up, girl! Right now!"

Sierra twisted around and gazed at the window. Probably wondering if she had enough time to climb through to escape.

More pounding.

"Open the fuckin' door!"

Her mother's voice: "Miguel, give her a minute, she's—"

"She's gonna open the fuckin' door or I'm gonna break it down and she won't *have* a fuckin' door no more! There's things I gotta do and she's pissin' me off."

"You're scaring her."

"I'll do more than that if she don't open the fuckin' door."

"Baby? *Please* open up, okay? I'm right here."

Sierra reluctantly crossed the room. With shaky fingers, she unlocked the door, then backed up quickly.

The door banged open, slamming into the dresser as Miguel bulled his way in. He grabbed Sierra by the arm and pulled her toward him. She tried to break free, but he had a death-grip on her. She squealed and finally wrenched free.

Miguel pulled his arm back to swat her. Sierra backed up toward the bed. I considered doing something interesting to one of his shoelaces. A slight tug would be all it needed. He'd trip and whack his head on the dresser. Then I could have the pleasure of telling him he was dead.

Sierra's mother grabbed his arm. "She won't do what ya want her to if you don't stop belting her around."

"I'll do more than that."

"Just tell her what ya want, okay?"

Miguel swatted the mother in the face. She stumbled backward, slamming into the dresser. She gasped in pain.

"That's what happens to a bitch, doesn't know when to keep her big mouth shut." He turned to Sierra. "See what I mean?"

Glaring at Miguel, Sierra massaged her stinging arm. "You okay, Momma?"

"I'm all right, baby..."

"You ready to listen now?" Miguel asked Sierra.

No response.

He moved toward her. She sidestepped, moving toward the open door.

"I *said*, you ready to—"

"I'm ready. Just stop hitting us!"

"I wouldn't have to, you quit fuckin' with me." He pushed a hand through his hair. "Now listen up. In about fifteen minutes we're goin' back out. I'm drivin' us to town. You're gonna walk over to a certain pickup and take a package from the driver. Get it?"

"Yeah."

"You don't say nothing, don't open that trap at all, understand? Just take the fuckin' package and bring it back to me. And that's it."

"That's all?" Sierra sounded skeptical. I couldn't blame her.

"I just said so, didn't I? Just take the package and get back in the truck. Then we drive back here. Short and sweet. You can come back to your room, lock yourself in it and stay here, long as you like. Get it?"

She nodded.

"Any questions?"

"How do I know which pickup?"

He pushed her against the door. "I'll let you know which fuckin' pickup when it's time for you to know which fuckin' pickup. Got it *now*?"

She turned away from him. "Yeah."

"I'm gonna have a beer. I come back, we go do our errand." He crossed the threshold and stopped. "You ain't here when I come back? Both you *and* your momma might as well dig your own holes."

75

I could easily tell from the back seat how tense Miguel was as he drove the pickup.

He puffed busily on his cigarette, pushing the smoke into the yellowed windshield while keeping an eye on the rearview and side mirrors. A can of Budweiser was wedged between his fleshy thighs on the seat. He lifted it frequently.

Sierra was silent. The fear and the anger surged through her, making her muscles quiver. Anyone could see how much she hated being with him. She sat as far away from him as possible, her right side mashed against the passenger door. Her arms were crossed, her head turned. She didn't even look at him.

"Just a couple more jobs," Miguel said, glancing at the side mirror. "Then we retire."

She didn't reply. She wasn't paying attention or didn't believe him. I didn't believe him, either. Anyone who dealt with drug dealers and beat up women and little girls didn't deserve my respect or trust.

"I don't like doin' this no more, neither." He stopped at the first traffic light and lit another cigarette.

Sierra watched the woman walking her toy poodle at the intersection.

"You think I *like* dealin' with these assholes?"

She didn't say anything.

"Can't stand this bullshit." He shrugged. "Wanna retire." He had a slug of Bud, belching loudly. "You know. Take it easy. The soft life. No worries."

Sierra just sighed.

"Can't do this shit forever, ya know." He pushed a thick cloud of smoke out the window. "I'm thirty-one now. Too goddamn old to let those jerks push me around. Most of 'em's twenty-two, twenty-three years old. Fuckin' *kids* pushin' *me* around." He shook his head. "I got zits on my ass older than those little fucks."

Sierra watched the woman with the poodle talking to another woman outside the laundromat across the street. Tuning him out was obviously no problem. She'd had lots of practice.

The light changed. We joined the flow.

"Rough business," he said. "Too many psychos right outa the pen runnin' things. They like hurtin' people. The cartel's one thing, but these boys? They're like right outa one of those slash'n gore flicks. Fuckers get off on pain." He swallowed more Bud. "Don't know how many times I been kicked around. Somebody don't like ya, don't like what ya did or how ya did it? They don't ask questions, they just kick ya around, make sure ya know ya fucked up so ya don't screw up the next time."

Sierra didn't reply.

"Listen. I know I slap ya around once in a while. But sometimes ya ask for it—ya know? Runnin' off, lockin' yourself in your room, givin' me all that grief? Just ain't right. You're the kid, remember? I'm the adult. You're s'posed to do as I say, when I say it, how I say it. That's the way it was down in Durango, where I grew up. My folks, they busted their asses in the fields, worked sixteen, eighteen hours a day six, seven days a week, pickin'

77

cotton, wheat, vegetables—whatever paid. They tell me what to do? I do it. I don't do it? I get the switch. But there's no need for that. Down there, kids do what they're told. Up here? Kids got it licked. They want somethin'? Daddy gets it for 'em. They don't wanna do somethin'? They don't have to. Kids wanna run things up here and their *loco* parents—stupid jerks—let 'em."

Sierra just sighed.

"Down in Durango?" Miguel scowled. "Things are way the hell different. I'm eight years old, bustin' my hump right alongside my folks. I'm workin' with 'em, then Papa keels over and dies of the heart. Later on Mama can't bend over no more 'cause of the authoritis and the blood clots. I'm out there with my uncles till they keel over, then I'm out there by myself. I'm eleven now, everyone thinks I can work harder cause I'm young and strong. So I continue bustin' my hump all day, every day. Then I hear about some guys comin' to Texas in the back of a truck. Texas. America. Land of Fuckin' Opportunities. I come up with 'em, sit in the bed all the way. It's a long damn trip, but I don't care. First thing you know, Border Patrol's on our asses. We get stopped. I slip over the side and crawl away and they don't see me. I'm skinny, so I crawl underneath the rocks and hide in the bushes all night, then two nights. Nothin' to eat. Nowhere else to hide."

Sierra made no comment.

"The rest of my family? My cousins, aunts, uncles? The ones able to come up here? They're migrants. Bust their humps twelve, fourteen hours a

78

day, pickin' oranges, grapefruit, melons. Make pennies."

Sierra looked bored.

"You got it real good, girl. You just don't know it yet. Got a roof over your head, got your momma and me takin' care of you." He stopped at another light and slurped more beer. "Two, maybe three more gigs like this one? We make enough money, we got the world by the *cojones*." He grinned, showing three gold teeth in front. "Then we retire."

***

The huge Walmart parking lot was packed.

Dodging the solid lines of creeping traffic, Miguel went down the first aisle, then coasted halfway down. In the next aisle, a light-blue Dodge pickup sat among a group of vans and another pickup in the center of the aisle.

He pulled into a space facing the rear end of the Dodge, put on the brake and switched off the engine. He flicked his cigarette out the window and turned to Sierra. "The blue Dodge Ram," he said. "Should be Ray but could be one of the other boys. Don't matter who it is, just take the package and bring it back. Get it?"

She reached for the door handle. Miguel snatched her left wrist and yanked her toward him until their faces nearly touched.

"I said, get it?" Slobber covered his lower lip.

I was tempted to play around with the beer can wedged between his thighs. Soaking his crotch would be hilarious. He'd be much too busy to bother bullying her.

I decided to hold off. If he had a spare brain cell to speak of, he wouldn't intentionally hurt someone about to do an important errand for him.

"I get it." Sierra wiped off some spittle from her cheek and pulled her arm free. Her anger returned, making her limbs quiver. She'd probably try to kill him if she had the chance.

"Don't fuck this up. I mean it."

She nodded.

"Little Anglo bitch..." Miguel pulled the can out of his lap and had another healthy slug.

Oh, what the hell... Why not have a little fun anyway?

I nudged his elbow a tad.

A rivulet of beer spilled down his chin, onto his gut, then his crotch. He uttered a soft string of heated Spanish and reached for a paper towel from the pouch on his door.

Ignoring him, Sierra pushed her door open and climbed down onto the hot pavement.

I followed her over to the grouped vehicles. She moved slowly, her head down, shuffling her feet much like she'd done the night before. I could tell she was afraid.

Once she crossed the aisle, she squeezed between two parked cars and stopped a few feet from the pickup. She turned back to Miguel's truck. Behind the dirty windshield, Miguel blotted his face and watched her closely.

The driver of the Dodge pickup was about thirty, long-boned and lean, dressed in a brown leather vest and faded jeans. He wore a battered black baseball cap pushed low onto his forehead.

His deeply-tanned chest glistened with sweat. His sunburned face was hidden beneath a large pair of wraparound sunglasses and a thick black handlebar mustache. He looked no different from many of the other male residents in the area.

That is, except for the shiny stainless automatic wedged in the waistband of his jeans.

Sierra slipped between a dark-green Saturn and the passenger's side of the Ram. She opened the door and stepped up onto the running board.

"Get in," the driver ordered.

She froze.

"Get in."

Reluctantly she slid in.

"Close the door."

With shaky fingers she grabbed the handle and eased the door shut without latching it. Smart girl.

"Close the damn door." The driver seemed bored.

She did as ordered. So much for being smart.

The driver grabbed her arm and pulled her close. "What the fuck happened yesterday? You weren't where you were s'posed to be."

She didn't reply.

"Asked you a question."

Sierra tried pulling away, but his grip was too much for her. With his free hand, he reached into his vest pocket. The clicking of a switchblade echoed loudly in the confines of the cab.

"You got to know what happens when you don't do as you're told," the driver said. "You're where you're s'posed to be? No problemo. You ain't? Big problemo. Big money depends on people being where they're s'posed to be. They ain't there? All kinds of important folks get angry. Then the money and the merchandise don't move like they're s'posed to. Unnerstand?"

She nodded, swallowing loudly. Her eyes didn't budge from the switchblade gleaming from the sunlight piercing the windshield.

"You're goddamn lucky we canceled the job at the last minute."

I moved closer, settling in back just behind the driver's right shoulder.

"Since that stupid Mex fuck don't know how to keep ya straight, I'm gonna have to do the job for him."

The blade moved toward her face.

"I ain't gonna kill ya, just put a friendly reminder on that pretty face. Every time you look in the mirror, you'll know not to piss us off again."

My ectoplasm erupting, I focused

(*pull*)

on the movement

(*over here*)

of the blade. I visualized myself grabbing his wrist and pulling, adjusting the path of the blade closer to his own neck.

Nothing. The blade kept moving toward Sierra's face.

Harder.

The arc suddenly changed, rotating in the opposite direction when his wrist twitched. A sharp gasp erupted from the driver's throat as the knife's razor-sharp edge sliced his own neck dangerously close to the jugular.

"*Goddamn son of a bitch!*" burst out breathlessly from his gaping lips. The spraying blood splashed his wrist and hand, covering his neck and chest.

The spray missed Sierra entirely. She'd already twisted around. Grabbing the door handle, she leaped out, jumped down and disappeared between the parked cars.

Chapter 8

Sierra apparently had a lot of practice running away. She'd made it halfway across the parking lot before I spotted her again.

I had mixed feelings about this. Since she was dealing with dangerous psychos who carried automatics and switchblades, eluding them was definitely a useful talent. But it was unfortunate that she should know these things at such a young tender age, when she should be sitting in a classroom, or acting silly in the cafeteria.

I found her crouched between a utility van and a tan Lincoln Town Car parked in a handicapped spot. She was trembling, her eyes darting everywhere. I remained close behind her as she scanned the scattered crowds moving all around us.

Fifty yards away, Miguel jumped out of his truck and ran up to the driver's side of the Dodge pickup. We could no longer see him.

Two men got out of the dark-green Saturn parked beside the pickup. They were both dressed in sport coats and dress slacks and walked unhurriedly to the other side of the pickup, where Miguel fussed over the driver.

The trunk lid of the Saturn suddenly popped open. The two men reappeared, half-carrying the slouched figure of Miguel. In one swift, coordinated movement, they dumped him in the trunk. One man pulled a small black pistol from his jacket pocket and leaned into the trunk. He extended his arm and held it in that position for about five seconds. His body barely moved. The barrel must have been fitted with a silencer because I heard nothing.

I saw that Sierra was already watching a different section of the parking lot. I wondered if she'd seen what they'd just done. I hoped not. She hated Miguel, but watching a mob execution would've been horribly traumatic for someone her age.

One of the men slammed the trunk shut. They then got into a shiny light-gray Cadillac parked two spaces down and eased out of their space. The driver of the Dodge pickup, his neck covered with a large blood-soaked towel, pulled out behind them.

From the other side of the lot, five young men in their early twenties climbed out of a glistening silver SUV. Each carried a cell phone. Three of them talked on theirs while walking briskly toward the front of the store.

They all scattered, three moving among the cars in the lot while the other two rushed into the store.

It wouldn't be very long before the three combing the lot spotted her. Knowing I couldn't suddenly appear beside her without turning this into a catastrophe, I planted the thought

(*find a crowd and go inside with them*)

into her head.

She didn't budge.

Oh well. It was worth a shot anyway. But it was obvious my ectoplasm was limited to manipulating the physical.

Or maybe Sierra was too frightened to interpret what she'd just heard.

85

But she had to make a decision, and fast. She was a sitting duck out here in the open. She'd stand a much better chance inside. Judging by the chaos in the parking lot, there were probably more than enough customers in the store to provide the confusion necessary to keep the young goons from nabbing her. If she had the presence of mind to hide in the ladies' room, the goons would grow tired of the chase and call their employer to tell them the girl had somehow slipped away.

She must have either figured this out on her own or finally received and interpreted my suggestion. She jumped up and joined the next small crowd of people filing into the store.

***

Walmart swarmed with its usual endless barrage of aggressive, inconsiderate, sloppy-dressed shoppers.

Sierra stuck close behind a group of chattering oldsters pushing their carts in slow motion, forcing everyone around them to swerve out of their way. Kids ran around the store, bumping into shoppers and acting like monkeys freed from their cages.

When I was alive, this sort of activity would have caused me to turn around and leave. I hated crowds, unruly kids and chaos. I also hated being around people who looked like they'd selected their clothing from the local Goodwill box.

Death tends to change your priorities. In this case it made things much more acceptable because I could walk through them without their noticing me.

Anyway, I was more interested in protecting a teenage girl from a group of psycho drug guys than a store filled with strange, confused people.

A tall young man appeared less than twenty feet straight ahead. He stood at the end of the aisle, watching everyone who passed. He kept his cell phone pressed against his left ear and talked into it while scanning the crowd.

Was he one of the fivesome I'd seen outside?

Judging by what had already happened, I decided to assume the worst. Now would not be a good time to become careless.

The boy was about twenty-one, six feet and broad-shouldered. He probably played football in high school and, like most young athletes nowadays, injected steroids before a game and snorted cocaine after. The glaze in his small blue eyes showed prominently.

I'd seen that glaze many times before, in the business arena. In just a couple of decades, drugs had reached both ends of the food chain—from street punks and prostitutes to Programmers, Software Analysts and CEOs.

My brain kicked into overdrive. Because of what I'd done to the knife guy in the pickup, this innocent little girl was going to be snatched by the same folks who'd just murdered Miguel.

If I hadn't messed around with that switchblade, she'd be horribly disfigured.

The pickup guy hadn't taken out his knife to clean his nails or trim his mustache. He hadn't intended to kill her, just perform a little graffiti on her face. To help her remember. To do what Miguel was unable to do. To make sure she knew not to "piss us off again."

Everyone knew that when you messed with drug guys, they had a nasty habit of sending disgusting messages to show everyone how tough they are.

Cutting up the face of a teenage girl doesn't show toughness. It only proves you're nothing more than a vicious sadist.

I strongly suspected the fivesome hunting her were no better.

In spite of the guilt I felt for getting Sierra into this, I'd saved her from something really bad. But in doing so, I'd put her life in jeopardy.

Time was running out. Once the oldsters passed the jock, Sierra's cover would be blown.

We were now just ten feet away.

The old women pushing their carts shuffled along, chattering away. Just as we were about to pass the jock, I visualized the old woman on the right accidentally turning her ankle, shifting her weight and bumping into the toothbrush display facing the aisle beside her.

Focus...

I directed my ectoplasm downward and straight ahead, imagining my hands wrapped around her ankle...

The woman stumbled, grabbing the cart and jerking to her right. The display cascaded into the aisle, tapping the jock's tennies and breaking his concentration. When he looked down to see what had fallen, he took his eyes away from our small

88

group. He muttered something into his cell and pocketed it.

Sierra must have been watching him as well. Just as the guy's shaved head came back up, she snuck around a heavyset woman coming down the aisle the other way, then disappeared behind the next aisle.

After maneuvering through half a dozen aisles, Sierra reached the other end of the huge store and ducked inside the ladies' room.

***

The door marked *WOMEN* posed a huge problem for me.

I didn't want to go inside. I realized I was dead, so there shouldn't be any reason why I couldn't just slip through the door and have a look to make sure Sierra was all right. I wouldn't be able to be seen, so I certainly wouldn't attract any unnecessary attention.

But I couldn't move closer.

What was the problem?

Thirty-six years of being a mortal male was the problem. It forbade me from entering a room in which women performed their bodily functions.

I realized that even if I knew for certain that the room was empty, I'd still have trouble slipping inside.

My dilemma was good—in a way. If the other guys felt the same, they wouldn't barge in there, either. Not even if they suspected Sierra had gone inside.

Even drug guys had standards, didn't they?

I was instantly proven wrong.

89

One of the boys I'd seen earlier passed right through me, heading for the door. As he reached out to push it open, I hastily thought of some tactic I could attempt to keep him from going in.

But before I could figure something out, the door opened.

An elderly lady around seventy-five appeared, giving her curly white hair one last fluff. She stared at him and scowled, then pointed a long, arthritic index finger straight ahead, where the door marked *MEN* faced the alcove.

He gawked at her helplessly, then turned around. Head down, he moped away.

The lady muttered something after him before shuffling away.

A stocky middle-aged woman with auburn hair emerged from the closed door a moment later and looked directly at me. "She's okay," she said. "She's hiding in a stall, but she's okay."

I looked around to see who she was talking to.

"I'm talking to *you*, honey," she said, cackling.

I stared. She appeared just as real as everyone else wandering about. But she obviously was not. Not if she could see me.

And certainly not if she just slipped through a closed door.

"You're dead?" I asked uneasily.

"You're good," she said, chuckling.

"You were in the *rest* room?"

She turned around and stared at the door. Then she turned back to me. "You can read, too..."

Damn, she was irritating. "You know what I meant."

90

"How else could I know that your little girl's okay?"

"She's not my little—"

"Why so worried, then?"

"How do you know I'm worried?"

"Do you *always* answer a question with another question?"

"Only when I'm confused."

She started to move away. "Take my word on it. Your little girl's okay."

"Tell me something."

"Sure."

"Why are you here?"

"Where? This store?"

"The ladies' room."

"I died here."

"In Walmart?"

"That's what we're talking about, ain't we? Unless you're one of those folks, can't keep focused..."

"I can keep focused."

"I figured as much. You're a tad young to have gotten Old Timer's."

"So why are you here?"

"I take it we're still talking about Walmart?"

"Yes. And why you're here."

"I died here. Right near this spot, in fact. Heart attack. Coming out of the ladies' room, then everything went black and I just took a dive to the floor. Just like that." She clicked her fingers. "Dead as a cooter."

"So you have to spend eternity here?"

91

"I can go somewhere else—just like you. You didn't die here too, didja?"

"No..."

She shrugged. "See there?"

This didn't make any sense. Why would anyone choose to spend the hereafter in *Walmart*, of all places?

"Then...why are you *here*?"

She shrugged. "Can't think of a better place to torment stupid morons, can you?"

***

Later, two thickset, sloppy-dressed women in their early thirties came out of the ladies' room with Sierra following them closely. One of the women wore a two-piece bikini over what looked like striped pajamas. The other had on a baggy gray sweatshirt and low-riding black sweatpants that revealed a pink thong bikini cutting into her crack.

Carefully watching the store activity, Sierra quickly joined a small crowd moving toward the automotive area. She cut through the line waiting at the checkout counter and slipped over to the EXIT door leading to the tune-up and tire-changing stalls.

As I followed her, the dead middle-aged woman I'd talked to earlier stood behind a young woman. The woman leaned over a cart, frantically searching her purse.

The dead woman turned to me. "Can't seem to find her receipt," she said, winking. She pointed to the tile floor. "She's standing on it." She giggled. "Just doesn't know it yet."

"That's cruel," I said.

She nodded. "Ain't it?"

92

"Tell me something."

"Sure."

"What did you do in life?"

"Whaddya think? Worked the cash register in this damned place."

I didn't know what to say.

"Answer your question?"

"Sure does."

"Stick around, baby. You'll see a bunch more of us messing around with these idiots." She shrugged. "Couldn't do anything about it when we were alive. We'd get fired."

I was speechless.

"You can do it, too, ya know."

"I know."

"You don't look like ya want to."

"I don't."

She shook her head and frowned.

I went through the crowd and quickly caught up to Sierra.

She crossed the huge open stall doors and disappeared around the corner. Using the wall of the garage as cover, she picked her way to the back lot, ducking down behind the three parked cars waiting to be serviced.

A man in his mid-fifties approached a late-model gray Mercedes parked on the other side of the lot. He wore a visor and sunglasses, checkered shorts, a baggy shirt opened at the neck and tennis shoes. He pulled his keys out of his pocket and used the remote to click open the door of the Mercedes.

Sierra cautiously approached him. "Mister?"

He turned.

"Mind giving me a ride? I only live a couple miles from here."

He stopped walking and watched her as she drew closer. His grin showed way too many teeth. "No problem. I'm headed for Orlando. I can take you wherever you want to go."

"Appreciate it."

I slipped into the back seat, directly behind her. The man kept grinning while he started up the ignition.

I hoped she hadn't made a big mistake.

***

We pulled out at the light and joined the eastbound traffic.

"So what happened to your ride?" the man asked. "Getting an oil change? New tires?"

"Huh?"

"How'd you get here?"

She shrugged. "Walked."

"Really?" He sounded skeptical.

"I only live a couple miles from here. I hang out. You know. The guys show up sometimes..."

"What about school?"

She shrugged.

"Don't you go?"

She turned away. "Sometimes."

He shook his head. "You really need to stay in school. Can't get a decent job nowadays without a high school diploma. One day you'll be glad you went."

"Yeah, whatever..."

He went silent for a few moments, glancing at her, then turning back to the road. "You really walked to Walmart?"

"Uh-huh."

"I didn't know kids walked anymore."

"You don't have wheels, you walk."

"In my day?" He laughed. "We'd all pile into a car and go out looking for action. We'd start out with three or four guys, then end up with six or seven."

"You went out looking for *guys*?"

"We'd look for chicks, but along the way we'd always bump into guys we knew and they'd join us and it would turn into a really wild ride."

She didn't reply.

"But that was thirty-five, forty years ago. Back then, not every kid had wheels."

"I don't."

"You're what? Fifteen? Sixteen? Plenty of time to get yourself some wheels."

She shrugged.

"Ask your daddy. He'll give you wheels. I would if I were him."

She turned toward the side window.

"Yeah, we'd go out looking to score, act real silly." When Sierra didn't say anything, he said, "You know what I mean. You're a big girl, right? You know what's what."

She must not have liked where the conversation was going. She moved closer to the door.

"You kids, you grow up so fast nowadays." He tapped her lightly on the shoulder. His hand stayed there longer than it should have. She pulled away.

"Pretty girl like you? On your own? You've seen and done things girls in my day didn't even know about until they were out on their own."

She pointed as we approached the strip mall at the intersection that led to her subdivision. "You can drop me off here. I live—"

"That's all right. I'll take you wherever you wanna go. Just tell me where."

"Just *told* you where."

A cop car whizzed past, its colors flashing. It weaved through traffic and made a sharp right at the intersection.

The light turned red. We slowed down and stopped.

"Maybe I could take you to the beach." He pulled down his sunglasses an inch. His eyes wandered. "I'm going there anyway—"

"Said you were going to Orlando."

"Well, I was just thinking, it's such a nice sunny day..."

Two more cop cars roared by, screeching as they took the corner.

"What the *hell*?" he said, mostly to himself.

Sierra stiffened in her seat. She stared after the squad cars. "Take me there," she said, pointing.

"Where?"

"Where those cops went."

"You don't really want me to—"

"I live down that street."

"But it's such a nice sunny day..."

"Take me there. I mean it."

"Listen, honey…you don't want to—"

96

She pushed open the door, jumped out and ran across the parking lot of the grocery at the corner.

***

Two fire trucks, four squad cars, an ambulance and two black Chargers sat at the curb in front of Sierra's house. Neighbors, mostly middle-aged women, stood out in their front yards in small groups, watching the activity. Many were talking into cell phones.

The blaze had obviously been caught in time. Most of the house hadn't been scorched yet. The shattered living room window, the smoldering couch and chairs and the activity in the kitchen made me suspect the fire had started in that section of the house.

A shapeless figure in a body bag was wheeled down the front walk in a gurney.

"*Momma!*" Shrieking, Sierra ran down the street, toward the rear of the ambulance.

A tall, well-dressed guy around thirty-five, his hair shaved down to black stubble, grabbed her before she could get too close to the gurney. "Just a minute, missy." He pulled her toward him, pressing her face into his chest and turning away to shield her from the sight. "No need to see something like that."

"Is that…is that my—"

"Her troubles are over, missy."

"*No!*" Sierra tried pulling free.

He patted her back. "There, there…"

"I wanna *see* her!" She fought hard to pull away.

97

He held her tightly. "Nothing you or anyone else can do, little lady."

Sierra went limp, sobbing into his chest.

Chapter 9

Sierra sat in the car, sobbing into a Kleenex while the ambulance eased away.

She glanced at it and immediately lowered her face. She was trying to come to terms with what actually happened but didn't want to face reality. Reality was the enemy. Reality meant death. And pain. And torment.

She knew her mother was dead but didn't want to believe it. Believing it would mean she would no longer be able to see her mother again. It also meant that she was suddenly all alone. A young girl facing a world where no one cared for her.

The detective leaned against the driver's door, talking softly into a cell phone. I tried listening to the conversation but he kept turning away and lowering his voice. I didn't know why he did that; he couldn't possibly see me or suspect someone was eavesdropping. He'd probably decided to be careful about anything he said. Neighbors, gawkers and firefighters still wandered around. Several people took pictures with their cell phones.

He pocketed his cell, got in behind the wheel and closed his door. He stared at Sierra for a few moments before he spoke. "I know this is a stupid question, but I've got to ask anyway. You gonna be all right?"

She blew her nose and sat back in the seat.

He nodded. "I know what you're thinking. You're thinking, my house is gone and my mother was just hauled away in a body bag. Now there's

99

this joker in a fancy suit asking me if I'm okay. Isn't that about the size of it?"

Sierra looked down at her lap.

"Got any other relatives living around here?"

She shook her head.

"What about your daddy?"

"Haven't seen him."

"Since when?"

"Since…I was little."

"Kid, I hate to burst your bubble right now, but you're still little."

"I was seven or eight, I guess."

"Where is he?"

"Left."

"Where?"

She shrugged.

"Florida? Or out of state?"

"Mississippi, I think. Or Alabama."

"That's out of state. Isn't there some guy— some Hispanic—living with you and your mom?"

She blinked. "How'd *you* know?"

"I'm a cop. I hear things. Your neighbors said something about a Hispanic man living with you two."

She didn't say anything.

"I called it in and they put the data into the system. They told me this Hispanic deals and runs errands. No other record of employment. No tax return filed last year. Know anything about that?"

"We don't…talk much."

"I also heard you work for him."

"For who?"

"This Hispanic—what's his name?" He pulled a notepad out of his jacket pocket and flipped it open. "Santos. Miguel Santos. Wanna tell me anything about that?"

She didn't speak.

"He the one gave you the shiner and the split lip?"

No reply.

"What's your name?"

"Sierra."

He consulted his notepad again. "Your mother's name was Florence, right?"

"Everyone calls—called her Flo."

"Flo Johns?"

A nod.

He found a pen in another pocket and scribbled something down. "So your name's Sierra Johns?"

Another nod.

"The man's good, isn't he?" He grinned, but Sierra's somber expression suggested that his joke had died instantly.

I personally thought he was wasting his shtick. The girl had just discovered her mother was dead and her home destroyed. She wasn't in the mood for snappy one-liners.

"Why aren't you in school, Sierra Johns?"

A shrug.

"Home-schooled?"

A nod.

"By who?"

"Momma…taught me social studies and stuff. Math, English…"

"You sure you wanna stick with that story?"

101

"Huh?"

He consulted his notepad again. "They also just told me that you haven't shown up at any of the local schools in months to—"

"Momma's been . . . busy."

"Doing what?"

No reply.

"Kid, this is serious. Your mother's dead. I have a strong feeling you know what's been going on."

"Going...on?"

"The fire. Her death."

"I wasn't even here." She turned away. "I was...hanging out."

"You weren't by any chance doing a job for Santos, were you?"

"I was hanging out. At Walmart."

"Why Walmart?"

"Everyone hangs out there."

"Why haven't you even asked what happened here?"

She shrugged. "It's a fire."

"Good call. But what bothers me is this. You haven't even questioned it."

"Huh?"

"Anyone else would be asking tons of questions. You haven't asked any."

No reply.

"Kid, I'm a cop. I get paid to ask questions. I also get paid to figure things out. In other words, I do other people's laundry. People do all sorts of stupid things. They also do stupid things when they're guilty of something. And one of the things they do when they're guilty, they don't ask any questions. What are you guilty of, Sierra Johns?"

No reply.

"Know what I think?"

Still no reply.

"Okay, since you asked, I'll tell you what I think. I think you know something about this. I also think you know what happened here, but you're afraid to tell me—"

"Ain't afraid of nothin'.."

"All right. Let's say just for one moment that you're not afraid. If you're not afraid, why aren't you talking to me?"

No reply.

"C'mon, kid. Say whatever's on your mind. Believe me, I've heard it all."

"I don't like you."

I wanted to laugh. I didn't know if they'd hear me, so I kept it inside.

He shrugged. "Okay, we'll go with that. Sure. I'm not a nice, outgoing, Ward Cleaver kinda guy."

"Who?"

"Never mind. The thing is, I never went in for that team spirit type of rah-rah bullshit. I was never elected class president in school and they sure as hell didn't vote me Most Popular. I've managed to live with it. I know my limitations. Isn't that what Dirty Harry once said?"

She sniffed. "He said, 'Do ya feel lucky?'"

"Well, yeah, he said that, too. But no—that's not what I mean. He also said that a man's gotta know his limitations. That's me. I know mine. But I also know something else. Know what that is?"

103

She didn't reply.

"I'm damned good at my job. I know how to get results. Like I said before, I get paid to figure things out. Let's look at this from my perspective. You live here with your mother. Your father made tracks years ago. Your mother gets lonely, so she hooks up with this Hispanic. Why? I don't know. Maybe he's a nice guy, maybe not. I think not because I see a little girl sitting beside me with a black eye and a split lip and I don't think her mother had anything to do with—"

"I tripped."

"Right. And ran right into the door."

"Doorknob."

"The doorknob split your lip and blackened your eye?"

A nod.

"Had to be one big doorknob."

"It was."

He shook his head. "Kid, why are you being such a hard ass? I'm trying to help you."

"Why?"

"You need it. Your mother just died in what looks like a kitchen accident, only no one here thinks it's an accident at all."

She stared at him. "It . . . wasn't?"

"Too damned convenient. And too pat."

"Pat?"

"Neat." He pulled a crumpled pack of Marlboros from his shirt pocket, lit one and blew the smoke out the window. "Here's what we think might've happened. Mind you, we're only going by how the evidence looks. Your mother's in the kitchen, doing whatever she's doing. She trips on something, falls and hits her head—probably on the back of the chair. Knocks her out cold. Her cigarette falls out of her mouth and rolls onto the floor. When she fell, she might've knocked the newspaper onto the floor, the coffee cup—everything on the table. Her cigarette rolls onto the paper. The paper catches fire. The flames grow, flare up one of the gas jets she just flicked on and *boom!* Room goes up like a torch. Luckily one of your neighbors phoned it in. Otherwise the whole house would've been toasted."

"That's how Momma died? She hit her head?"

"As I just said, that's how it looks. Why?"

"How do you know somethin' else didn't happen–"

"Your mother cook much?"

A nod.

"Most people using a gas stove know how it works, how to flick it on. They also know how dangerous gas jets are. Even if you're just using a gas stove for the first time, you learn fast. It doesn't take a rocket scientist. You don't just turn on a jet and walk away—which is what your mom did if this fire happened the way it looks."

"Maybe she tripped before she could—".

"How'd she trip? Room was mostly charred black and all, but no one found anything on the floor that would've made her fall."

"Maybe she spilled some grease."

"That's possible, I guess. Anything's possible, when you come right down to it. But we didn't find evidence of a grease fire on the linoleum. Know what that means?"

She shook her head.

"No one could actually find a good, slam-dunk reason why she tripped. Which tells us maybe someone *helped* her to the floor."

The girl looked down at her lap.

"Let's get back to this Santos fella." The detective took one last puff of his cigarette and flicked it through the open window. "When'd you last see him?"

A shrug.

"I know this can't be pleasant for you, but believe me, we're trying to do our job here. Santos dealt with some bad people. Word on the street says Santos was running coke for someone straight out of Colombia. Pipeline came directly here through Miami. One of the bigger ones, too. Know anything about that?"

She didn't say anything.

"Those Colombians, they're animals, kid. Worst of the worst. They make the Mafia guys look like a bunch of fun-loving pansies. Colombians are only a notch or two below the Russian Mob—which should tell you something, too. Colombians think you're causing them trouble? They'll whack you just as soon as look at you. And they don't care if anyone else is around. They think you're on a bus? They'll blow it up. They'll blow up a goddamned *train* if they think someone's on it they need to get rid of. A building. A plane. Whatever it takes. Now...you wanna tell me what you know?"

Silence.

"Kid, if Santos is still around, he's probably not facing a bright future. He pissed off someone? He's probably in pieces or about to be filleted. Colombians like to take their enemies out on a boat, chop them up as bait and use the pieces to catch sharks. Someone probably came here to ask your mom about him. They did her in when she didn't give them the right answers. They're funny that way. They don't like to waste their valuable time on someone giving them trouble. But something tells me they were looking for something other than the Hispanic."

"Like what?"

"You tell me."

"I don't know anything."

"Kid, we know how they operate. They're thorough. If they don't get the right answers from your mother or Santos, they're gonna look for you."

"Me?"

"Santos might've stiffed them, for all we know. He have any secret place you know of?"

"Secret *place*?"

"Somewhere he could dump money? A little coke?"

"Why would he do that?"

"A lot of runners and street dealers skim from the top—especially if the line they're running is big. They figure they'll take a bill here and there, no one'll notice. It works most of the time. These big shits don't count their money, they weigh it. A missing bill or two here and there won't register on the scale. But somewhere down the line, someone's bound to find out. The bigger the setup, the more sophisticated the operation. Some of these outfits use certified bookkeepers. The really high-class ones use CPA's. They might not find a discrepancy right off, but eventually they will. They're bean-counters. They work all day long, checking for things. And they don't stop until they find something that doesn't look right or add up right. Ever see Santos doing anything suspicious? Burying something? Hiding something? Maybe in the attic? The flower garden?"

"Don't *think* so..."

"That backyard's a mess. We've got our guys looking around, but it'll take a while. It would really help if you gave us a heads-up."

She shrugged.

"Think about it, okay? You might remember something later on. You're under a lot of stress now. Just try to get past this, okay? Don't worry too much about anything. You'll find when you're a little older that things tend to take care of themselves."

"My mom's *dead*," she whispered hoarsely.

The heat coming from her made him pull back. He sat there, slightly dazed. He hadn't expected such a violent reaction. "I know, kid. I'm really sorry about that. I mean it."

"Then don't tell me to get *past* this."

"Sorry, kid. I didn't mean it that way. All I meant was, sure, right now things seem as bad as they can possibly get. But take my word for it, you'll get through this. Okay?"

Sierra pushed a hand roughly through her hair and sat back.

The detective started up the ignition. "You got anyone? Someone who'll look after you?"

She shook her head.

"I need to head back to the office. But before I do, I'd better drop you off somewhere."

"Where?"

"Kid, we don't know who's watching us right now. Could be no one. Could be the same folks that did your mother and torched your house. Since we don't have a lot of time, I'll tell you what I think we ought to do. I think I should take you back to my place for a little while. My girlfriend can watch you until we figure out who's responsible for this. I won't feel comfortable taking you to the courts because some of these characters have informers and other connections all over the damned place. Understand? I have to figure out what we really need to do about this first. When the air clears, I'll get in touch with Child Welfare and we'll see about sending you somewhere safe. How's that sound?"

She didn't reply.

"If *you've* got any ideas, I wouldn't mind hearing them."

"If someone's watching, can't they follow us?"

"I've got three of my best men out here, questioning your neighbors and doing a perimeter check. If anyone's still lurking around, he's awfully stupid. Anyway, I can spot a tail a mile away."

Sierra said nothing.

"It won't be bad, I promise. I'll drop you off with my girlfriend and come back a few hours later, after I get some things done. We can figure out what to do then. All right?"

She nodded, but I could feel the fear building within her.

I could also feel the suspicion building within me.

Something about this just didn't feel right.

But I could tell this detective was absolutely right about himself.

He was no Ward Cleaver.

Chapter 10

Heading east on 192, the detective passed the Orlando turnoff, staying on the long straight stretch that would eventually take us to the ocean.

Sierra sat hunched over in her seat, her arms crossed. She kept her eyes straight ahead but snuck glances at the door from time to time for reassurance. The door handle was her only true friend at the moment. Her ally. Her means of escape. It remained within easy reach if she needed to grab it in a hurry. I caught her rubbing it with her elbow at least twice since we left St. Cloud.

I could only imagine what she was going through. In a single morning she'd lost her mother, her house and the only family life she ever knew. She was now riding in a car with a total stranger, a man who'd frightened her by telling her bad people were looking for her.

I had money in my bank accounts, a 401(K) fund and stock portfolios as well. If we could get back to my apartment before Jenna or my lawyers helped themselves to my papers, I could try to figure out a way of signing it over to Sierra in some form of trust. Or maybe just gather up enough cash that would enable her to flee this area and look for her father.

Money might help her out of this predicament. I might be able to use my ectoplasm to sign over my beneficiary forms to her, put a bogus date on them and slip them through the system. Or write her a personal check and find a way of getting her over to the bank to cash it.

A brainless plan at best...

But I had to do something. This detective hadn't been entirely honest with her. I suspected he was taking her somewhere he shouldn't be taking her.

This definitely didn't feel right. He should be taking her somewhere safe. Some place with cops. And people who worked with displaced kids.

If I were working this investigation, I'd use every available resource to find her father. And I certainly wouldn't have hinted at the Colombian cartel tracking her down.

About five miles east of the Orlando turnoff, the detective made a right, turning onto a narrow dirt road that went south. We passed a few ramshackle homes sitting in overgrown lots. A trashy-looking trailer with the husks of three stripped cars resting on blocks cluttered a front yard. Crushed beer cans littered the dirt path. An old block home in dire need of a new roof sat by itself in a yard overrun by weeds.

Definitely an isolated area.

This didn't make me feel any better.

He coaxed the big car down a winding path for about another mile, then pulled up the dirt drive of a small frame house. He parked in a sandy circular drive in front of the house and flicked off the ignition.

"Marla's good people," he said, winking. "She'll take care of you."

He got out, circled the front of the car and opened the passenger door.

Sierra didn't budge.

"C'mon, kid. Nobody'll know you're out here."

He'd said that to make her feel safe, but with my growing suspicions, it made her situation even more hopeless.

"Aren't you hungry?"

She shrugged.

"I'll bet you haven't eaten since breakfast."

She said nothing.

I hadn't seen her eat anything since I'd stumbled upon her. Her world had been destroyed in just hours—food wasn't her primary concern right now.

"There's a spare room and TV and food—anything you need. I'll bet we can find you some clothes as well. Wouldn't you like a shower?"

Sierra reluctantly got out of the car.

He slammed the door shut behind her. Then, nudging her forward, he led her up the stone walk.

***

The small, cluttered living room hadn't seen a fresh coat of paint in a long time. The couch and armchairs were old and well-worn. The ceiling had yellowed from years of cigarette smoke. The reek of smoke and dampness hung heavily in the air.

A tall, slender brunette came out of the kitchen, wiping her hands with a red-and-white checked dishtowel. Her red halter top and blue shorts showed off her deep tan. Several silver necklaces covered her neck. Bracelets dangled from her right wrist; an expensive watch covered her left. Rings decorated several long-nailed fingers. She was probably a year or two shy of thirty and looked like a model by the way she stood.

113

"Who's the kid?" she asked flatly.

"This is Sierra. We're putting her up for a few days."

She blinked. "We're *what*?"

"I'll tell you about it later. What's going on in the kitchen?"

"Not a damned thing. Why?"

"Sierra can use some food."

A scowl covered her fine-featured face. "Oh, she can, can she?"

"See that she gets some."

Her large blue eyes grew. "See that she *what*?"

"Fix her something to eat."

"Are you out of your fucking—"

"You heard me. Kid hasn't eaten all day."

The woman just stood there. She obviously wanted to get mad. She also wanted to ask questions. She must have seen something in the detective's face that discouraged both. She stared at Sierra a few moments, then sighed. "C'mon, kid." She led the way back into the kitchen.

***

Five minutes later, Sierra sat at the table, eating a ham and Swiss on rye.

A soap played from the portable TV sitting on the hutch in the corner next to the window, but Sierra wasn't paying attention. She kept glancing at the stack of dirty dishes in the sink and the half-eaten apple turning brown on the counter.

Marla had slipped out of the room and caught the detective outside the bedroom down the hall. She walked right up to him and stopped less than a foot away, her hands on her hips, sparks shooting

114

from her eyes. Her voice, breathy and low, sounded venomous. "Just what the hell do you think you're—"

He slapped a hand over her mouth, pushed her into the bedroom and closed the door behind them. "Keep your voice down. She'll hear you."

I slipped through the door and situated myself just a couple of feet from them.

"Don't you *dare* put your hand over my mouth again, asshole." She gingerly touched her lips. I suspected she was worried about her lipstick smearing.

He blinked. "You told me you liked that."

"You know damned well when I like it. This isn't exactly the time, bucko."

"You sure?" He grinned and slapped the side pocket of his jacket, causing a small clinking noise. "I brought along the cuffs. Just in case you change your mind."

She took a breath. The valley between her breasts deepened. "Like I said, it isn't the right time…"

"It isn't the time to get on that little girl's bad side, either."

"Really. And I'm supposed to give a rat's ass that she hears me because…?"

He moved closer to her and lowered his voice. "That little bitch knows where there's half a million and change."

I knew at that moment that I'd been right about this man.

It also told me Sierra was in deep trouble.

115

Marla sat on the edge of the bed. She pushed some long black hair away from her face. "And you know this how?"

"Simple math." He lit a cigarette and went over to the yellowed window, which overlooked the palmettos in the overgrown backyard. He blew smoke at the window. "She lives with a bag man."

"So?"

He turned around. "Bag man's stupid. He's that Spic, always liked being in fast company. A Mexican Barney Fife."

"And this concerns us how?"

"Asshole Spic does something stupid and gets his shit splattered early this afternoon. Kid's old lady pisses off the wrong people and gets *her* shit splattered as well, about an hour ago. Who's left?"

Marla jabbed a thumb toward the kitchen. "What makes you think *she* knows anything?"

"Little bitch has been making runs for the Spic the last six months. You don't think she knows where that stash is?"

Marla shrugged. "Just 'cause she knows doesn't mean she'll tell you."

He grinned through his cigarette smoke. "She'll tell me."

"What makes you think so?"

"Baby, I been a detective fifteen years. You don't think I know how to ask questions?"

She snorted. "Oh, I'm sure you know how to ask questions. I'm just not so sure you know how to get the right answers."

"You don't think I can get the right answers from a stupid thirteen-year-old bitch?"

116

Thirteen. Sierra was thirteen. She definitely acted older. But based on what she'd been going through, it was no wonder.

"I don't know, Parker..." Marla pushed some hair away from her face. "Kid doesn't look stupid at all."

"Doesn't matter. I've been around the block. I know my way around. She's a kid. How smart can she be?"

"She also looks tough."

"Course she's tough. Why else would the Spic use her?"

"But if she's *that* tough..."

"I'm tougher, babe." He ground out his smoke in the tin ashtray on the scratched surface of the dresser. "*You* know that. *I* know it. Anyone who's ever crossed my path knows it."

"How's that gonna get her to talk?"

He slapped her ass on his way to the door. "You can get anyone talking once you convince them they can trust you." He opened the door a crack and patted his pocket again. "Last chance for the cuffs."

"I'll take a rain check."

He winked. "You've got yourself a date, babe."

***

Out in the kitchen, Sierra had finished her sandwich.

She'd changed the channel, replacing the soap with a sitcom, thus lowering the quality of material a smidge. Instead of three well-dressed women arguing about which of them a certain doctor

117

wanted, three teen girls in skimpy clothes discussed the attributes of some cute guy on the football team.

Parker came in, snatched up the remote from the table and flicked it off. "Looks like you're gonna have to stay here with us a couple of days, kid."

Sierra frowned at the remote in his hand and said nothing.

Parker lit a cigarette and sat down facing her. "I just talked to my boss at the Department. Seems your momma's boyfriend Santos is dead."

Sierra made no comment. She'd either seen what happened at Walmart or just didn't care.

But that wasn't what concerned me. Parker hadn't used his phone at all during the last few minutes. So how did he know Miguel was dead?

And why the lie about calling his boss?

"Kid, both your guardians are dead, and unless you've got relatives we can contact, you're on your own. I know it's tough and all, but you've got to face facts. You've got no one now. Whether you know it or not, there are some tough customers after you."

"Who?"

He shrugged. "The bastards that wasted your mother and Santos. They were obviously after something. Why else would they order a hit?"

"Why me?"

Parker pushed some smoke toward the ceiling. "You're in the way. Maybe you know them. Or maybe you've got something they want."

"What?"

118

"Let's not bullshit one another. You worked for one of the cartel's top bag men in the area. They know that. They're missing some money. What do you think that tells them?"

Sierra said nothing.

"It tells them that maybe it would be worth their while to find out where their money is."

"But I don't *know* anything."

"They'll find out, one way or the other. Like I told you, these boys don't play around. They have ways of getting to the truth. And they're not sentimental."

"Huh?"

"Let's just say they're not as hung up about your fingers or toes as you are. In other words, they won't mind messing you up if they think it'll help them get what they're looking for."

"You mean—"

"You know what I mean." He stared at her for a few moments, letting it sink in. He wanted to make sure she understood what he'd just told her. Judging by her paleness, her stiff position in the chair, she knew exactly what he meant.

His smug expression told me the worst. He'd just scared her half to death and was damned proud of it. I wanted to flip the cigarette around in his hand, making him put the hot end between his lips. That way, he'd carry around an impressive blister for a few days and wouldn't be able to do his best work with Marla.

I decided to be more subtle. I focused on keeping the cigarette stuck to his lips while he reached up to pull it out.

119

His fingers slid down to the hot end.

"God*dam*mit!" He jumped up, shook his hand and looked at it.

"What the hell?" Marla asked.

"Damn, damn, *damn*!" He angrily squashed the butt, then stomped over to the sink, splashed cold water on his fingers and gently dabbed them dry with a towel. Once he'd calmed down, he turned back to Sierra. "Just think of that for a while, kid. Meanwhile, I've got to get back to the office. You stay here with Marla and do everything she says. I mean everything."

"How long before I can--"

"Kid, if I were you, I'd just shut up and let us do whatever it takes to keep you safe. Because that's exactly what it amounts to."

The two of them left the room.

I followed.

Once they were outside, Marla whispered, "What the fuck am I s'posed to do with a teenage girl?"

"You were a teenage girl once."

"Fifteen years ago!"

"You don't remember what it was like?"

"Things were a little different when I was her age."

He chuckled. "Hey, the parts are the same and the attitude's the same, so what's the problem?" He shrugged. "You two will get along. If she likes you, she might confide—know what I mean? Two babes sharing secrets?"

"What kind of secrets can a teenager share?"

"I'm only interested in the ones involving Santos."

"And you think she's gonna open up to *me* about that?"

"Who knows? You might get lucky. She might even like you. Then she could spill the beans and—"

"And what?"

"And we'll be rich."

"I don't know about this..."

"Make the best of it, babe." He kissed her and patted her ass. "But don't sweat it. I'll be back in a few hours."

"Then what?"

He pulled the keys from his pants pocket. "I've got to make a few calls, get some of my connections working on a few things. It shouldn't take long. Once I find out what I need to know, we'll be able to handle this better. But keep your eye on her. Whatever you do, don't let her get away. That little bitch could earn us half a mill. That's *cash. Tax-free*. Know what a cool half-million'll buy you?"

"Yeah. I know."

"Then why the attitude?"

She shrugged. "We don't have it yet."

"We'll get it."

"You think so?"

"Trust me." He winked.

Marla went back inside.

Parker slid behind the wheel and flicked on the ignition. He pulled out his cell and pressed some buttons. After a brief pause he said, "I got her." Another pause. "Yeah, at my place." Pause.

"Marla's with her." Pause. "Sure, I don't mind. Just don't hurt Marla, okay? Have them tie her up and stick her in the bedroom or something. Tie her loosely, so she can get free. Make sure she knows who you are. I don't want her to think she's in any danger. She freaks real easily. I should be at the Department for the next couple of hours. Your guys'll have plenty of time to work." Pause. "Yeah, I'm sure that kid knows. She's just being a hard ass. Tell them she'll probably eventually crack, but it might take a little while. Break a finger or two, see what that does then." Pause. "I'm leaving now. Wait fifteen minutes before you move in." Pause. "And don't forget—I get half of whatever we find. Since there's a million missing, my cut adds up to five hundred K. I've been working on this for months and no one's gonna fuck me out of it. Understand?"

Parker pocketed the cell, put the car in park and eased down the drive.

I hurried back to the house.

Fifteen minutes isn't very long.

Especially when you're dead.

***

Marla was fixing a drink in the kitchen.

She filled half a glass with Bacardi Rum, added a splash of Coke, grabbed two cubes from the freezer and dropped them in. She had a big swallow and sighed. "You drink, kid?"

"I'm thirteen." Sierra had flicked the TV back on.

"You never had a *drink*?"

Sierra shrugged. "Some tequila Momma gave me a couple times."

122

Marla sat down beside her. "Like it?"

Sierra frowned. "Tasted weird."

"It's s'posed to." Marla covered a belch with her hand. "Listen, kid. Things'll go a lot better if we understand one another."

Sierra remained staring at the set.

Marla grabbed the remote and flicked it off.

Sierra glared.

"I'll turn it back on in a sec, okay?" Marla put the remote down and drank more rum. "Kid, Parker wants me to keep an eye out for you, but I'm really not cut out for stuff like this. You'll have to help me. I know when someone's in trouble, and from what he says, you're in a shitload right now."

"Sounds like it."

"But we'll take care of you. You'll be all right. You just have to do as I say, understand?"

Sierra nodded.

I checked out the smiley clock on the opposite wall. Five minutes had already elapsed. Going by what Parker had said on his cell phone, someone else would be here in another ten minutes to do some terrible things to Sierra.

I didn't know what to do, so I started pacing. I used to pace in my office when facing some major problem. It always helped me then, so I figured it would help me right now.

"We won't tell you to do anything we wouldn't do ourselves, understand?"

Sierra shrugged.

"So anything we make you do will be for your own safety."

I stopped pacing. It wasn't helping.

123

I had to get Sierra out of here. I still wasn't sure of my ectoplasm talents, but I knew I didn't have the luxury of thinking about it right now. I could just stand here like an idiot until I heard them coming, then turn away so I wouldn't have to see what they did. Or maybe I could just grit my teeth—or whatever I had left—and try and figure out something that might help.

One thing was certain—I had to do something *now*.

Marla said, "You can have that spare room. Parker won't mind. He only uses it to store his guns and his fishing equipment. But there's a couch in there, so you can—"

"What about clothes? I've had these on all day." She wrinkled her nose. "They're starting to smell funky."

"I can let you try on some of my things. You're smaller than me, but our waist size seems about the same. You'll probably be able to wear my shorts. My tank tops might hang a little on you but no one'll see you, so there shouldn't be a problem there, either."

Fear was the only thing I could use right now. People responded instantly to fear. If I wanted to get Sierra out, I had to scare both of them half to death. I didn't mind scaring Marla—I didn't have much respect for her. I couldn't respect women who picked dirtbags for their partners.

But I didn't want to do anything to Sierra. She'd already been through too much and didn't need to be traumatized again. But even with my

124

good intentions, I knew I didn't have the time to stand around and consider other options.

I moved over until I was standing behind Sierra, then focused.

"How about if Parker and I—"

Appear....

"*Whoa*!" Marla spilled some of her drink and jumped up from her chair.

Sierra spun around in her seat and gawked at the doorway. "What's wrong?"

"I *saw* something..." Marla stood stock-still, her eyes filling the sockets.

"What?"

"Some *guy*..."

"Some *guy*?"

Marla glared. "Guy. You know. Like us? Only male?"

"Where did you see this...guy?"

"He was standing right behind your chair..."

Sierra jumped up and quickly joined Marla near the sink. "Right *there*?"

"There."

"A *guy*?"

"You hard of hearing, girl? Yeah. Guy. Man. Dude."

"Standing behind my chair?"

A deep sigh. "Yeah. Your chair. Get the picture?"

"What was he doing?"

"Just standing there."

"What did he look like?"

Marla swallowed. She was pale with fear but her glare shot right out, nonetheless. "How the hell should I know? Isn't it bad enough there was a guy standing there? Anyway, what difference does it make what he looked like?"

"Are you sure? I mean, like, did you really see an actual *guy* there?"

"No, dammit. I imagined him. There. Satisfied?"

Sierra forced out a smile. "You so totally scared me. I totally thought you did see a—"

"I did, dammit." Marla was still looking around.

"But you just said—"

"I know what I said."

"Then—"

"This has me messed up, kid."

"You *look* messed up."

"Thanks. That asshole Parker didn't tell me this rat hole was, well, haunted."

"Haunted?"

"What would *you* call it if *you* just saw a guy standing there in the kitchen, five feet away? And as soon as you blinked, the sucker disappeared?"

"You okay?"

She cringed. "Of *course* I'm not okay. What makes you think I'm okay? I just saw a fucking guy standing there. Only a nutcase would be okay after that. I'm not a nutcase. I'm *not* okay, dammit."

"You're drinking..."

"Yeah. I'm drinking. You shack up with a guy like Parker, you'd be drinking, too. Listen, girl. I don't know about *you*, but I'm getting the hell out of Dodge."

"Getting *out*?"

126

"Splitting. I'm leaving. Cutting out. Right now." Marla moved cautiously toward the doorway, then peered out into the hall.

"But what about *me*?"

"You can either come with me or stay here. One thing's certain. I ain't staying in this shack if it's fucking haunted." Then she disappeared around the corner.

I glanced at the smiley clock. Just six minutes left.

Sierra left the kitchen and went into the living room. A minute later, Marla hurried down the hall, lugging a suitcase. "You coming or what?"

"But what about—"

"What about *what*?"

"Your boyfriend."

"What about him?"

"You gonna call him?"

"Why the hell *should* I? He didn't bother to tell me this place was haunted, did he?"

"Maybe he didn't know."

"It's his house. Wouldn't *you* know if your house was haunted?"

"I don't know…"

"Well, I do." She hurried over to the front door.

"But won't he freak when he comes back and we're not here?"

"Fuck him." She pushed the screen door open. "I sure as hell didn't sign on to this gig so I could mess with ghosts or haunted houses!"

127

Chapter 11

Sierra and Marla ran frantically through the overgrown grass.

About a hundred yards behind the house, an old two-car block garage with a rusty tin roof sat in a grove of scrubs at the end of the bumpy gravel drive.

A late-model tan Honda Accord slept in an open stall. Marla opened the trunk, tossed her bags into it and slammed it shut. She yanked open the driver's door and jumped in. Sierra slid in beside her.

I drifted in back, settling behind Sierra.

Marla slammed it into reverse, backed out, spun around and raced to the front of the property.

I hoped that whoever was on their way here to interrogate Sierra wasn't close enough to watch us leave.

Luckily, I'd scared Marla enough to get her scrambling. She pulled out onto the main road and headed west, quickly accelerating to seventy. At the turnoff she took a right and made her way north, toward Orlando.

"Where we going?" Sierra asked.

"I got this condo in South Conway. Just twenty minutes or so from here. It's nice. I grabbed it when I was making big bucks modeling swimsuits for J. C. Penny's a few years back. I should never have let Parker talk me into moving in with him." She shivered. "Always hated that place. Damned house looks like it's been there since before Disney. And those neighbors out there?" She groaned.

"They're right out of *The Hills Have Eyes*. They got meth labs all over the place. Grow their own pot, too. There's a field just down the road from Parker's place, growing wild with plants. Then those stupid hicks have dog-fighting on Saturday nights. You can hear that shit for *miles*." She sighed. "If only Parker wasn't such a good talker..."

"What about *me*?"

Marla nervously lit a cigarette. The Honda bumped the curb. "Kid, I didn't count on someone like you showing up. My life's messed up enough. I've got this problem—booze and coke. I really need the stuff. Can't get through the day without it—know what I mean?"

Sierra nodded. "Momma needed her cigarettes and tequila—especially at night."

"Your mother...she didn't do any blow?"

"Only once in a while. She didn't like what it did to her sinuses. She has—had—a deviated septum."

"Well, I can't get by without it. Fuck my sinuses." Marla shivered. "Gotta have it. *Got* to."

"Does Parker do it with you?"

"He likes his booze. He gets me whatever blow I need and I'm okay for a while, but when I don't get it, I sorta, well, it's like I—"

"Freak?"

"Basically."

"Is that why you and he—"

"Parker gets me all sorts of stuff. He's a cop, so he can grab basically anything I need. And he does look pretty good, cleaned up and all. I have to admit he's not that bad in bed. You'll find out when

129

you're older, no one guy can do it all. Some guys are good in bed. Others give you enough money and presents, so you don't care *how* good or bad they are. I went around with a doctor a while back. Never saw him much, but he always gave me money. Good thing. Asshole was horrible in bed. I mean *horrible*."

Sierra nodded but said nothing.

I thought it sad that she'd been exposed to so much at such a young, impressionable age. I didn't learn about sex until junior high school. I imagined that Sierra, at thirteen, had known about it for several years already.

Marla puffed on her cigarette. "Parker's decent in bed and gets me whatever I need, so right now he's a keeper. He can be a serious butthole most of the time, but a girl's gotta get her priorities straight if she wants to make out in life."

Marla sounded very much like Jenna, possibly because Marla used the same terminology, such as "keeper," "decent in bed," and "butthole." Or maybe because both Jenna and Marla were beautiful women, had worked in the public eye and personally knew every conceivable type of man.

"But here's what I'm trying to say," she told Sierra. "I gotta go back to my place and think all this out. I'm not ready for stuff like this, you know? It's got me whacked out." She tilted her head and went silent for a moment. "Maybe…maybe *that's* what really happened back there."

"You mean you're not sure you actually saw an actual guy?"

"Mighta been all this excitement, I don't know. Things tossed to me all at once, you know? I was out of my element, for one thing. I'm not a country girl, to begin with. Grew up in Atlanta, went to modeling school in New York City. Now here I am in the sticks, surrounded by weird people who fight dogs and walk around in tight jeans pulled down to show their hairy cracks. Then *you* show up."

"I didn't mean to—"

"I know you didn't. Parker told me. Your mom's dead?"

Sierra lowered her head and nodded.

"Sorry about that, kid. I mean it. It's tough. I know it is."

"Your mom, too?"

Marla frowned. "My mom's a stupid, crazy bitch. Can't stay away from the bottle long enough to take a bath. A real class act. Anyway, those are the breaks. I left home when I was fifteen and haven't been back since. Been doing okay, too."

"You make a lot of money modeling?"

"Not anymore. Money's great while you're young and skinny, but once you hit the big Two-Five, develop a line or two on your face and no longer look cherry, that's it. The ball game. Those fucks just stop calling. But I'm okay. I got some money saved. I'll make it. Plenty of rich guys out there that would love to mess up the sheets with an ex-model."

"What about Parker?"

"He's okay for now. But these surprises of his are gonna kill it for us. You, for example. It really freaked me. And whenever I freak, I have to get

131

back to my place. Familiar surroundings and all that crap—you know? I like doing all my thinking by myself. I always seem to think better in my underwear—especially without shoes. I'm much more relaxed in my bare feet. Then, after a line or two and a couple of drinks, I have an easier time figuring what everything means."

"So you wanna be…by yourself?"

"Sorry, kid, that's just the way it is. Can't take care of someone if my own head isn't on straight—know what I mean?"

Sierra sighed. "Yeah…"

She looked like she wanted to cry. I could tell what she was thinking. After losing her mother and being taken to a strange place by a strange man, she was about to be dumped so she could fend for herself again.

"Where would you like to go? I mean, where can I leave you off? Got any kin out this way? Friends? Someone you can crash with?"

"Nope."

"I'll take you to my place. You can have a shower and I can maybe let you have some of my old clothes. Like I said before, you'll probably be okay wearing one of my shirts. And I have a million pairs of shorts. That okay? No offense, but you really need a shower, girl."

"That'd be cool."

"Then you can do what you want, go where you want. I could give you a little jack—not much, mind you, since I really don't have all that much to toss around. But I can let you have some carrying-

132

around money, help you get somewhere. Sure you don't have any kin close by?"

"My momma...she's got an older sister..."

"Where?"

"Somewhere up north. I think maybe in North or South Carolina."

"Shit."

"They never got along. I never even met Aunt Barbara. Don't even know her last name. She's been married three or four times, Momma said."

Marla pulled off Conway Road, onto the winding paved drive leading to a sprawling complex of Spanish-style condominiums.

"Well, like I said, I can only do so much to help you out. I can make sure you're clean, have a change of clothes, some food and a little cash. Other than that—*shit!*"

The Honda swerved, bumping the curve.

"What's up?"

Marla stopped in the middle of the road, sat back and shoved her hair away from her face. "Some dirtbag's parked in my space."

A sparkling black Olds sat in the space in front of Bungalow 12.

It looked like it just came from the showroom. I didn't know who owned it, of course, but I suspected that someone who could afford such a car was also capable of reading the signs

PRIVATE PARKING
VISITORS
DESIGNATED SPOTS ONLY

posted every sixty feet or so from the front entrance of the complex.

A heavy wash of warmth shot up where my spine used to be. This also smelled, but not in any way I could easily pin down. Since the fire at Sierra's place, I'd grown suspicious of everything and everyone I'd seen. The Olds parked in Marla's spot didn't make me breathe any easier.

Marla eased into the guest space next to the Olds and slammed it into park. She was already boiling and ready to do battle.

I couldn't blame her. I'd gone through similar situations at my Winter Park apartment complex. The offenders were usually relatives of my neighbors, arrogant realtors or insurance salesmen who parked their Lexus or Cadillac wherever they pleased.

And, of course, the bug man, who didn't care who he blocked with his truck.

This had a different feel altogether. Judging from what I'd already learned about Parker, what I'd heard him arrange on his cell phone and what Marla had said about him, he was most likely involved with the local drug runners. If the owner of the Olds was in some way connected to Parker or his associates, this wasn't going to go well at all.

Marla slammed her door shut and pulled the strap of her handbag over her right shoulder.

Sierra opened her door. "What's going on?" she asked uneasily.

"I'm about to feed some asshole his own balls for lunch," she growled, snatching her hair away from her face.

Sierra got out.

Marla stomped toward the front steps of the bungalow.

I suspected that Parker's friends had already arrived at his house. It wouldn't take them very long to check the house and the garage. They'd probably already called Parker and told him the women were gone. Parker most definitely had gotten the word out quickly and sent someone here.

Or maybe someone else—someone Parker didn't know about—had come here for some other reason. Either way, Sierra was just as vulnerable.

As Sierra crossed the walk, I focused on a lace of her tennis shoe, visualizing myself unraveling it.

Marla rushed up the steps.

Sierra's shoelace loosened, straightened, then fell underneath her other shoe just as she brought it down, and she tripped on the curb.

Luckily, she didn't fall on the concrete slab. She looked down at her shoe, bent over and re-laced it.

Marla reached the top of the steps. I heard the tingling of keys, the sound of a door opening.

A moment of silence.

Then, Marla's loud voice: "Who the hell are *you*?"

The sound of a slap.

A gasp.

A scuffle on the deck.

Her handbag flew over the rail, thumping to the concrete a few feet from Sierra. Sierra jumped and spun around. She craned her head up.

Someone fell roughly to the deck floor. The deck and steps shook. A flower pot fell onto the deck floor, knocking dirt through the wooden slats and onto Sierra's shoulder.

A hard-faced man with a dark brush-cut peered over the rail. His eyes immediately fixed on Sierra.

In that instant, time stopped. Realization of the situation turned her face a deathly pale color. She stiffened. Her body shook.

Time resumed with the force of a rifle blast.

The man raced down the steps, two at a time.

Her terror propelling her forward, Sierra dashed through me and shot around the corner. Her pursuer leaped the last four steps, landing on the concrete slab. Without losing a beat he spun expertly to his left, taking off after her. As he rushed through me I figured him at around six-one and one-ninety, broad-shouldered and obviously athletic, as evidenced by the ease in which he moved.

I followed. My spiritual form enabled me to easily keep up with him. For a moment I thought I actually had wings. I moved with explosive bursts and was able to stay in a straight line without worrying about bushes, wooden posts or parked cars.

Sierra darted past a throughway, turned left and disappeared around the corner.

I reached the same corner about five seconds later. The sign *RECREATION HALL* was posted on the side of the adjacent building. Her pursuer stopped abruptly, scouring the surroundings. He was hardly out of breath, which told me I'd been accurate about his athletic ability. It also told me he wasn't about to abandon his pursuit of Sierra.

Seeing nothing out of the ordinary, he walked up to the door of the rec hall and reached for the doorknob.

It opened before he could touch it.

A short elderly man blocked the doorway.

Sierra's pursuer reached into his jacket pocket, instantly producing a badge—

Badge? A *cop*?

The elderly man nodded and awkwardly stepped aside.

Sierra's pursuer disappeared inside the building.

I realized only then just how much trouble Sierra was in.

***

Inside the rec room, a couple of old men in shorts and tank tops played ping pong while two others busied themselves at the pool table. Two young boys, both around ten or twelve, sat in the far corner, playing video games.

Badge moved off toward the left.

Down the hall, the sign *SHOWERS* showed prominently along the concrete wall. *RESTROOMS* appeared farther down, halfway to the *REAR EXIT* sign designating the pool access.

Badge paused in front of the door marked *MEN* and pushed it open. An elderly man in shorts, Hawaiian shirt and tennis shoes washed his hands in front of the mirror. Another man about the same age, wearing an oversized pullover, Bermuda shorts, ankle socks and tennis shoes, crowded a urinal,

137

whistling. The four open doors revealed empty stalls.

Badge let the door close and moved quietly down the hall, to the door marked *LADIES*. He listened for a moment, looking around to make sure no one was close. When he was reasonably certain he was alone, he cracked open the door. An inch, then two inches. He glanced up and down the hall once again and listened. Then rushed in and let the door close softly.

Apparently Badge didn't share my reluctance about entering a ladies' room.

The door of the third stall was closed. No feet showed in the gap beneath the door.

Badge reached into his pocket. "All right," he said in a soft, low-pitched voice. "C'mon out."

Silence.

"C'mon out. I don't have all day."

A soft thump. Sierra's scuffed tennis shoes appeared on the floor behind the stall door. A sharp clicking noise. The door squeaked open.

Sierra stood in the doorway, trembling.

"C'mon out." Badge removed a small automatic from a jacket pocket and a silencer from another. His eyes stayed on her as he screwed the silencer onto the short barrel. "I don't have much time."

Sierra couldn't take her eyes off the gun. "You gonna...*kill* me?" she asked softly.

"Listen carefully. I'm only gonna say this once. We're leaving here through the back and you're walking in front of me."

"Where?"

"All you need to know is that I'm following you out. My car's parked right outside the woman's condo. We can get to it from the back. If you do anything I don't like, I'm gonna have to cap you. I'm not supposed to because we need you to answer some questions, but if you act stupid, I'll just have to handle this my way and explain what happened later. Understand?"

Sierra swallowed loudly. "Who *are* you?"

"Like I just said, don't have the time to explain." He motioned with the gun. "Just move on over to the door and don't piss me off."

She crossed her arms in front of her and raised her head. "I'm not going anywhere with you."

He groaned. "Listen here. I'm not gonna argue with you—"

"I'm not going with you."

I couldn't believe how stubborn she acted with a gun pointed at her. I knew she was tough—I just didn't realize she was *this* tough. Living in such abusive conditions had created a thick, rough exterior.

I could only wonder if she'd seen the wrong end of a gun barrel before.

Badge sighed. "Don't make this any harder than it has to be."

"I don't know how hard it's s'posed to be. You won't tell me shit."

"Listen to me, now..."

"I don't *wanna* listen to you. I want you to go. You're not allowed in here anyway. This room's for girls. You're not a *girl*, are you?"

The muscles in Badge's thick neck tensed like taut cables. "You're asking for it, you little bitch…"

It was time to intervene. Acting tough wasn't exactly a good tactic in this situation. I didn't like the way Badge kept his pistol aimed steadily in her direction. Or how his neck muscles had tensed up. Or the red blotches standing out on his broad cheeks.

I moved over to his right and a little to the left of the sinks. Since I hadn't used my ectoplasm lately, I figured I should have quite a bunch stored up. I wasn't sure if it worked that way. I hadn't been given instructions when I woke up dead. But it sounded reasonable.

I concentrated on using every bit of ectoplasm I could muster to show myself. I looked down.

My legs materialized. Then my arms.

"You really don't want to do anything stupid," I told him.

Sierra turned sharply and gawked at me. Her jaw dropped.

Badge cringed. The gun instantly moved in my direction. His shaking hand accidentally tugged on the trigger, forcing out a quiet round thumping into the tiled wall. A light-blue square shattered, forming a jagged white star. "What the *fuck*—"

"I saw your badge," I said. "You a hitter or a cop?"

He didn't reply. He fought hard to keep the gun aimed at me, but his shaking made the effort extremely difficult. His eyes bulged. His cheeks had paled.

140

"If you're a cop, you shouldn't be doing this. Cops don't pull their guns on little girls. I don't even think they're allowed to carry silencers. That *is* a silencer, isn't it?"

His shaking worsened.

I decided to keep up the pressure.

"You must be a hitter, then. A cop would've already called someone and told them he'd found the girl."

No reply.

"You found the girl. You just didn't bother calling anyone, right? I could be mistaken, but I don't think so. I didn't see you make a call, and I've been with you since you did that number to Marla on her balcony."

His eyes grew even larger. "What the—"

"You're a hitter, then. Right?"

The gun still shook, but remained pointing in my direction. This was good. In his nervous state, I didn't want him aiming it at Sierra. I moved a couple of more inches in the other direction to widen the distance.

"If you're a hitter, you're way overpaid. Anyone who can't hit their target at this distance is either blind or drunk."

The insult made him tense up. He straightened and aimed. Another slug thumped into the tile directly behind where my back used to be, forming a long jagged crack extending toward the floor.

I could feel my energy draining a little even though I'd been conserving it. But at least it hadn't waned as much as it had at the cemetery.

141

"Son, you need to go back to the firing range and spend a few hours working on that rear sight. No offense, but you're really a piss-poor shot. I didn't think a hitter could be a piss-poor shot and stay a hitter very long, but what the hell do I know?"

He emptied one more into the tile. It slammed into a fresh square, sending serrated cracks fanning outward like frightened ants.

"A *little* better, but still no cigar."

Gasping, he bolted for the door. He had trouble pulling it open—his hands shook badly. The gun in his right hand also gave him a slight problem. The tip of the silencer kept bumping the door. He glanced at me to make sure I was still there.

I let my legs fade a tad for his benefit—and, of course, to conserve energy.

It must have worked. He pocketed the gun, then clawed at the door again, this time with renewed vigor. He finally slipped through the narrow opening.

Sierra couldn't take her eyes off me. Her mouth was still open but she wasn't shaking very much—possibly because I'd just saved her life. Whatever the reason, she stood there in shocked silence.

"You busy right now?" I asked.

She scrunched up her face. "Huh?"

"He might've brought along a buddy or two."

"What?"

"There are probably others in on this."

"Huh?"

142

Too much had happened for her to concentrate, obviously. Her young brain was trying to process too much too quickly.

"Pay attention, now. If you'd like to live long enough to have kids and maybe even a husband, you're gonna have to stick with me."

"Who *are* you?"

"The name's Jason. Jason Mild. But that isn't important right now. Actually, my name is the least of your worries."

"But who…where'd you come from?"

"My mom's name was Lillian. My dad answered to James." I guessed that if I kept my tone light, she wouldn't freak as easily.

"That's not what I—"

"Listen, if I told you what was really happening, you wouldn't believe me."

"But I didn't even see you come *in*—"

"I always thought that grand entrance thing was highly overrated."

"But where…how…when—"

"Are you interested in making it through the rest of the day?"

She nodded.

"Follow me. Maybe we'll be able to get you out of here in one piece."

"We?"

"Figure of speech."

She shrugged. "Know something, Mister? You're totally weird."

I knew right then that she was even tougher than I'd thought.

143

Chapter 12

We reached the main road without incident.

A hundred yards behind us, three OPD squad cars sat behind Marla's Honda outside her condo. Two cops questioned four elderly residents while two other cops sniffed around Marla's deck, talking to their cell phones.

An ambulance hadn't shown yet. I didn't know if Marla was dead or just injured.

Sierra stayed beside me as we hurried down the private road. She kept glancing at me as if trying to determine how much of what I'd told her was true. She probably had a ton of questions to ask. She probably also wondered if I was crazy, judging by the distance she kept between us.

We reached the complex entrance, then crossed Conway Road and headed north.

About half a block later, she turned back to the complex—possibly to see if anyone was following us. There was no one. She stopped walking, then shifted her gaze back to me. Her expression was one of urgency. "Are you gonna tell me who you are?"

"Are you sure you're ready to know?"

She sighed. "Mister—"

"Mild. You can call me Jake."

"How'd ya spell that?"

"J—A –"

"Your other name."

I spelled it for her.

"That spells mild."

"Not mild. Mild. Like mildew."

"*Ewww...*"

144

"Tell me about it. Growing up with that name was a real treat. High school especially was interesting."

"No shit."

"Watch your language."

"Why?"

She brought up a good point. Why worry about proprieties when your life had just come apart?

Since I was dead, I ought to feel the same way. I just didn't know why I still cared about the same things. Maybe it was because I felt sorry for this girl and wanted to set a good example. The concept sounded ridiculous, but I didn't know how else to explain it.

"Let's just say it makes you sound...well—"

"Like a little slut?"

"Basically."

She shrugged. "I don't care."

I didn't reply. I couldn't blame her for feeling that way. Not at all.

"What's everyone call you?"

"My friends used to call me Jake."

"*Used* to?"

"You can call me Jake."

"*Used* to?"

I didn't know exactly how to respond to that. I just nodded.

"Mister....Jake...if you knew what I've been through—"

"I know."

She frowned. I could tell she was trying to understand that one.

"I've been following you all day."

145

Her frown remained. I knew where she was coming from. What I'd just told her sounded like a heavy-duty crock of bull.

"All day?"

"Since last night, when those three rocket scientists picked you up. I even watched you when you were trying to sleep in your tree house."

She gasped. "H-How did you...what...who...how'd ya know about...*them*...the tree house?"

"I told you. I've been with you quite a while."

"But...I haven't *seen* you..."

"There's a good reason for that."

She waited.

This was probably the perfect time for a detailed explanation, yet I couldn't think of one. If I told her I was dead, she'd probably freak. I didn't want her to freak. We were much too close to the road and the traffic was too heavy. If she lost it and ran out in the middle of the road, I'd never forgive myself.

Maybe she'd decide I was a mental patient who'd escaped the local nuthouse. That would be easier for her to grasp than walking around with a dead guy.

I could lie, but if I did, what could I tell her that would sound reasonable? How could I explain how I'd just appeared in the men's room back at Marla's complex? I just happened by? I was there all along but neither her nor Badge had noticed me right off?

This was going to take some thinking. But I suspected I didn't have much time. It might have been her tense expression. Or the way she kept tapping her tennis shoe on the ground.

The tapping suddenly stopped.

"Gonna tell me or what?"

There. I'd already run out of time.

"I'm thinking up a really good explanation."

"Why?"

"So you won't freak or think I'm a nutcase."

"Why think it up if it's true?"

"The truth can be hard to swallow sometimes."

"Maybe I'm in the mood for it."

"How's that?"

She turned away. She appeared to be staring at the complex straight ahead, but I suspected she wasn't really looking at anything. "Momma lied to me. Miguel lied to me. That Parker dude lied to me. I'm pretty sure Marla even lied. Those dudes in the TransAm lied, but I expected them to. They were real jerks. Everyone lies and I'm getting fucking tired of—"

"Watch your language. You're too young to talk like—"

"Dammit." She spun around. Her eyes were wet. "Gonna tell me what's going down? Or you gonna lie, too?"

She had a point. And as she'd proved a couple of times before, she was one tough young lady. If she couldn't handle the truth, no one could.

"You really want the truth?"

"Well, duh…"

"All right, then. Here goes." I took a breath. "I'm dead."

She blinked.

147

"Did you hear me okay? This traffic's kind of loud, and—"

"You're dead?"

I nodded.

"You mean *dead*?"

I nodded.

"And you're right here? Talking to me?"

"Just the two of us. Me and you."

"Prove it."

"Huh?"

"Prove you're dead."

"Touch me."

"Huh?"

"Go ahead. Have a feel."

Her eyes narrowed. "You a pervert?"

"Not really, although a couple of my ex-wives might disagree." I held out my arm. "Here. Knock yourself out."

Tentatively she brought up her hand and held it over mine. She watched me to see what I'd do. I did nothing. Then she lowered her eyes and brought her hand down.

It went right through the empty air.

"See there?"

She gasped. Her eyes filled the sockets. Without a word she spun around and bolted up the street.

I let her run, watching her as she grew smaller in the distance.

A passing Ford pickup slowed down, pulled onto the shoulder a few yards in front of her, then stopped.

The pickup was covered in primer and patched with Bondo. One of the taillights was cracked. Two big blue foam dice dangled from the rearview. The silhouette of two naked, kneeling women covered the silver splash guards. The personalized license plate said *GOOBER*. A *PARTY NAKED* and two NRA stickers covered portions of the rear window.

The driver pushed open the passenger door.

Sierra climbed in.

I turned invisible again. And not a moment too soon, either. I'd already begun fading.

Moving quickly, I caught up and raised myself into the bed of the truck, then into the cluttered back seat directly behind Sierra.

We eased back onto the road and roared away.

***

The driver wore a stained green baseball cap, black tee shirt and faded jeans. He was about forty, long-limbed and skinny. He smelled of B.O., cigarettes and booze. A pint bottle of Jack Daniel's was wedged between his skinny thighs.

He yanked the bottle from his lap and had a hefty swallow. He offered her the bottle. She took it eagerly.

Remembering what I'd heard her say about drinking, I'd obviously upset her. Or maybe it was the combination of her mother dying, her house being torched, Parker taking her away from civilization, a strange man with a pistol approaching her in a strange ladies' room and a dead guy popping up in her life—all in one afternoon.

"Easy, now," he said. "How old are ya, sugar?"

149

"Eighteen." She had another small slug. Then sighed and turned around in her seat. She was looking right at me, she just didn't know it. She stared at the place where we'd been walking, probably wondering where I'd gone.

"Really? Eighteen?"

"Just had a birthday."

"Look younger."

"I get that all the time. It sucks."

"What's happening? Look like ya just seen a ghost."

"Did. Sorta."

He snatched the bottle from her.

"I'm with this guy, he just sorta shows up, giving me all kinds of bullshit. Weirded me out, ya know?"

"Maybe he just wanted to score with ya."

"Too old."

"Old guy?"

She nodded. "About your age."

"Hey, I'm thirty-five. That ain't old."

"Look older."

His right eyelid twitched. "Want out now? Next light?"

"Sorry. Just weirded out."

He had another sip of Jack's and stuck the bottle back between his thighs. "So where ya headed?"

She shrugged.

"Where ya live?"

"St. Cloud."

"St. Cloud's south a here."

"I know."

"We're headed north."

"I know that, too."

He gave her a quick once-over. "You ain't...runnin' away, are ya?"

"From what?"

"Home. Your folks." He shrugged. "You know."

"Got no folks." She stared straight ahead.

"You an orphan?"

"Momma's dead. Daddy left home."

"That's tough." He brought the bottle back up.

"You get used to it."

"So who you staying with?"

She shrugged.

He pulled off his cap and rubbed his tanned scalp. Then stuck the cap back on and frowned. "Listen, sugar, I got my own problems. Old lady took off with some clown, sells life insurance. Got this other female, wants to move in. Bitch goes nuclear when I tell her my place is too damn small. Goes all kinds of apeshit, accuses me of being a homo." He sucked down more Jack's. "Got more than enough problems."

"That where you're going now? Your place?"

"Have something in mind?"

"I need to get drunk."

He stared at her. "*Sure* you're eighteen?"

"I oughta know how old I am."

He shook his head. "Last time I hooked up with an eighteen-year-old, she turned out to be fifteen. I did time."

"What'd you do to her?"

He snorted. "What *didn't* I do? Shit, she asked for it. Damn straight. I didn't do nothin' she didn't ask for. Fuckin' courts, they don't care about *any* of that shit. Don't care that she begged for it, or that she looked like she was twenty fuckin' years old. Or that I wasn't even the first guy she'd scored with. All they care about was her fuckin' age. Sucks. Sucks real bad."

"Sounds like it."

"Whaddya need a drink for? Bad day?"

"You might say that."

"What happened?"

"Too much."

"And ya say your momma's dead?"

"Died in a fire. Kinda think her boyfriend's bosses killed her."

He stiffened. "What kinda bosses?"

"The kind that beat you up or blow you up when they're pissed."

"No shit?" He drove a little while in silence. "They don't, uh, know where you are, do they, sugar?"

"I'm with you. On the road. How could they know?"

He snuck a quick glance at his rearview, then his side mirror. He scratched the back of his neck. "They ain't…lookin' for ya, are they?"

She shrugged a shoulder. "Might be."

He swallowed. "Say they killed your momma?"

"Yeah."

"Think maybe we both need to get drunk."

***

152

Bud's Place on East 50 was an old two-story frame house recently painted a gray-blue and treated with better windows framed with white shutters. A tin roof topped it. A white wooden porch spanned the front. It resembled Cracker Barrel on a much smaller scale. A rocking chair, beat-up wooden table and an ancient wine barrel brimming with artificial flowers added a little class to the porch. The building was almost hidden among the plethora of tune-up shops, strip malls and eateries that had literally taken over that stretch of highway.

I followed them in. Goober waved at the crowd of local boys gathered around the pool table. They waved, laughed and exchanged a few mock insults, most of them involving Goober's mother, his breeding from inferior stock and his lack of sexual prowess.

They knew him at the bar, too. When the barman saw him, he grabbed a bottle from the shelf in front of the mirror, poured a double shot into a glass, added ice and slid it over to the tall, skinny waitress.

She brought it right over.

He took it, sipped and patted the waitress on her flat rump.

She put her hands on her hips and stared accusingly at Sierra. "How old's this one?"

"Says she's eighteen."

"Uh-huh. And I'm the Queen Mother."

"I am," Sierra said proudly. "Last week."

Goober sighed. "You told me last month."

Sierra shrugged and reddened. "Time goes so fast..."

153

The waitress shook her head. "What *is* it with you, boy? Wasn't one stretch enough?"

"Fuckin' A. Not enough alone time and I didn't appreciate the sleepin' arrangements one fuckin' bit. I think I'll pass on doin' another one."

"Then stop looking for trouble."

He shrugged. "It always finds *me*."

"Take her somewheres else. We just got done paying our last fine." She went back to the bar.

Goober shrugged. "Sorry, kid. Them's the breaks."

Sierra got up to leave.

"Got some place to go?"

She shook her head.

"Listen, I got a couch—"

"Don't need your help." She marched over to the door, pushed it open and went back outside.

For the next few minutes, she stood on the front porch, watching the heavy traffic as evening approached. She sniffed, then wiped her eyes. "This sucks," she said softly. Then, a little louder: "Sucks big-time." She went down the steps and crossed the front lot.

I decided to make another appearance. She'd probably be desperate enough to listen to me this time.

"Want some company?"

She spun around. "You again?"

"Can't help it. I end up everywhere I go."

"How'd you...how'd you get *here*?"

"Hitched a ride with Goober."

"You were in the truck?"

I shrugged. "Can't use my own car anymore."

154

She shoved her hair away from her face. "Why won't you leave me alone? Who *are* you? And don't give me that dead shit again."

"I told you the truth. You wanted it and I figured you deserved it. I can't help it if the truth sounds like something out of a George Romero movie. But it's how things are. I thought you were mature enough to handle it. But I won't leave you alone. I can't. You need help. You need it right now. I know I can help if you just let me. I don't know how, I just know I can. But I can't help being dead. Like I said, it's how things are."

"Really?"

"Really what? That I'm dead?"

"You're really dead?"

"Yes."

"And you really wanna help me?"

"My last mission on earth."

"Then leave me alone." She started walking toward the end of the lot, which led to an auto body repair and painting shop that was closed.

"But you do need help."

She spun around. "Maybe, but I sure don't need it from some creepy guy, says he's dead. Doesn't that weird you out? It's totally weirding *me* out."

"I want to help you."

"Then stop saying you're dead."

"Okay. I'll stop." If that was all it took, I'd do as she asked. "I won't say it again."

"Then you aren't? Really?"

"Aren't really what?"

"Dead."

"Sorry. Can't help it. It's the truth."

155

She shook her head.

"How do you explain what happened in the rest room?"

"Don't wanna."

"Why not?"

"I'll weird out."

"Why's that?"

"It doesn't make sense!"

"It happened, didn't it?"

"Maybe. If I keep thinking about it, I'll freak. I know it. I'll fucking freak!"

"But if you'll just give me a little time—"

"Then what?"

I shrugged. "I'll probably grow on you."

"Leave me alone." She turned and walked away.

"But—"

"Leave me alone!"

"You okay, girl?" shouted a booming low-pitched voice coming up behind me.

A huge bearded guy in filthy overalls lumbered toward us. He held a bottle of beer in his right hand. His left gripped the taped handle of a large ball-peen hammer.

For the very first time, I was really glad I was dead.

"Hell, no," she said. "I don't look okay, do I?"

"This guy bothering you?"

"It's all right. He's just weird." She waved and kept walking away.

He stopped a few feet from me and sized me up. I smelled the beer and the sweat and knew he was eager to show off. "You want trouble, Jack?"

"Jake. And no, I've had more than enough the last couple of days. But thanks for the offer."

"Leave the little chick alone, Jack."

"Jake. And no can do. She needs help and I'm gonna help her, regardless of what she wants."

"Listen, Jack..." He moved closer. "I told ya, get lost. Leave her alone. She doesn't want your help."

"Jake." I wasn't in the mood for this. "Listen here...I've just had a rough couple of days, and I don't need any more grief from you or anyone—"

"If you don't get the fuck outa here, your rough days ain't seen nothin' yet." He had a slug of beer and watched me closely. The huge, grease-covered hand holding the hammer twitched slightly.

"I honestly don't think you can make things any worse than they already are."

"Oh, yeah?"

I couldn't help chuckling. "What *is* this? The playground? What's next? You going to tell me to step over a line?"

His small dark eyes glistened in the haze of the street lamp. "I'm gonna have your shit for supper, pal."

"You'd be much better off with your usual double cheeseburgers, pancakes and fries. Besides, I'm not your *pal*."

"A wise guy, eh, Jack?"

"Jake. Listen, fella—"

"*You* listen. Drift, and I mean it. Now."

"Now?"

"Yeah. Right now. Make tracks. Disappear."

157

"What exactly should I do first? Drift? Make tracks? Or disappear? I can't do all three. It's very confusing."

"Yeah, a fuckin' wise guy." He had more beer. "Listen, asshole. Just disappear and you might save yourself a giant case of whup-ass—get it?"

"Disappear?"

"Fuckin' right."

I laughed.

Then I disappeared.

The big ape's jaw dropped. So did the beer bottle. Then the hammer.

He backed up. And kept backing up. When he was about ten yards away, he disappeared behind an ancient VW bus up on blocks. The sound of a trash can lid banging against metal reverberated off the wall of the brick building.

I turned.

Sierra was gone.

PART TWO
THE DESTINATION

Chapter 13

I found Sierra at the next busy intersection.

The tears staining her cheeks glistened in the haze of the streetlamps. She made no attempt to wipe them or even push the hair away from her face.

I had to comfort her somehow. I'd failed miserably twice already. I knew she wouldn't be receptive to another try. Despite my good intentions, she needed more time. Maybe after another couple of hours, once she'd accepted what had just happened back at Marla's and at the bar, she'd be in a better frame of mind. As it was, too much had happened. Now, in addition to everything else, she had someone popping into her life who'd just told her he was dead.

I decided to follow her as before, staying close. I'd only show myself when totally necessary. She'd probably breathe much easier if she didn't think I was tagging along behind her.

But just then she sighed and looked around. "You there? Somewhere?"

I hesitated.

"If you're there, I'd really like to know. I feel totally weird standing here, talking to myself."

"I'm here."

She looked around. "Doing your dead thing? I can't see you."

159

"Yep. My dead thing."

"I wanna see you."

I showed myself.

Someone in the passing traffic must have seen my sudden appearance in his headlights. The screeching of brakes filled the night air just before the red light at the next intersection.

She looked me up and down, wiping her eyes. She pushed her hair out of her face so she could see me better. "I guess you're okay," she said.

"You mean my looks?'"

She shrugged. "For an older guy."

"I'm...thirty-one." I'd met my demise a few months after my thirty-sixth birthday but felt the need to defend myself. I'd often considered it ridiculous that people had to justify their age as if it were some sort of crime or malady.

But I realized where she was coming from. To someone her age, anyone older than twenty was ancient.

"Thirty-*one*?"

I nodded.

"Look older."

"Gee, thanks. And you look slightly younger than eighteen."

She smiled.

Her reaction surprised me. I'd never seen her smile before. Two small dimples appeared at each corner of her mouth. She was actually a very pretty girl. Her smile even eclipsed her black eye and swollen lip.

"I didn't know you could do that."

"Do what?"

160

"Smile."

"Not much to smile about."

"I know."

"That's right, you've been following me."

"Long enough."

"For what?"

"To see why you don't smile."

"You didn't happen to see…the fire, did you?"

"I was with you."

"At Walmart?"

"I helped you."

"When? I mean, what didja do?"

"A couple of things."

"What?"

"First, I made sure you didn't get carved up."

"*You* did that?"

"It's this phobia I've got. I don't like to see people get their faces slashed. Or beat up. I get kind of squeamish."

She automatically reached up and covered her eye, then thought better of it and lowered her hand. "Wondered what happened. Ray uses that blade a lot. Thanks."

"No problem."

"What else?"

"Let's just say I influenced a few things to happen to help you get away."

She studied me a little while. "You a guardian angel or something?"

That hadn't occurred to me. "I don't *think* so..."

"Don't you know?"

"No one's actually told me anything since my accident."

161

"You don't see any other guys flying around?"

"Just a few. Nothing big. And they're not flying, they're walking."

"How'd you...I mean, why are you dead?"

"I was hit by a truck."

She grimaced. "*Bummer* . . ."

"Yeah, it didn't exactly make my day."

She shook her head. "Your day's worse than mine."

"In some ways."

She turned to the passing traffic. A shadow passed over her fine features. The darkness of the night had intensified, but the streetlamp provided just enough light to enable me to see the sadness filling her eyes.

"Life sucks. Big-time." Her voice became a whisper.

Her sadness brought about a heavy throbbing inside me. She'd been forced to grow up much too quickly, skipping much of her childhood entirely. Her tender impressionable years had been taken away, along with her innocence and her sense of wonder.

I'd grown up slowly and naturally, remaining a boy as long as I possibly could. I had toys, boyhood friends and dreams. I played ball, wandered off by myself in the woods behind our house and frequently lost myself in daydreams even while in a classroom, when I was supposed to be studying. I was stupid and silly and carefree and happy well into my teen years.

I wouldn't trade my childhood memories for anything.

162

Sierra, I suspected, had very few childhood memories. Because of her father leaving and her mother bringing home someone who'd only wanted to use her for his own benefit, she experienced no carefree days. No school. No friends. No sunny afternoons where she could run around the neighborhood, acting like the kid she actually was.

I snapped myself out of it and focused on more urgent matters.

My apartment, most importantly.

Now that we'd reached Colonial Drive, it wouldn't take us long to get to Winter Park. Although I still wanted to see what had happened there—as well as find the moron who'd turned me into road kill—now I realized it would be a good place to take Sierra. I didn't know how long I'd been dead, so I had no idea if the place was even still available. It would take a while to go through the proper legal channels—even longer, since I had no beneficiaries. If the condo manager hadn't yet surrendered it to Probate or turned it over to my software company, we could use it temporarily. Sierra could have a shower and something to eat. She'd also have a place to stay for the night. She looked exhausted.

"We need to go somewhere," I said.

"Where?"

"My place."

She didn't reply, but I could see the trace of a smile.

"I didn't mean it to sound that way."

"What way?"

163

"You know. My place? You and me, baby? Let's have a few drinks, tear up the sheets and boogie?"

A frown. "Huh?"

I'd obviously just handed her something she might not be familiar with. Kids nowadays spoke a different language. "I didn't mean anything funny."

"What did you mean?"

"I meant my place. But not for what you think."

"What do I think?"

"You know. Shacking up. That sort of thing."

"I know *that*."

"You do?"

She shrugged. "You're dead."

"What was I thinking?"

"I don't know. I can't even read my own mind sometimes."

"So here we are, back to square one."

"Where's that?"

"Trying to decide what to do."

"You said your place."

"At least you could crash there, find something to eat. We can figure out what you can do in the morning."

"You really have a place?"

"Of course I have a place."

She blinked. "Didn't think dead guys had a place of their own."

"I had it when I was alive. It's probably still there. I just—"

"Haven't been back?"

"Haven't had the chance."

"Why go back?"

164

"I'd like to see if my ex picked the place clean."

"So?"

The way she said that made the whole thing sound lame. But she was just a kid and hadn't learned about such complications yet. "I'm curious."

"Why?"

"I also want to find the guy who killed me."

"Then what?"

"Good question."

"Got an answer?"

I didn't—not really. So I just said, "Closure."

"Huh?"

"It's one of those hang-ups grownups invented to help them cope."

She nodded. Then looked down.

"What's wrong?"

"You're fading."

She was right. My feet and lower legs were already absorbed by the darkness.

"That okay?" she asked.

"For who? You or me?"

"You."

"I guess so. I'm still new at this."

"New at what?"

"This ectoplasm stuff."

"Huh?"

"Appearing and disappearing. Sticking around."

"So where's your place?"

"Winter Park."

"How do we get there?"

165

"How else? You're going to hitch a ride."

"By myself?"

"I'll be with you, silly. You just won't see me."

"How come?"

"I'll be conserving my energy."

"Cool."

"Besides, you'll stand a better chance of getting picked up."

"Yeah. Guys don't like picking up chicks with other guys hanging around."

"Exactly."

"Especially older guys."

"Ouch."

She shrugged. "You're old enough to be my dad."

"Your dad's thirty-one?"

She shook her head. "Nope. Neither are you."

"Show someone your thumb," I said.

"Huh?"

"Start hitching."

I hated smartasses. Especially when they were female.

***

The highway continued its loud chaos and erratic explosions of headlights.

Sierra seemed oblivious to the noise, the traffic, the bright lights and the catcalls. She'd withdrawn from the cold, nasty world, where she was safe. In her own world, people didn't force her to do things she didn't want to do. Didn't hit her when she hesitated or turned away. Didn't yell at her. Or curse at her. Or threaten her.

166

She was probably thinking of my apartment as some sort of sanctuary where she could have a shower, a bite to eat, then relax for a few hours in a real bed for a change. She probably also wondered if she could trust me. If I'd lied to her. If I was truly dead. If I could help her at all.

A Toyota Supra stopped at the next light. The window eased down. A well-dressed guy around forty-five sat behind the wheel, grinning. "Got far to go?" he asked.

"Not really."

"Get in."

As Sierra slid in beside the driver, I oozed into the back behind her. The car was sparkling-clean and still had that new-car smell to it. A leather briefcase sat on the seat beside me. It also smelled new.

"Where to?" the driver asked, looking her over.

"Winter Park."

The light changed. He eased into the turning lane and made a right. "I'm going there myself, actually. Whereabouts?"

"Park Avenue," I whispered in Sierra's ear.

"Park Avenue," she said.

"That where you live?"

"A friend of mine lives there."

He nodded. "Anywhere near the mall?"

She half-turned, tilting her head toward me.

"That new complex across the street," I whispered.

She repeated my message.

"Something wrong with your neck?" the driver asked.

167

"Why?"

"You keep tilting it funny."

"How am I s'posed to tilt it?"

He laughed. "You definitely have a point there. This friend of yours. Male? Female?"

She nodded.

"Which is it?"

"He's a guy, I guess."

"You *guess*?"

"Well…he *used* to be…"

"Watch it," I whispered.

He nodded. "I think I understand. These days, you never know. I take it he's young."

"No, he's old. *Real* old."

"I'm thirty," I whispered, slightly miffed.

She turned back to me. Without thinking, she said, "I thought you told me—"

"What's that?" The driver jerked the car, twisting in his seat.

"Just talking to myself."

"You sounded like you were talking to someone else."

"No one else is here, right?"

"Right." He glanced in his rearview. "Right," he repeated uneasily.

He immediately went silent. He probably thought she was a fruitcake or just some weird female he didn't want to antagonize while she sat in his sparkling new vehicle. Some weird kid who talks to people who aren't really there. Occasionally he glanced in his rearview—possibly to make sure no one was actually sitting behind him.

168

Less than a mile later I caught him eyeing her chest. Even though the cab was dark, I could see that his expression had changed. I knew how most guys operated. What they thought and felt. I'd been a guy myself all my mortal life. We all acted basically the same with females.

This man had the unmistakable look of someone who wanted sex. This was okay if the woman was a decent age and willing. But it *wasn't* okay if the woman was actually a thirteen-year-old and the guy was old enough to be her grandfather.

"Much farther?" he asked.

"The next intersection," I whispered.

She repeated what I said.

"You live with your folks?"

"Not no more."

"On your own?"

"Sort of."

"Kinda young for that, aren't you?"

"Maybe."

"This friend of yours. You guys tight? Close?"

"I don't know him that well yet."

"How well do you know him?"

"Just met him an hour ago. Why?"

"Just wondering if you'd like to go to my place first, maybe have a drink."

"No, thanks."

"Don't drink?"

"Once in a while."

"It might loosen you up."

"Not in the mood."

"Wait a minute." He rubbed the back of his neck. "You say you just met this guy an *hour* ago?"

169

"Yeah?"

"Something doesn't make sense."

"That's all right. You can drop me off right here."

He coaxed the Toyota into the front lot of the 7-Eleven at the corner. He pulled over to the air pump, stopped and put it in park. Then he turned in his seat. "Right here?"

"This is great. Thanks."

"I can buy some beer and—"

"I said I wasn't in the mood."

His eyes changed again, filling with that dull blackness of aggravation a horny man gets when he's turned down. It's like a sharp knee to the midsection. Most men can't handle it. The ones who can don't like it. This jerk was obviously in the first group.

"What's wrong, chickie? I thought girls like you were *always* in the mood."

"Huh?"

"Look at you."

She looked down at herself. "What's wrong with me?"

"Nothing. You look just great."

"Then whaddya mean?"

"Like I said, look at you. How you're dressed. That top. Those jeans."

"I always dress this way."

"And you're hitching. At night."

His tone made it sound like she was a hooker doing something despicable.

"So?"

170

"You going to tell me you're not looking for trouble?"

"I'm not looking for trouble."

"You're old enough to know the score. What are you? Seventeen? Eighteen? Nowadays, chicks know the score by the time they're ten. I'll bet you've already been—"

She reached for the door knob.

"Where do you think you're going?"

"Thanks for the ride."

He grabbed her arm and pulled her back in. "I'll let you know when you can leave."

My anger fired up quickly. It took all I could not to make him stick his own thumb in his eye. "She wants to leave," I said. "Let her leave."

"Who's there—what the hell?" He jerked his head toward me, his eyes darting everywhere. "Who's b-back there?"

"My friend. That guy I told you about." Sierra pushed the door open. "Thanks again for the ride."

I wasn't quite finished with him. "A guy your age can get into serious trouble trying to force an underage girl to do something she doesn't want to do. You should be ashamed of yourself."

He gasped and jerked back, his elbow thumping the door.

"Anyway, you're old enough to know better. You probably have grandkids her age." I moved out of the car as Sierra slammed the door shut.

The Toyota peeled rubber jerking out of the lot, cutting in front of traffic and zooming through the intersection on red. The honking of protesting horns resonated in the muggy night air.

Sierra laughed.

"I've actually made you laugh," I said.

She turned to where I was and squinted. "You gonna stay that way all night?"

"What way?"

"Invisible."

"Until we get to my place."

"How far is that?"

"Just on the other side of this 7-Eleven."

"Why?"

"Why what?"

"Why stay that way?"

"Conserving energy."

She nodded.

"You don't mind, do you?"

"It's a bummer, talking to someone you can't see."

"Never thought of it like that."

"Like talking to God, only he never talks back."

"That's one way of looking at it. Just do me one large favor."

"Sure."

"Never confuse me with God."

Chapter 14

The rage swept over me like a fireball.

Jenna's emerald green Camaro sat in the visitor's space in front of my condominium.

Damn. I knew she'd come here. She wasn't the type to walk away from a situation that might earn her money. Nor was she the type to pass up the chance to pick her dead ex-husband's bones clean.

I didn't think she'd wait very long before racing here in the car I gave her for her thirtieth birthday two short years ago. She lived in Casselberry—it would only take her fifteen minutes, even in heavy traffic. She probably spotted my name in the obituaries. Or maybe one of my business associates gave her the news.

"Both those rides yours?" Sierra asked as we crossed the well-trimmed path.

"In a manner of speaking."

"Huh?"

"I bought both of them."

"You drove both rides?"

"Just the Mustang."

"How 'bout the Camaro?"

"I bought it for my ex."

"How come?"

"Her birthday."

"Nice guy. That mean she's here?"

"Unfortunately."

"Going through your stuff?"

"I'd bet on it."

"You pissed?"

173

"Actually, I'd have to be a lot happier and more relaxed to be pissed."

"What's *that* mean?"

"I'm way beyond pissed."

"Just because she's here?"

"Yeah."

"But you're dead. She can't hurt you anymore."

"Technically, you're absolutely right."

"But you're still pissed."

I couldn't take my eyes from the living room window, wondering what she was doing at the moment. Who she'd brought along to help her. If she'd used my bed. If they'd used my bed.

"She's probably inside, helping herself to whatever strikes her fancy."

"So?"

"She'll eat my food and use my bed and bathroom and—"

"You don't need that stuff anymore."

"She'll also make sure there's nothing in there she doesn't want. And I can't do a damned thing to stop her."

Sierra scowled. "Makes me not wanna have anything when *I* croak."

"You've definitely raised a valid point."

Sierra was silent for a few moments. She pushed some hair away from her face and turned to where she thought I was. "She's your ex, right?"

"The divorce was finalized three months before I died."

"Then how can she come back and just take your stuff?"

174

"She's got a good nose for finding the best lawyer."

"So?"

"She's been shacking up with one for months. She's got him by the...she's got him, well—"

"Pussy-whipped?"

It bothered me that a thirteen-year-old knew such language. But at least I didn't have to waste time explaining things to her. "You got it."

"So what'll we do?"

I had no idea. Nor did I have any sort of backup plan. I didn't think I'd even make it back here. I'd once heard on a cop show that most people planning murders always neglected to plan past the actual murder. As a result, they were always caught.

I hadn't planned to murder Jenna—although right now, that image brought about an instant plethora of happy thoughts. But my situation was no different. I'd only thought of getting here—not what I'd do once I'd returned.

"You don't know what to do, right?" Sierra asked.

"Not a clue."

"If it was me? I'd go in there and scare the shit out of her."

"What would that accomplish?"

"You don't want her in there, right? Besides, it'd be cool."

Sierra's idea sounded just about as mouth-watering as my image of murdering Jenna. Sending Jenna out into the night screaming and wetting her pants would be worth the trip here. "It would be, wouldn't it?"

"Why not do it, then?"

"It seems so…juvenile…"

"I'm thirteen. I'm s'posed to be that way."

"I'm not."

"You're dead."

"Still, it somehow seems, well, wrong."

"How about what she's doing to you in there right now?"

The anger flared inside me once again. "That's *very* wrong."

Sierra shrugged. "Then what's the problem?"

"The problem, I guess, is me. How I feel about doing things like this."

"Don't worry about that. Just do it and worry about how you feel about it later."

She did raise a good argument. But somehow coming all this way just to scare Jenna reeked of tackiness. "I don't know…"

"Why not?" Sierra was grinning, stirred up for the first time since I'd known her. "It'd be totally cool."

"Maybe…"

"What's your problem now?"

The problem was Jenna. Knowing her as I did, I suspected she'd probably take this a lot more seriously than Marla had. She'd get a bunch of people involved and might even coax her boy-toy lawyer to cut a deal with the local TV stations to do a story on the paranormal or a possible haunting.

Jenna could easily turn this into a freak show.

I just wanted to do something that wouldn't backfire.

176

"Scaring her just wouldn't be enough for me," I told Sierra.

"Then tell me what you wanna do. I don't even know why I'm here."

"You're here because I'm here."

She frowned. "You keep following me."

"And because I saved your life."

She didn't reply. She lowered her head.

"What's wrong?"

She looked up. Her wet eyes glistened in the darkness. "You *really* think you saved my life?" she asked softly.

Damn. I'd been so wrapped up in my own problems that I'd forgotten how difficult the last twenty-four hours had been for her. "Are you saying I should've *let* that knife guy cut you up?"

"I've got nowhere to go, no mother and no one who cares about me. There's a bunch of bad guys after me because they think I know where Miguel stashed a bunch of money."

"I care."

She just sighed.

"I do. Otherwise—"

"I know." She turned away.

"Now *you* sound pissed."

She shrugged.

"What's *that* mean?"

She spun around. "I'm not sure I wanna live anymore."

Her statement sliced right through me. It made me realize how low she'd sunk. How lonely she was. How desperate. How frightened.

I had to make this right. Somehow.

"Momma's dead, Jake." Her voice a harsh whisper.

"I know."

"I'm…all alone."

"I know that, too."

"I don't even know how I feel. Momma, she changed. She was never the same once Daddy left. She…went away, too."

"It was probably easier for her to cope that way."

"She was never the same. Never Momma again. It hurt. It *totally* hurt."

"I understand."

So much hurt for one so young. So much emotion and anguish.

It just didn't seem fair.

My mortal life had been spent focused on my software business, acquiring money and independence. I'd been married twice and had a slew of ex-girlfriends and business acquaintances. I knew people everywhere.

But now that I was finally able to look back on my life, I realized that I never really actually *cared* about anyone.

Until now.

I didn't know why Sierra had become so important or special to me.

It made me wonder if it was because of her vulnerability, her loneliness. The bad breaks she'd been dealt. Or maybe a strong sense of guilt on my part for enjoying the childhood she never had and would never have.

178

I couldn't forget why I was attracted to her the first time I saw her. I'd seen myself in her as she plodded down the road, alone and depressed. In my own case, I'd felt sorry for myself because I had no glove. I had a home, two parents who loved me and security, yet I felt sorry for myself.

It never occurred to me back then that if my parents had split up, I would have had a legitimate reason to experience genuine self-pity.

But it occurred to me right now. And I knew right then that if I wanted to help Sierra, I had to start right at the source.

"You want to live," I told her.

"Why?"

"You were given life. The least you can do is live it."

"But—"

"Let's stop this arguing and just go on in there. Once we get rid of Jenna, you'll have a place to stay for the night."

"Then what?"

"What do you mean? I've got a nice bed in there—"

She started.

"*Now* what's wrong?"

A shrug.

"What're you worried about? I'm dead. Doesn't the fact that you can't see me tell you anything?"

"I'm not thinking of that."

"What's bothering you, then?"

"I can't see you."

"That's because I'm dead."

"You can see *me*."

179

"Okay..."

"I would like to take a shower..."

"I've got a shower in there. A tub, toilet, sink—all the modern conveniences."

"What about privacy?"

"It's got a door as well."

She frowned. "You see through doors."

Suddenly she'd turned back to being a young, impressionable, vulnerable little girl. One with real fears and anxieties. If I'd been able to, I would've hugged her and told her not to be afraid.

"You'll be okay. I promise."

She didn't reply, but I could still see the doubt in her eyes.

"I wasn't a peeping Tom when I was alive. Why would I change when I'm dead?"

"'Cause maybe you can?"

"I promise I won't sneak into the john, okay?"

"Really?"

"Really."

"But...you're still a guy. Sorta."

"And?"

She shrugged. "Guys. You know. "

"I'm a spirit. I have no body."

"But you're still a guy."

"Without a body."

"You don't...don't still..." She pointed to the spot where my crotch would be.

"Don't still what?"

"You know."

"Yeah, I know. And no. I don't."

"Bummer."

"I'm getting used to it. But listen...even if I did, I wouldn't try anything with you."

"Why not?"

"You're a kid."

"You don't think I'm hot?"

"Maybe. For a kid... If I was another kid. A live kid."

She didn't say anything.

"Look at this." I made my arm appear, then reached out to her. My hand went right for her breast, then disappeared. "How's that?"

"How's what?"

"Feel that?"

"Feel what?"

My arm disappeared. "That ought to make you feel less apprehensive."

"Does that mean afraid?"

"Basically."

"All right. So you can't cop a feel. But what about the lady in there? You still haven't told me what you want me to do."

"Why don't you just knock on the door and we'll take it from there?"

"But you're not gonna do the scare thing?"

"I don't know yet. Let's see what happens, okay?"

"You didn't change your mind, did you?"

"I'm more interested in finding you a place to stay for the night. We can't do that as long as Jenna's in there."

"Can I do a number on her?"

"What sort of number?"

181

She shrugged. "I can probably totally freak her out."

"Do what feels right, okay? Don't go overboard."

"Why not?"

"We don't want to put her in a coma."

"Why not?"

Good point. "Let's take it nice and easy for a while first. If she gets us riled up, the coma thing might just be the way to go. But not right away. And just remember, I'll be right here with you."

"Gotcha."

"One other thing."

"What's that?"

"You're wrong about Jenna."

"Whaddya mean?"

"She's no lady."

***

A tall, thin guy around forty opened my door.

He wore dark blue shorts and a white sleeveless tank top and appeared tennis-fit. His thinning light-brown hair, combed straight back from his high forehead, accentuated a near-perfect line of hair transplants. He held a drink in one hand, a cigarette in the other. He looked Sierra over curiously, then raised one thick sandy brow. "Yes?"

"I came to see the lady," Sierra said.

"Are you selling something? It's kind of late for that."

"I'm a friend of Jake's."

"Jake?"

"He just got killed the other day. He used to live here."

He turned sharply around. "Jen? Someone to see you, says she's a friend of Jake's."

Jenna, fashionably slender as ever, came down the hall tugging the robe of the red terrycloth housecoat I'd bought her two Christmases ago. Before she closed it I could see the laced pink bra and sheer panties she had on.

I also caught a glimpse of a rose tattoo covering the top of her left silicone breast.

A small diamond stud pierced the left side of her nose as well as a larger one at the end of her left eyebrow.

She knew I hated studs and tattoos. She'd probably had these done before our divorce was even finalized. I was glad she was able to spread her wings—or whatever else—and do what she wanted once she no longer had to worry about my approval.

She stopped just a few feet from the doorway, making the guy beside her back away to give her center stage. Her slender arms were folded beneath her perfect breasts. She studied Sierra as a scientist examines something interesting in the lab. Jenna had always been the suspicious type. Right now she was trying to decide why a thirteen-year-old girl had come here at this time of night.

"What's this about Jake?" She turned to her male companion. "You did say Jake, didn't you?"

The man nodded.

Jenna turned back to Sierra and gave one of her quick shrugs, which had always resembled a nervous twitch. "You knew Jake? What's this about?"

183

I was pleased my ex-wife had calmed down and learned to take things easy since our divorce.

Sierra said, "Jake and me, we were tight."

"Tight? You and Jake? You're just a *kid*, for God's sake." To the guy: "She's just a *kid*."

The man nodded. "I see that."

"How tight?" Jenna asked Sierra.

"I'd do errands for him."

"Errands?"

"Yeah."

"Nothing else?"

Sierra glared. "I'm thirteen. Jake was old. Even older than you."

I wanted to laugh, but knew better. Even so, holding it in presented a major challenge.

Jenna stepped back. She hadn't expected that. Her companion covered his smile with his hand holding the cigarette.

Jenna took a deep breath and recovered. "So…what kind of errands?"

"I'd run down to the store, buy him some magazines. Stuff like that."

"He didn't pay you, did he?"

"Sure did."

Jenna turned to the man. "Jake paid her for errands like that."

"I heard her."

"Jake was stingy with his money," Jenna told Sierra.

"How come he kept giving me some, then?"

Jenna turned to the man. "How about that?"

"Maybe he wasn't as stingy as you thought," the man said.

She glared. "You're an idiot, Ralph." To Sierra: "Why're you here? To tell me what you did for Jake?"

"I thought I'd come over. You know. One last visit."

"Why?"

"He was my bud. I wanted to see his place one last time. Before they sell it to someone else."

Jenna stared at Sierra a few moments, this time to determine if she was speaking the truth. If there were any angles she should know about. She finally said, "C'mon in."

Sierra stepped inside.

Ralph closed the door, went over to the couch and sat. He flicked some cigarette ash in the glass ashtray on the end table and drank some of his drink.

I wanted to pick up the ashtray and sprinkle the ashes on his transplants. The added gray flecks would give him a more distinguished look.

"How long did you know Jake?" Jenna asked.

"Couple months. My mom and me, we moved here."

"You *live* here?" Jenna wrinkled her nose as if something foul had drifted past.

Times like these forced me to remind myself why I'd married her.

The answer never took very long.

Being a damned good stripper, looking flashy and turning heads is important to a man. But just because a woman looks great and can pull chrome from a fender doesn't mean she'd make a good soul mate.

185

Jenna didn't even have a soul.

"Momma and me…we moved in about three months ago."

Sierra was good. Everything flowed out of her mouth smoothly, as if she actually was speaking the truth. I was proud of her.

I was also sad for her. Being able to lie so easily was never a good thing.

But when you were forced to live in such a horrible environment, you used whatever means necessary to survive.

Jenna went over to the wet bar and fixed herself a Scotch rocks. Ralph had been guzzling my bourbon. They didn't know it, of course, but they were lucky I was dead. Otherwise, I would've strangled them both. Not only for sucking down my booze but also for conning themselves into my place and making themselves at home.

Jenna brought her drink over to the couch and sat on the other end. She put her glass on the end table. Neither invited Jenna to sit down.

"Your mother." Jenna lit a cigarette and blew the smoke toward Sierra. "What's she do?"

"Huh?"

Jenna gave another of her quick shrugs. "As in work? A job? In some cases, even, a career? Things people do when they become adults and go off on their own. You know, to pay the bills. You'll learn stuff like that when you're older. What's your mother do?"

Ralph smiled at the battery of insults.

It made me want to gouge out their eyeballs and drop them in their drinks.

"Nothing," Sierra said.

"Nothing?" Jenna wrinkled her nose again. "She just sits around? Does nothing? Collects Welfare checks? Isn't this place a little ritzy for that?"

"Momma doesn't have to work. She won the Lottery. The Power Ball."

I couldn't help smiling. It wouldn't take long for the fireworks to begin.

Ralph's smile vanished. His gaunt cheeks turned bone-white.

Jenna coughed out a small gray knot of cigarette smoke. "Power Ball? She win it here?"

"Ohio."

"Ohio?" Jenna turned to Ralph and scowled. "Ohio."

"I've heard it's pretty big up there."

"We moved here right after we won. Momma said she always wanted to live in Florida. She's got this cough, this really gross sinus thing. It gets totally funky when she—"

"The Power Ball?" Jenna obviously liked saying it. She was probably already calculating. The sounds of the gears grinding in that beautiful, demented skull were almost audible. It took her a few moments to collect herself. She needed a big belt of her drink and a deep drag of her cigarette to help settle her. Then she sighed and cleared her throat. "How much...that is, how much did she...how much *was* it?"

"A lot."

"How much is a lot? Thirty, forty million?"

"Ninety."

187

Jenna gasped. Ralph coughed.

Jenna shook herself out of it. She took another healthy swallow of her drink. Then, just as I expected, the *on* switch of her charm came on full. Her smile dazzled the room.

"Have a seat," she said, gesturing to the armchair.

***

Sierra cautiously approached the armchair, watching them as if she expected them to do something. But her smug expression told me she was having fun.

So was I. This was much better than scaring Jenna.

Jenna got up. "You won't mind if Ralph and I leave the room for a minute, would you? We have something to discuss."

Sierra shrugged.

"Just don't touch anything," Jenna warned. Then she and Ralph went down the hall. The sound of a door slamming echoed, making one of my small winter scenes twitch on the living room wall.

"You around?" Sierra whispered.

"Right here," I said.

"Why'd she tell me not to touch anything? This isn't even her place."

"That's just how she is."

"Whaddya think they're doing in there?"

"She's probably having a frantic discussion with Ralph about how to spend your Power Ball money."

"How's she figure she can get someone else's money?"

188

"She's done it before."

"We're not even related. She doesn't even know me."

"You're not giving her enough credit."

"Why'd you marry her?"

I just sighed.

"Gives good head, huh?"

"That's no way for a thirteen-year-old to talk."

"Is it true?"

"Yeah."

Sierra shook her head. "Guys sure are dumb."

"That's the way you females want us, isn't it?"

"I haven't had much experience with guys yet."

"We'll talk later."

"Ya leaving me here?"

"Just for a few minutes. I've got to find out what's going on in there."

"Don't be long."

"You're not nervous, are you?"

"Sure am. This place is creepy."

"I thought it was a pretty nice, comfortable home."

"Prob'ly was."

"They *are* pretty scary, aren't they?"

"It's not that." She shivered. "A dead guy lived here."

"Save the funny stuff for later." I drifted down the hall and into the last room on the right, which was my bedroom.

Jenna sat on my bed. It was unmade and disheveled. The pillows were scattered, the sheets shoved onto the carpet.

This pissed me off even worse. My ex-wife and her boyfriend going hot and heavy in my bed not long after I died.

How tacky.

"Ninety million," Jenna whispered. If her eyes had grown any larger, they would've popped out of her skull. "Ninety fucking million."

"Even after taxes, that's quite a chunk of change." Ralph sat in my rocker, holding his glass on the polished wooden arm. Water from a wet ring dripped down its side but he didn't notice. Or care.

"Talk to me." She sucked on her cigarette.

"In simple terms, you don't have access to that money, so don't even get yourself worked up about it."

"Why not?"

"You'll make yourself sick again, run out of your meds and I'll have to go out looking for that pervert dealer connection of yours."

"I don't mean *that*, asshole. I meant—"

"The kid's not even a relative. She's just a friend of your dead ex. And quit calling me asshole. I'm a respected attorney."

"I thought you liked that."

"Only when we're having sex. And when you're on top, being nasty."

"Don't go all sensitive on me, now. There's more important stuff at stake here."

"Like I said, that kid was only your ex's friend."

"A good friend."

"She obviously knows you and Jake were divorced."

190

"She'd have to be a moron not to. I mean, we're staying in his place. I'm wearing this housecoat, just my underwear on underneath. It doesn't take a rocket scientist to know we're having sex in his place."

"I'm sure he told that kid about you."

Jenna stared off into space. "She said they were tight."

"You think he told her…everything?"

"You mean our sex life?"

He shrugged.

"She's a kid. Why would he?"

"If they were as tight as she just said…"

She let out another lungful of smoke in a long, slender plume. I could tell she'd already come up with something. "That could actually help us, you know."

"How so?"

"When you're tight with someone, you quite naturally feel guilty when something bad happens."

"Just what're you getting at?"

"We pump her. Get her to talk, find out a few things. How well they liked one another, what they used to do."

"Why so interested?"

"She just doesn't feel right. I don't know if I believe that errand shit. Or about the two of them being tight. Jake never even liked kids."

"Neither do you…"

"So the hell what? Neither of us did—which made our marriage pretty damned uncomplicated. While it lasted, that is. So why would he suddenly buddy up with a trashy kid from Ohio?"

Ralph shrugged. "Maybe they just hit it off."

"I never saw Jake hit it off with anyone. Jake wasn't a nice guy. He was a die-hard taskmaster that stepped on anyone who got in his way while he was running his company. The turnover there was really high. He was a taskmaster at home, too. Bastard pushed me around all the time."

Jenna was an expert at turning the facts around to make herself appear as pitiful as a Holocaust victim.

"Why'd you marry him?"

"I told you. He had a bank account and owned his own company. And he looked good in a suit. Looked good naked, too."

Jenna was never one to mince words.

"What's all this have to do with that little girl out there?"

"The kid's trash—anyone can see that. She's messy and smells like she hasn't showered in weeks. I'll bet her momma's trash as well. She did say they were from Ohio, didn't she?"

Good ol' snobby Jenna...

Ralph scratched his jaw. "I happen to know some nice people from Ohio."

"Really?"

"As odd as it sounds, Jenna, there are nice people in Ohio—just like everywhere else."

"Whatever. But take my word for it. That kid and her mom are trash."

"So?"

"Trash like them wins the Lottery all the time. Then they're flat-broke within a year. You're an attorney..."

192

"A divorce attorney."

"You can provide financial advice, right?"

"But what does that have to do with—"

"Give me half an hour. I'll get that little twit and her momma on our side. Together, we can convince them to sign over their Power Ball money."

"You're not serious."

"Ralph, how long have you known me?"

"Since about a week before I became your divorce attorney."

"Have you ever known me not to be serious about money?"

Chapter 15

Sierra was leaning over one padded arm of the chair so she could stare down the hall. I could tell she was anxious about what was going on in the bedroom.

"I'm back," I whispered as I drew closer.

She jumped up. "Scared the crap outa me!"

"I whispered, didn't I?"

"You're still invisible."

She was right. I had much to learn about sneaking around as a spirit. "That makes sense. Sorry about that."

"What're they talking about in there?"

"Just what I figured. Trying to con you out of your Power Ball money."

"Can they do that?"

"Her boyfriend's an attorney. They're going to try and convince you to let him handle your legal stuff."

"*What* legal stuff? I didn't win the Power Ball. That was just a story. Besides, I'm just a kid."

"It doesn't matter. You've got Jenna's blood up. Once she's grabbed hold of something, she's like a dog with a bone."

She shivered. "This is creeping me out."

The sound of a door clicking open made me stiffen.

"Just keep playing it by ear, like you've been doing."

"By why are we even doing all this?"

"You need a place to stay, don't you?"

They came back in. Jenna looked around. "Who were you talking to?"

Sierra shrugged. "I talk to myself when I'm alone and nervous."

"You nervous?"

"I'm always nervous when I'm with strange people."

"We're not so strange." Jenna took her place on the couch and lit a cigarette. "*You're* the strange one, talking to yourself like that."

"I can even do impressions."

"What kind?"

She shrugged. "Guys."

"Why?"

"They're harder to do."

Jenna shook her head and frowned. "Still sounds weird."

Ralph finished his drink and crossed the room to get a fresh one at the wet bar. If I wasn't dead, I'd make him buy me a brand-new bottle. Good booze isn't cheap.

"So I guess you and your mom are sitting pretty about now," Jenna said.

"Pretty?"

"You're in really good shape."

"Oh. Yeah. You could say that."

"Have you started collecting the money yet?"

"We need to find an attorney. Someone told us that."

Good girl...

Jenna laughed.

"What's up?" Sierra asked.

"Ralph's an attorney."

195

Ralph brought back his glass and sat.

"You're an attorney?"

"For the last fifteen years."

"That's convenient," Jenna said.

"Huh?" Sierra asked.

"You and your momma need an attorney. Ralph could work out a few things for you, make sure you don't get stiffed. Get the tax man off your backs. Right, Ralph?"

"Sure. No problem."

"How much does he charge?"

They both laughed.

Jenna winked at him. "Ninety million and she wants to know how much you charge."

Smiling, Ralph drank more of his drink.

"Why's that funny?" Sierra asked.

"Baby, with *that* much lettuce, you can afford O.J. Simpson's entire legal team."

"Momma wants to find her own attorney."

The laughing stopped.

"What?" Jenna asked.

"It's Jake's idea."

Jenna sat up in her seat. "What the hell's Jake have to do with your winning the Power Ball?"

"Well, when we were hanging out, he'd tell me a few things."

"Like what?"

"About life and other things you should know when you're grown up."

"Now why would he tell you about things like that?"

"When Momma and me came down here, Jake was the first guy we met. Momma thought I should do odd jobs—"

"Even with all that money?"

"Momma wants me to learn responsibility. She doesn't want me to, you know, get in with the wrong crowd. Do drugs and all that other stuff."

"Wasn't that considerate of Jake?" Jenna wasn't smiling.

"One day he told me he had to go somewhere for a few days on business. He mentioned Miami."

"Probably one of his stupid conventions."

"Anyway, he paid me to take care of his place. I picked up his mail—stuff like that. I guess he sorta liked me, so when he came back he asked me to do other stuff. I came over one Saturday when he was washing his car and helped him. We talked a lot that day. He told me all about dishonest people and what they'd do for money, how they hurt one another—"

"*Jake* told you that stuff?"

Sierra nodded.

"Jake *Mild*?"

"Jake was smart."

"Girl, Jake knew about dishonest people because he was one of the most dishonest assholes I ever met." Jenna said it calmly—as though she'd just said something about the garbage man coming in the morning.

I wanted to kill her.

Sierra sat there in tense silence. I had no idea what she'd say. I hoped she wouldn't totally believe Jenna. In business, I'd been forced to be dishonest because I dealt with dishonest people all the time. I

197

didn't like it, but it's the way things are done everywhere. People who deal with you always have an impressive story to tell. They exaggerate, color things, omit details they don't want known and lie about their contacts, their assets and their lifestyles. Everyone does it nowadays. If you don't, you don't get anywhere.

I just hoped Sierra would consider how I'd been treating her and sum up Jenna's evaluation as resentment from someone with an axe to grind.

But I knew that would be difficult for a thirteen-year-old. Even someone with Sierra's world-weary experience.

Sierra sat back and shrugged. "I don't care."

"How's that?" Jenna asked.

"I don't care what you say. Jake was good to me. A good friend."

"Kid, you're young. You don't know about life yet. You haven't—"

"I don't know you, either. But I knew Jake and he was cool. Even saved my life a couple times."

I moved closer to Sierra. I wanted to tell her to cool it. Her story was becoming a little too involved. At this rate, Jenna would see through it.

"He…saved your life?"

"He looked out for me when I needed help. I was mixed up with the wrong crowd…at school. Even got beat up and pushed around. Jake told me what might happen and what I oughta do to get away. I listened to him. So I don't care what you say."

198

I was very touched. I didn't know if she realized it but she'd just told me what I'd done for her and how much she appreciated it.

"Kid, I was married to him. For three long years."

Actually, it was only two years and eight months, but that didn't really matter.

"That's why I don't trust you," Sierra said.

"What?"

"You're mad at him. You'll say stuff to make him look bad." Sierra got up. "I'm leaving."

"Listen. Kid." Jenna jumped up. She didn't want the vision of ninety million bills dancing in her head to vanish right out the front door. "You don't have to go."

"Don't wanna stay if you're gonna diss Jake. He's dead. Can't defend himself."

"You're right. I was way out of line. Ralph and I both were. Sorry. Listen...since you're leaving... Why not call your mom? We'd like to meet her."

"Why?"

"As I said before, Ralph's an attorney. You'll need one. Anyone who wins the Lottery needs a good attorney."

"Is he good?" Sierra asked.

Jenna smiled. "Ralph's the best attorney there is. He can smell a loophole a mile away."

"Momma's out of town right now. She's visiting her relatives in Dayton. Won't be back for a few days."

"She left you by yourself?"

"I can take care of myself."

"By the way, why'd you really stop by?"

199

"I told you. I wanted to—"

"That's the only reason? To come here one last time?"

"There was another one, but you wouldn't be interested." Sierra turned back to the door.

"C'mon, now. You can tell us."

"Jake was seeing someone. I saw the strange car, so I came over to see if it was her."

Jenna and Ralph exchanged curious looks.

Jenna said, "Tell us about his new girlfriend."

"Jake was really stuck on her. I figured she'd be the one he'd leave everything to. I came over to see if she stopped by to pick up some of her stuff. Jake said she sold jewelry."

Jenna's face tensed at the last word. "Jake didn't even *like* jewelry."

"He liked the stuff she gave him."

An immediate sparkle blazed in Jenna's blue eyes. "Good stuff?"

Sierra nodded.

Jenna's look of total skepticism told me she'd been over my place with a fine-tooth comb. "You *sure* he kept the stuff he got from her?"

"He told me he did."

"He say where?"

"Not really."

"If you two were so tight, how come he didn't tell you?"

"I never asked him about, you know, personal stuff."

"How come I don't know about this? Ralph and I are taking over Jake's estate—that is, what there is of it."

200

"You and Jake, you're divorced."

"So?"

"Then why're you here?"

"We...pulled strings. Jake had no next of kin, and since I was recently married to him, Probate considered me the logical—"

"Jake told me he didn't even like you.'

"What?"

"He said your divorce was bad."

Jenna stiffened. "Our divorce was very amicable. In fact—"

"Then why didn't he like you?"

"Jake, he was funny about things." Jenna glanced at Ralph. "He was angry with me for divorcing him. Why else would he say something like that?"

Sierra shrugged. "Maybe you weren't as nice to him as he thought."

"Kid, you don't know what you're talking about."

"I only know what Jake told me." Sierra turned back to the door.

"Let us know if you and your mother want to talk to Ralph. Like I said, he can give you all sorts of great financial advice—"

"Can he give us the name of another attorney?"

Jenna practically choked on her drink. She cleared her throat. "If that's what you'd like. Right, Ralph?"

Ralph fidgeted. "I've got...tons of contacts."

"I'll talk to Momma when she gets back."

Outside, Sierra went down the steps and kept walking toward the recreation hall. "You there?" she whispered.

"Keep looking straight ahead," I whispered back. "Jenna's watching from the living room window."

"What'll we do now? I didn't want to come right out and ask if I could spend the night. I don't like her. She's a total bitch."

"She is. But watch your language. You're just a kid."

"I'm getting tired. I wanna lie down and sleep forever. It's been a really…a really long, bummer of a day." She sighed. "But at least our little visit helped."

"Helped?"

"It…kept me from thinking."

"Thinking?"

"About Momma."

I couldn't reply at first. The realization of what she'd just said hit me hard. She was truly one strong, resilient young lady.

"Give me a few minutes and those two will be long gone."

"What'll you do?"

"I intend to scare the living shit out of them."

"That's what I wanted you to do in the first place."

"I know."

"Then why didn't you do it?"

I didn't want to tell her that I didn't want to put her through any more stress. Even so, I was looking forward to unleashing my new powers. "I wanted to find out a few things first," I said.

"Like what they're doing here?"

"Among other things."

"Think you can scare them? She's pretty scary herself."

"If you can't scare someone when you're dead, you're in pretty bad shape."

"How can you be in any shape at all when you're dead?"

"Figure of speech."

"You sure say that a lot."

"Sometimes I tend to be boring."

"Just sometimes?"

As I said before, I didn't really care for smartasses.

Chapter 16

To my relief, the rec room was deserted.

At this time of night, only a few of the younger residents or relatives of the older residents would come in occasionally to play pool, ping pong or video games.

Sierra rushed right over to one of the couches against the window overlooking the well-lit pool. She propped up a pillow, then stretched out.

"Don't get too comfortable," I said. "I won't be gone long."

She propped up on an elbow. "Sure this'll be okay?" She glanced around the large dimly-lit room.

"No problem."

"I'll freak if I see another dude with a gun."

"The guards aren't allowed to carry guns."

"How come?"

"The Association's afraid of lawsuits."

"Huh?"

"They're afraid the guards will accidentally shoot one of the residents."

"Must be old."

"Even older than me."

"Wow..."

"Don't be a smartass. Now listen. You'll be okay. If anyone comes in, no one'll even ask who you are."

"You sure?"

"There are too many people in this complex to keep track of. You're my guest."

"So…if someone comes in and asks who I am, I can tell them I'm visiting a dead guy who used to live here?"

"Um, I don't think that would be a good idea."

"No?"

"You should try and adjust your wording a little if you want them to go away."

"It's the truth, isn't it?"

"Actually, it's a little *too* truthful for most people to grasp, if you get my drift."

"I shouldn't say anything, then?"

"Just relax. I'll be back as soon as the apartment's empty."

"Don't be long, okay?" She suddenly looked frightened.

I didn't want to leave her. After all she'd been through, her being alone in a strange place wouldn't help. I considered staying with her rather than return to the apartment.

But Jenna and her boyfriend had to get out. In my present mood, it wouldn't take me very long to get rid of them. "I'll be back as soon as I can."

***

Ralph and Jenna were in my bedroom, arguing, when I got back. I could hear her agitated voice long as soon as I drifted in through the front door.

"There's no girlfriend. I'll bet money on it." Jenna posed in front of the mirror in her bra and panties, admiring herself as always. She arranged her hair neatly over each shoulder, pushing it in one direction. She patted the skin under her chin to test its tautness and frowned. I could see another facelift in her immediate future. Then, sighing, she turned

205

away and sat on the edge of my bed. "Nope. No girlfriend."

"How can you be so sure?" Ralph, in his tighty-whities, slipped into bed.

"Just a hunch. A really strong hunch."

"Jake wasn't a bad-looking guy. You even said so yourself."

"He was just too hung up with work to bother looking for another female so soon after our divorce."

"He could've met someone at a convention."

"Let's get one thing straight. I don't believe much of what that kid said. She sounded like a con artist to me."

"Why'd she even come here?"

"How the hell should *I* know? For all we know, Jake was banging her."

Ralph frowned. "She's a kid."

"Jake was an asshole. How many times do I have to tell you that?"

"But…a kid?"

"Didn't I tell you some of the disgusting crap that man used to do to me? How kinky he got? Especially after watching those disgusting porno flicks he rented on weekends?"

Jenna was the one who'd picked up the porno flicks on her way home from shopping on the weekends. She said the movies excited her, made her feel uninhibited.

"You told me he liked bondage flicks."

She groaned. "Every time I turned around, that jerk was forcing me down on the bed, tying me up and ravaging me."

Jenna was the one who insisted on being tied up. She enjoyed being manhandled—even liked being slapped and spanked. It made her feel like a "bad girl."

"You told me you liked that," Ralph said.

"Taking his side now?"

"Just trying to make sense of this. You never told me he liked little girls."

"I had no idea what he liked. He was pretty messed-up. Just like those other weirdos he worked with."

"Then why'd you put up with him?"

"He owned a software company, for God's sake. It was worth more than five mill back then. We had a nice place, too. I had all the clothes I could ever want and went to dress-up gigs with him all the time. We went to the finest restaurants. Hell, if he wanted to strap me down six or seven times a week and feed it to me while I was totally naked and helpless, why shouldn't I let him?"

Jenna had demanded kinky sex nearly every day. If I didn't express an interest, she suspected me of cheating on her.

Ralph blinked. "Six or seven times a week?"

"Sometimes more. Why?"

Ralph scratched the back of his neck. "You must not have minded very much."

"Like I said, he was worth more than five mill. Besides, the sex was pretty damned good."

"Then why bring it up? If he was kinky and you liked it as well—"

"I was humoring him, dammit."

207

Jenna had a strange way of remembering the past.

"How come we never do that?" Ralph said suddenly.

"Let's talk about that later, okay? I've got other things on my mind much more important than half an hour of rough sex."

"Half an hour?" Ralph's eyes filled the sockets.

She scowled. "You having trouble hearing?"

Ralph thought this over. "Tell me why you divorced this guy again?"

"You trying to be funny?"

"Like I said before, I'm having trouble making sense out of this."

"Don't bother. Jake's dead. Now we've got other things to consider."

"Like that Power Ball business?"

"Something about that kid really bothers me."

He shrugged. "She's a street kid. They all act like that these days. She didn't mention a father. I'll bet there isn't one in the picture. Broken families have been the norm for a couple of decades, now. A broken home messes up kids. That's why they're smoking, doing drugs and having sex by the time they're twelve."

"That's not what's bothering me about her."

"What is it? The Power Ball? Or the fact that she seems to know so much about Jake?"

"Both." Jenna lit a cigarette and lay down with her back against the pillows. "I just can't see Jake doing the buddy routine with any female. Especially a kid."

"Why?"

"Jake never could treat a woman like a human being. She always turns into a sex object. And he hates kids. Always has."

"I take it that's why you never had any."

"I never wanted any, either."

"Then why even bring this up?"

She shot him a glare. "Would *you* like gaining forty pounds and waddling around for nine months, bloated and ugly, throwing up every damned morning?"

"It wouldn't exactly be something I'd dream about."

"Besides, Jake was always busy working. He didn't have the time to help me bring up a child. I would've had to raise the damned thing myself." She puffed on her cigarette. "No, something's definitely wrong about all this."

"What do you suggest?"

"Tomorrow morning I wanna see the complex manager and find out if that kid even lives here. I have a feeling she was lying to us."

"About what? Living here? The girlfriend? Or the Power Ball?"

"Everything."

"What if she was?"

She shrugged. "I intend to find out why."

"What difference does it make?"

"If this kid was somehow involved with Jake, I need to find out about it. She might fuck up my plan."

"She can't do anything to hurt you. I've already told you, I've got all sorts of connections in Orange County. I know three judges. How do you think I managed to get the papers necessary for coming here in the first place? Taking over his—"

"I know, I know. But if you don't mind, I need to find out about this first. It'll bug the tits off me if I don't."

"Wouldn't want *that*."

"What the hell's *that* supposed to mean?"

"Nothing." He grinned sheepishly. "Just that I wouldn't want anything to happen to those beauties…"

"Oh, stop it, Ralph. I'm not in the damned mood."

***

I waited about half an hour before making my move.

I had no idea what kind of sleeper Ralph was. However, Jenna slept lightly, so I planned my strategy around her.

I crept over to her side of the bed. When I was just a few inches away, I blew in her face.

Gasping, she sat bolt upright. Then turned to Ralph, who lay beside her, snoring softly into his pillow. "You being funny?"

No response.

"You'd better not be playing games. I told you, I'm not in the damned mood."

Still no response.

Jenna lay back down. "If you didn't have such rich friends," she muttered, "I would've parked your scrawny butt to the curb." She squirmed into a comfortable position and pulled the covers up to her neck.

"That wasn't a nice thing to say," I whispered.

210

"What the—" She instantly shot right back upright. The covers slid back down, exposing her bra and her rose tattoo. "Who the hell…said that?" Twisting around, she squinted at Ralph, then swatted him on the shoulder.

He sputtered, pushing himself up on an elbow. "W-What's wrong?"

"You didn't hear that?"

"Hear what? I was sleeping."

"Someone's here."

"What?"

Jenna groaned. "Dammit, someone's in this room." She groped for the light on the nightstand and switched it on, nearly knocking it over.

Ralph sat up and shielded his eyes with a forearm.

Jenna nervously peered around the room. When she reached the area where I was, I summoned my energy for a brief appearance.

I smiled pleasantly, then winked.

"Jesus God!" She rolled over Ralph, driving a surprised gasp from him. She fell over the edge of the bed and thumped to the floor. Scrambling back up, she peered over his sheet-covered form.

"*Now* what's wrong?" he asked. "Why the hell'd you do that?"

"You didn't see that?"

"See what? Jen, what's going on?"

"He was there."

"Who?"

"Jake."

"Who?"

"Jake, you idiot."

211

"You don't mean—"

"Yes, dammit. I mean Jake. My ex-husband. He's standing there."

"Where?"

She pointed to the opposite wall. "There. Right there."

"Your ex-husband...he's *standing* there?"

"That's what I said."

"Jen, Jake's...dead."

"Tell me something I don't know, brainiac."

"C'mon, now. You're having a bad dream. It's probably because of that kid. Or because you're in his apartment, sleeping in his bed."

"Jake was standing right over there, bigger than shit."

"What was he doing?"

"Standing there, you idiot. Smiling. Even winked, for God's sake."

"He...winked?"

"I just said he did."

"You're sure?"

"I know what a damned wink is, thanks very much."

Ralph scratched the back of his neck. "He smiled and winked."

"Yeah. Smiled and winked. I'm *so* glad you're paying attention."

"I didn't see him."

"But I did."

"Listen...you're just overwrought. I think—"

"Of course I'm overwrought. I just saw my dead ex-husband. Wouldn't you be overwrought if you just saw your dead ex-husband?"

Ralph blinked.

"You know what I mean, dammit."

"He'd dead, but he appeared right over there, smiling and winking..."

"You think I'm crazy."

"No I don't."

"I see it in your eyes."

"Listen, Jen—"

"Jake's in this room, dammit."

"Now why would your ex-husband come back from the dead? Give me one good reason why he'd come back. And while you're at it, tell me how he could come back. He's dead."

"I have no idea. But he's here. In this room."

"Even if he *did* come back, why would he come here?"

"How would *I* know? Maybe he came back for his stuff."

"Why would he need his stuff? He's dead. You don't need anything when you're dead. Get real, Jen."

"How should I know why he came back?"

"Maybe I just want to make sure you two don't steal anything while you're here," I said.

They both froze.

I showed myself again, this time longer. "Or maybe I came back just for old time's sake. But when I saw you both here, making yourselves at home, it kind of set me off—know what I mean? So I decided to stick around long enough to make sure you can find your way back out."

Jenna's jaw dropped. "J-J-*Jake*?"

"You remembered me. I'm touched."

213

Without taking her eyes off me, she whispered, "R-Ralph? S-S-See him? Tell me you see him. Please? Don't tell me you don't see him. I'll go absolutely nuts if you tell me you don't see him. Please tell me I'm not…seeing things."

Ralph's lower lip quivered. He couldn't take his eyes off me. I truly enjoyed the sensation. "I…s-see him, Jen."

"You're not just saying that?"

"Believe me. I see him." Ralph's lip continued to quiver. He swallowed noisily. "O-Over there? In front of the…the closet?"

Jenna nodded. "Uh-huh…there…the closet… Right there…"

"Y-Yeah… I…I see him…"

Turning invisible, I crossed the room and stood behind the rocker. After a few moments, I showed myself again. "Now I'm over here."

A tiny mouse-like squeak trickled out of Jenna's gaping mouth. She bit her lower lip. Her face paled instantly.

"What are you doing here, Jenna?" I asked.

She backed up, nearly tripping. Her bulging eyes stayed on me. She groped for her clothes, gawking at me as she pulled them on. Her jaw rested on her breastbone.

"You really shouldn't be here, you know."

She slipped her tennis shoe on the wrong foot, then fumbled to get it on right.

"We're divorced. You're not entitled to anything that belongs to me. I'm surprised your boy-toy attorney here went along with you on this."

Ralph pulled on his shorts and tank top, his gaze on me all the while. He hurriedly slipped on his tennies but didn't lace them.

"I should demand that you make my bed before you leave," I said. "But you probably wouldn't do a very good job, would you?"

Ralph didn't reply. Still staring at me, he grabbed his suitcase from the metal stand in front of the window. Gripping it clumsily in front of him, he sidestepped on his way to the open doorway. A tiny "excuse me" escaped his lips as he eased his long, trembling frame out into the hall.

I heard him bumping into the wall and knocking over something out in the living room.

"This was extremely tacky, Jenna," I said. "Even for you." I clucked. "Shacking up with your boyfriend in your dead ex-husband's place. You should be ashamed."

Jenna managed a soft, low-pitched moan. She snatched up her suitcase, overnight bag and handbag and tiptoed past, keeping as far away from me as possible. Her yellow scarf fell silently to the carpet. She didn't notice.

"You dropped your scarf."

She froze, gulped, and looked down at her feet.

"You wouldn't want me to hand it to you, would you?"

She muttered a soft, incomprehensible reply. With shaking fingers, she picked it up, dropped it, picked it up again, then resumed her arduous journey to the open doorway.

The slamming of the front door shook the walls.

The roar of the Camaro outside broke the silence.

***

Sierra was sound asleep when I went back for her.

I hated to wake her but didn't want her to spend the entire night out in the rec hall. Our Security wasn't exactly a well-structured operation. The guards were supposed to make their rounds every hour but on a good day managed one or two walk-throughs each night. I didn't want them stumbling on Sierra, waking her and asking questions.

But even if the guards didn't come in, the oldsters usually showed up early in the morning for their daily card games, pool, ping pong and gossip sessions. Sierra had been subjected to more than enough trauma for one day.

Since she was dozing so soundly, I suspected she wouldn't freak as badly if she saw me, rather than just hearing my voice.

Gathering my strength, I showed myself, then bent over the couch. "Sierra?"

She turned over and rubbed her eyes. "Hey…"

"Ready to sleep in a *good* bed?"

She looked me over. "You're all there."

"As much of me as I could find."

"Did you *do* them? Your ex and the dude with the funky hair?"

"They're gone."

She yawned and sat up. "How'd you do it?"

"I used my charm."

She pushed her hair out of her eyes and smiled. "Scared the shit out of 'em, huh?"

216

"Damned straight. And watch your language."

"Only if you watch yours."

"I'm dead. I don't have to watch anything anymore."

"Not fair."

"You wanna be dead?"

She sighed. "Sometimes, especially lately—"

"Don't even go there. Come on. You need to get to bed."

***

While Sierra slept soundly in my bed, I hung around in the living room, feeling as if I'd just been dropped off in some stranger's home.

I didn't know why I should feel this way. This was my own place. My sanctuary. I'd been living here several years, had shared this apartment with two wives and several girlfriends. This place had a history, a personality. I remembered where I'd bought the couch, the recliner. When the deliverymen had brought them in. What I'd been doing when they rang the doorbell.

I remembered the winter scenes I'd picked up at the Winter Park Art Show several years ago. The artists I bought them from. The conversations we had.

But now everything felt strange. Unfamiliar.

Worse, I felt like some sort of voyeur. As if I'd broken into someone else's home and was walking around, taking inventory.

I shouldn't feel this way. Not at all. But I did. Possibly because I was no longer the person who lived here.

217

My life had ended here. And when my life ended, my connection to this apartment and everything in it had been broken.

The situation was extremely daunting. I was back home but could no longer stay here. This place now belonged to the living.

And it would be the living who'd force me away.

Who knew what Jenna and her boyfriend would do after our last encounter? Knowing her as I did, she'd milk this for all it was worth.

I could imagine the headlines in the papers once Jenna's busy mouth had done its damage:

LOCAL HAUNTING IN WINTER PARK

She'd turn the complex into a freak show— maybe even a tourist attraction. With Ralph's legal help, she'd purchase the condo herself and hire people to conduct daily tours. And when the excitement caught on, she and her boyfriend would pull in droves of wide-eyed thrill-seekers and bask in luxury. My belongings would become souvenirs bringing high prices to fortune hunters. And once the novelty had worn off and they'd accumulated as much wealth as possible, they'd sell what was left on eBay.

Movies like *Beetlejuice* and *The Canterville Ghost* came to mind, and I was suddenly extremely angry with myself for doing what I did in the bedroom.

But my actions had been necessary. Sierra needed comfort for the night. I'd gotten rid of them

218

but knew they'd be back. And they wouldn't return alone.

The world was filled with fanatics and all sorts of crazies. Ghost hunters and paranormal freaks abounded. So did thrill-seekers, adrenaline junkies, death-mongers, groupies, souvenir hunters—every conceivable form of weirdo.

No matter how much I justified my actions, I realized that in chasing Jenna away, I'd done the worst thing imaginable.

I shouldn't even care. Once I'd found the best way to help Sierra, we'd both be long gone.

I decided to wait until she'd awakened, then ask her to check my apartment, from top to bottom. I kept my important papers in my filing cabinet in the spare bedroom. In it, I kept my will, stock portfolio and other legal forms.

My checkbook lay in the top drawer of my desk. The last time I checked, my bank balance hovered just above the five-thousand range.

Once Sierra and I found what we needed, I'd find some way of getting her money. Once she had it in her pocket, we could make plans. I didn't know what these plans were, but I was determined to figure out something.

I'd been moving blindly since I'd stepped out of my grave. Those spirits I'd bumped into at the cemetery hadn't given me a clue. Neither did the dead lady harassing the customers in Walmart.

Many other spirits were wandering around even though I hadn't come across them yet. I had no idea where everyone had gone.

But there had to be someone who could give me answers. Someone wandering around this planet had to know something…

And until some greater power appeared and personally told me where I needed to be, I was going to stay close to Sierra and see this thing through.

My television sat on the table in front of the picture window. I wanted to turn it on but quickly realized I no longer had the substance necessary to manage such simple functions.

Depression instantly set in.

I was dead. A spirit. No longer among the living. Lacking a body. And, most important of all, an index finger necessary to operate the remote.

Stop this. Remember what you've done since you came back.

Yes. I'd done quite a bit. I'd scared off three spaced-out morons in a TransAm. I'd spilled coffee, beer, an entire breakfast table and a sizeable toothbrush display. I'd made a phone ring and even performed a few nasty tricks with lit cigarettes and switchblades.

How difficult could switching on a remote be?

Renewed with a sudden surge of self-confidence, I concentrated on the on/off switch.

The lamp clicked off.

I wasn't concentrating. My mind was had focused on too many things.

I tried again.

Moments later, the microwave beeped.

Damn. This was getting ridiculous.

Once more should do it.

220

The TV, thank God, finally came on. The channel was set for the Home Shopping Network. Jenna, no doubt. She watched that channel religiously and bought many of her outfits and jewelry from it.

I focused on the Movie Channel—

And a Spanish soap came on.

This wasn't going well at all.

Once again. *Focus. Movie Channel*....

Finally, it worked. *Bringing Up Baby*. I recognized the movie instantly. It had always been one of my favorites. Katherine Hepburn dragged around a leopard, chattering away hysterically while Cary Grant, in bottleneck glasses, spent the entire movie wondering what catastrophe was going to befall him next.

It was a funny, crazy movie, but I couldn't concentrate. I was worried about what Jenna and Ralph might be planning to do. Sierra's Power Ball tale, then that bit about my fictitious girlfriend, had undoubtedly vanished into the darkness of Jenna's mind once I'd made my miraculous appearance in my bedroom.

Jenna was probably back at her place. Or Ralph's. No doubt babbling about what happened. I could visualize her drinking and smoking. And pacing. And plotting what to do. She'd be fighting with herself, struggling with my return from the dead and Sierra's fairy tale about winning ninety million dollars.

What should she do? Find out about Sierra's story? Or get someone to find out about me? What would be worth her time? Finding out about a ninety-million-dollar jackpot that might be totally fiction? Or getting qualified professionals who dealt with the occult interested in something that could turn into instant megabucks?

I shouldn't worry about that for now. The important thing was that I'd found Sierra a place to stay.

What I did from this point on was another matter.

Sierra needed a place to live. A home. People to care for her and love her. She deserved such things.

The same things I'd taken for granted while I was growing up.

According to what she'd told Parker and Marla, her father lived in Mississippi or Alabama and hadn't been in the picture for some time.

That was it. The solution to Sierra's situation.

I had to act on this.

And judging by what had happened in my bedroom, I had to act quickly.

Chapter 17

Just before nine o'clock, Sierra came out of my bedroom in her bra and panties, yawning and rubbing her eyes. Her hair was a mess.

"Hey." She looked around. "Here anywhere?"

"Right here," I said from the couch. "And why are you dressed like that?"

"Like what?"

"In your underwear."

"What's wrong with my underwear?"

"You're almost naked."

She shrugged. "No one's here. Who gives a crap?"

"I do."

"You're dead."

"I can see you."

"Can't see *you*..."

I showed myself briefly. "How about now?"

"Doesn't count."

"Why not?"

"You're dead."

"What does that have to do with this?"

"Don't have any parts."

"So?"

"Wouldn't matter anyway. I'm a kid."

"Yeah..."

"And you wouldn't wanna do anything anyway."

"You're right."

"So why're ya freaking out?"

"You're almost naked."

223

"But you can't *do* anything. You told me that yesterday. What's different?"

"Nothing."

"Then why're your panties in a knot?"

I guessed it had something to do with my compulsion to protect her. Judging by her reaction, I was obviously overdoing it. She was right. I was beginning to feel almost like a nervous father on Prom Night, rather than just a self-appointed guardian.

But I couldn't help it.

"I just don't like you walking around almost naked. And don't talk like that."

"Like what?"

"You sound almost like Jenna and Marla. You're too young to sound like that."

"Why so bummed-out this morning?"

"You shouldn't parade around nearly naked in front of a middle-aged man."

"You mean a middle-aged *dead* man?"

"Yes."

"I'm not parading. I'm walking."

"Same thing."

She squared her shoulders, stuck her chin out, raised her head and marched down the hall like a runway model. Then she turned around and came back the same way. "*That's* parading. This is *walking*." She slouched down and shuffled around in a little circle. "See?"

I wanted to laugh. It was a good thing she couldn't see me. My grin would clearly suggest that she'd won the argument.

And she had. With very little effort, she'd completely taken my mind off my hang-up. I knew then that she was more equipped to handle life than I'd been at that age. She'd had no problem manipulating me, and I'd dealt with people nearly all my life.

She knew exactly what she was doing. It made me wonder if she even needed my help in the first place.

"Still there?"

"Still here."

"Why aren't you saying anything?"

"I'm thinking of a good way of asking my next question."

"What question?"

"Where'd you learn to walk like that?"

"The parade thing? Or the walk thing?"

"Guess."

She shrugged. "TV shows. Especially the ones with the Hollywood hotties all dressed up, showing off."

"Doesn't matter. You're still almost naked."

"You're totally weird."

"Go put some clothes on."

"Why?"

"Because it's proper."

"Let me see you."

"Why?"

"Just for a sec."

I showed myself again. "Now what?"

"I want to see your face when I tell you you're going all creepy on me."

"Because I want you to act proper?"

225

"Because you're dead and want me to act proper."

I vanished again. "I guess that *is* creepy."

"Can I have some breakfast? I'm starving. Haven't had anything since that sandwich Marla made."

"I would like you to put something on first, though. It's all right to eat breakfast naked when you're alone, but not when you've got company."

A deep sigh. "I'm not naked."

"You almost are."

"And you're not company. You're dead."

"Humor me, okay?"

"Why?"

"What else do I have?"

She didn't say anything but I could tell by her eyes that she was feeling sorry for me. She suddenly looked confused. "You know what naked is, don'tcha?"

"Of course."

She shrugged. "Figured you forgot. Or wanted to see it again—just to make sure."

"I didn't forget. And I don't need a reminder, thank you. But would you like to know what I'd really like to see?"

"What's that?"

"I'd really like to see you putting on your clothes before you have your breakfast."

She shook her head. "You're scaring me, Jake."

"Hey, I'm scaring myself."

***

When Sierra came out of my bedroom a few minutes later, she wore her jeans and tennies and

226

one of my red tee shirts. It was a little big on her—not bad, since it had shrunk a tad from its last dozen or so trips through the dryer—but looked good anyway. She held out her arms and did a little spin. "Okay now?"

"Much better."

"Okay that I took one of your shirts?"

"I can't wear them anymore, can I?"

"Just making sure."

"It looks good on you."

"You're not gonna freak out again, are you?"

"I think I'm okay for now."

She didn't reply. She was staring at the three rows of hardbacks in the corner hutch. "Those are *all* your books?"

A strange question. "I've got a couple of boxes of paperbacks in my bedroom closet."

"Why aren't they out?"

"No room for them."

"You don't—didn't—read much?"

"Too busy working."

Sierra looked disappointed.

"I didn't know you liked to read."

"I *love* to read. Used to read a *lot*." She sounded angry.

I remembered the paperbacks scattered on the floor of her tree house. It was her only sanctuary. She probably read whenever she wasn't running errands for Santos. I imagined that since working for Santos took up much of her home-study time, it also took up much of her reading time as well.

"What happened?" I asked.

A shrug. "Miguel moved in."

I felt sorry for her all over again. I wanted to ask her what she liked to read but decided against it. It would depress her. Besides, we couldn't stay here very long.

She went into the kitchen.

I was glad Jenna and her boyfriend hadn't had enough time to raid the fridge. I was also glad I'd bought groceries just a couple of days before I died. Since I frequently ate out, I'd never spent much time in supermarkets. I kept the usual staples on hand for breakfasts and snacks—eggs, milk, butter, lunch meat, bread and cheese. And, of course, a few bottles of wine and dark beer.

Sierra opened the fridge. "You want anything?" she asked.

"Don't be funny."

"Just trying to pull you out of your weird."

I switched the channel to a local news station. "I said I'm okay."

Judging by her tone, I guessed she was doing okay under the circumstances. A good night's sleep had done wonders. And the fact that she had me as an ally had obviously lowered her stress level. I hoped I could keep her occupied so she didn't slip back into a serious depression.

Sierra found milk, an onion bagel and a tub of cream cheese. She smeared the bagel with cream cheese, nuked it then brought it and a glass of milk over to the couch. She looked around. "Where are you?"

"Over here," I said from the armchair.

She put down the milk on the coffee table and began nibbling on her bagel. "I didn't want to sit in your lap."

"I don't have a lap anymore."

"Whatever you have, I didn't want to sit on it."

"Now that's weird."

She drank some milk. "No weirder than you not wanting to see me in my underwear."

"I was just being a gentleman."

"You're dead."

"Thanks for sharing."

"You know what I mean. *Shit*." She stiffened on the couch.

"Watch your—"

"Look." She grabbed the remote and turned up the volume.

On the TV, an enlargement of Sierra's face filled the screen.

"Shit." I couldn't believe it.

An attractive brunette in her early thirties sat behind a desk, trying to look both official and glamorous—which I'd always thought ridiculous when I was alive.

But that wasn't what caught my attention now.

"...And St. Cloud police are still looking for thirteen-year-old Sierra Johns, who disappeared right after her mother was found dead in their Virginia Avenue home, the result of a house fire..."

Sierra's photo was then substituted with an inset of her mother.

Sierra put down her bagel. Her eyes welled up.

"I'll turn it off," I said.

She shook her head. "I...have to hear this..."

229

"...Florence Johns, thirty-four, was found dead when St. Cloud firefighters arrived on the scene. Johns, divorced, had been living with Miguel Santos, thirty-one, the last eight months. Santos is also missing. Police think Santos, a rumored local drug dealer, took the little girl following a drug burn. Detectives are conducting an intense investigation into the incident..."

Sierra lowered her head and covered her face with her hands. She'd gone back and found a little more grief to shed.

Knowing it was necessary, I let her. But only for a couple of minutes. We didn't have time for this. Later, if circumstances permitted, I'd let her grieve as much as she wanted.

When I decided she'd had enough, I said, "I know this is difficult, but you've got to focus. Put it somewhere in the back of your mind, in a safe place. Just for a little while. It'll still be there when you go back for it. And if it isn't, you're much better off. We have more important matters we need to concentrate on."

She sniffed and wiped her eyes. "They haven't found Miguel yet?"

I materialized in the armchair. This certainly sounded fishy. "Strange. You wouldn't think Walmart would tolerate abandoned vehicles cluttering up their parking lot. Surely someone was curious enough to have the cops check it out by now."

"Why haven't they, then?"

"I wish I knew."

The newswoman continued: "...St. Cloud detectives arrived on the scene once the fire was under control..."

Parker showed on the split screen, smart and shiny in his pressed blue suit, his sparkling grin playing havoc with the TV cameras.

Sierra gasped, stiffening in her seat.

This interview looked like it was filmed in front of the Courthouse in Kissimmee. Two uniforms strolled by as the female reporter moved in closer for the shot.

The newswoman continued: "Detective Parker Tibbs, Chief of Detectives in the St. Cloud-Kissimmee area, was asked about the progress in this case."

My God. I'd known Parker wasn't an honest cop. I also strongly suspected he was involved in Santos's murder. I just didn't know someone like him could become Chief of Detectives.

"We're doing all we can," he said, his expression quickly shifting to solemn. "We're dealing with drug people, and the safety of a thirteen-year-old little girl is at stake—"

"That asshole kidnapped me," Sierra whispered hotly, her eyes glistening.

"He obviously did it so no one else could get to you." There was no use trying to shield her from harsh reality. She'd already seen entirely too much of it.

"What about that other asshole? The one who wanted to shoot me in the ladies' room."

"He was probably one of Parker's men."

"This totally sucks."

231

Tibbs said, "Once we find out where Santos is, I'm sure we'll find little Sierra."

"Will a reward be issued?" asked the newswoman.

"At the present time, we're uncertain about the details. If we don't find her in the next twenty-four hours, more extreme measures will have to be taken. We regard such matters very seriously."

"Is he for *real*?" she asked.

"I'm afraid so. One thing really disturbs me about all this."

"What's that?"

"He knows about Santos."

"You sure?"

"Positive."

"Why didn't he mention him?"

"A good cop keeps certain details from the public."

"He's not a good cop."

"I'm talking generally."

"Huh?"

"All cops keep as much as they can from the public. It helps them solve cases by letting the bad guys think they've gotten away with something. When the perps are in custody, they slip up by saying the wrong thing."

"Think that's why he didn't mention it?"

"In this case, he didn't mention Santos because he doesn't want the cops knowing about the hit."

"Why not?"

"I strongly suspect Parker was directly involved."

"Figured he was a bad dude."

232

"I had a feeling you knew."

She nodded.

"Did you hear anyone mentioning Marla on that newscast?"

Sierra's eyes grew. "You think she's—"

"Possibly."

"Parker's as creepy as Miguel. Parker just dresses better."

"I'd say that would be a safe assumption."

She tilted her head. "That mean yes?"

"It sure does."

Chapter 18

The local news station presented another report of the incident later on. Still no word on Miguel Santos, but the mention of a possible reward for Sierra's safe return was discussed again.

I visualized crowds clamoring to find her. I sincerely hoped I was worrying over nothing. For one thing, Sierra didn't even attend school. She wouldn't know many people in town. The only people she did know were involved with drugs. Someone into drug trafficking wouldn't volunteer for a reward when his picture could already be posted in police stations and post offices.

I was more concerned about Jenna and Ralph. If either of them had seen the newscasts, Jenna would be back in a heartbeat—even faster if a reward was involved.

I felt even guiltier for bringing Sierra here. The stakes had increased as soon as Jenna had entered the picture. Now I couldn't even provide shelter for Sierra because she couldn't stay here. In addition to the Association working with Probate to get the papers ready to put the condo on the market, I now had to worry about Jenna, Ralph and anyone else the two of them decided to bring into this.

Sierra came out of the bathroom. She'd showered and washed her hair. It looked great. A thick, shiny honey-blonde that covered her shoulders.

She'd put my red tee shirt back on as well as her faded jeans. I didn't know if she had on anything underneath. It would have been nice if

Jenna had left some of her stuff, but that was not an option. Sierra might be able to buy some clothes if Jenna hadn't already gone through my checkbook. Even if she had, I kept some cash in a large pickle jar in a corner of my bedroom closet, behind a pile of old blankets. I probably had about three or four hundred dollars in twenties in the jar. I made a mental note to ask Sierra to take some bills first chance we got.

"Feel better?" I asked.

She ran a hand through a tangle in her hair. "I don't know about your shampoo, though..."

"Your hair looks great—trust me. Come here. We need to talk."

"Where are you?"

I materialized on the couch.

She sat beside me. "About what?"

"Your dad."

"What about him?"

"What happened?"

"Whaddya mean?"

"Why'd he leave?"

She sighed. "Stupid stuff."

"Be more specific."

"I'm not real sure. They never fought when I was around, but I sorta got the idea Mom cheated on him."

"Any idea where he is?"

She shrugged.

"You must know something about where he went."

"I was little when he left, but I heard them both mention Gulfport a couple times."

235

"Mississippi? Right off the Gulf?"

She nodded. "I even got a birthday card from him once. A few months after he split. It was from Gulfport."

"Why there?"

"Shrimp fishing. He always wanted his own boat. His mom was from around there. I think he said he went to school up there somewhere."

"What's his first name?"

"Why?"

"I'm curious."

"It's really weird."

"More information, please."

"Hiram. Everyone called him Hi."

"That helps."

"Helps what?"

"There are probably a thousand Johns' in the phone book. But probably not too many Hiram's."

"You gonna try taking me back to my dad?"

"It might not be that difficult."

"We gonna take your Mustang?"

"Don't be silly."

"It's a cool ride. I can drive."

"I said, don't be silly."

"I'm serious."

"That's what I'm afraid of. But like I said, his first name should narrow down our search. And Gulfport isn't that huge. At least not as big as Orlando or Tampa. If we can just get up there—"

"Why can't I stay here with you?"

"I'm dead."

"No one's perfect."

"Be serious."

236

Her eyes grew, telling me her fear had returned. In spite of her independence, her boldness, it still dominated her. And it didn't take much at all to bring it back.

"We get along, don't we? You're pretty cool...for a dead guy."

"Thanks, but I really don't think that'll go over very well."

"With who?"

"Neighbors. The meter reader. The grocery—especially if I try pushing the cart."

"*I'll* push it."

"Listen. Sierra..."

She turned away. "I just don't think he'll want me."

"How do you know?"

"He hasn't tried to get in touch with me at all."

"He probably has a good reason."

"Bet it's a doozy."

"I can think of one."

"What's that?"

"Your mother."

Her eyes flashed. "Momma was all right before...before she met that...him. Miguel."

"Sierra, I know you love your mother and I'm really sorry about what happened to her. I just can't understand why she made you do errands for drug guys."

"She didn't make me. Miguel made me."

"She should've protected you."

Sierra got up and paced. I could tell she was upset, but she had to know certain things.

"She should have never let him make you do anything that involved—"

"She…couldn't help it."

"Believe me. She could have if she'd wanted to."

She spun around. Her eyes glistened. "What was she supposed to do? Every time she tried arguing with him, he belted her."

"She could've taken you and left."

"She didn't have the money. Besides, Momma had problems."

"What kind of problems?"

"She…she was afraid."

"Of what?"

She shrugged. "Being alone. Not having anyone." She went over to the window and nudged the drapes aside.

"There are certain things a grownup shouldn't expose his child to. One of them is—"

"That bitch."

"Pardon me?"

"Your ex. The one who was here last night?"

"Jenna?"

Sierra continued looking out the window.

"What about her?"

"Her car's out there. In the parking lot across the road."

A knot of heat flared up where the back of my neck used to be. "You sure?"

"Emerald green Camaro."

"Lots of folks have emerald green Camaros."

"She's standing beside it."

238

Dammit... The heat instantly grew into a basketball-sized knot pressing against my spiritual form. "Are you *sure* that's her?"

"That dude's right there with her. The one with the funky hair."

"What're they doing?"

"Talking to a cop."

***

Jenna, wearing one of the many expensive business suits I'd bought her during our marriage, stood beside the Camaro, which was parked in front of the small one-story stucco building marked *Office* two streets down. A cop car sat beside them, its driver facing Jenna. He towered above her, looking bored as she chattered on.

I could only imagine what she was telling him. She'd obviously seen the local news report and had gone into serious overload when the word "reward" was mentioned.

Jenna's senses were expertly tuned in to such details.

"We in trouble?" Sierra asked.

"Probably." I didn't see any reason to hide the truth from her. Particularly when three cops were gathered outside, staring at my apartment and talking to their radios.

"What'll we do?"

"Stay here. I'll be back."

"Leaving again?"

"Back in a flash."

I drifted outside and moved down the walk. I was about to pass the cluster of mailboxes when I paused, looking down at the pavement.

It all came back. The deafening roar, the enormous wall of brilliant heat slamming into me, the coffin I was standing on when I finally came back as a spirit. It had all happened right here. In this very spot.

The rage took hold of me instantly.

The image of Sierra drifted back, and I shook myself out of it.

Now was not the time for such anger. There were much more important things to deal with.

I drifted farther down the road. To my right, another squad car had pulled into the complex. I could also see a third cruiser farther down, parked on the other side of the office, its driver talking to the president of the Association.

Terrific. This would probably reach every news channel in the country. I was surprised CNN hadn't brought their choppers out here yet.

The cop talking to Jenna switched off his radio. "Lady, they just told me no one's seen the Johns girl. We even showed her picture around. The one they used for the news report. The Association said she doesn't live here."

Jenna got behind the wheel of the Camaro and slammed the door shut. She glared at Ralph. "That little bitch lied to us. It's just like I figured. Didn't I tell you that Power Ball story was a crock? And that bull about Jake's girlfriend. Everything that little bitch told us was bullshit."

The cop said, "Well, if she showed up at your dead husband's place—"

"Dead *ex*-husband."

240

"She's got to be around somewhere," Ralph said.

"You did say there was a reward," Jenna said to the cop. "They said something on the news about a reward. A *cash* reward. There's a reward, right? Cash money?"

"It hasn't been confirmed yet," the cop said tiredly. "You asked me that before, lady."

"But the fact that they're considering it tells me—"

"Doesn't mean anything. Not really. I told you that before, as well."

"Then why'd they mention it? They wouldn't have mentioned it if—"

"Who knows why they say anything on the news?" The cop sounded disgusted. Jenna was obviously getting to him just as much as she got to anyone else she decided to pester. "Reporters go for the drama angle. They don't worry too much about getting the facts down when they can milk drama out of the story."

Jenna scowled. "They don't care about facts?"

"Drama gets ratings. That's all the news people care about."

"This does involve an open drug case," Ralph said.

"Yeah." Jenna nodded eagerly. Her excitement level had jumped back up several notches. "An open drug case. Everyone gets really hyper whenever you mention drugs. And when there's a minor involved—"

"Let's just take this one step at a time, okay?" The cop's radio crackled. He snatched it from his shoulder. "Copy?" More crackle. "Gotcha." He switched it back off. "Someone said they saw a young girl sleeping in the rec room last night."

Damn. One of the older residents suffering from insomnia probably spotted her in the window when he was walking by.

"What was she doing there?" Jenna asked.

"Sleeping." The cop frowned.

"That's not what I meant." Jenna sighed impatiently. "I meant, why was she sleeping in that rec room right after she visited us to feed us a cock-and-bull story about the Power ball?"

"Maybe she did know Jake," Ralph said.

"What's that have to do with anything? This whole thing is weird."

The cop said, "We'll be going into your dead husband's condo—"

"*Ex*-husband."

He sighed. "We'll be going in there to check things out, make sure she's not there. You'd better stay here."

"No problem," Jenna said. She and Ralph exchanged nervous glances. "You won't catch us anywhere *near* that damned condo."

***

Sierra was still peering through the living room drapes when I got back.

"Bad news," I said.

She jumped and spun around. "Damn, I wish you wouldn't do that."

"Sorry. Can't show myself for a while."

"What's going on?"

242

"Cops are on their way. We've got to get you out."

"There's only one door."

"Two, actually."

"There's a back door?"

"They both open to the front."

"Bummer."

"I didn't design the place."

"Not what I meant." She turned back to the drapes. "Guess what? They're on their way."

Two cops crossed the street on their way over. One of them spoke to his radio as he walked. The cop who'd been talking to Jenna stared approvingly at my Mustang.

"So now what?" Sierra asked.

I thought about it a moment. A moment was all we had. There wouldn't be time for her to look for my checkbook or the cash I kept in my pickle jar. There might be a slim chance later on—if I could get her out of this. But I didn't have the luxury of thinking about that, either. There was no time at all for any other sort of plan.

"Stay right here and watch."

"For what?"

"The moment you see pandemonium out there—"

"Panda-*monium*? What's *that*?"

"Chaos. Confusion. People running around like idiots. And commotion."

"Like, at a theme park? Or rock concert?"

"Pretty much, only less organized."

"Cool. Then what?"

243

"As soon as things turn crazy, sneak out through the other door. It takes you out through the kitchen and onto the side porch. Keep low. You can use the glider as cover. Crawl past it, then go down the back steps. The bushes out front conceal part of the deck. Go around back and try to reach the road, using the bushes and trees for cover."

"What'll I do if there's no panda-monium?"

"There will be."

"How d'ya know?"

"Trust me."

***

The cops were halfway to the condo when I passed them. When I was about twenty feet behind them, I muttered, "Assholes."

They both stopped abruptly and turned. They glanced at the two cars, then at one another.

"Say something, Ernie?"

"No. You?"

"Wasn't me. Lady?" He yelled at Jenna. "You say something?"

"No. Why?"

"You sure?"

She frowned. "I ought to know if I said something, don'tcha think?"

They continued looking around.

I reached Jenna's Camaro.

Jenna said in a soft voice, "Cops sure as stupid."

"Generally," Ralph agreed.

"No doubt about it. Look at them gawking at one another. I'll bet they don't have ten IQ points between them to spare."

"They manage to get things done once in a while. Don't forget, if they find the girl, we can really make out in this."

"I still like my medium idea."

"Mediums are whackos."

"They know how to get people riled up," Jenna said. "I still intend to look up that one I heard about at the nail salon. She's really good, too. Has a connection with a TV station. I'll bring her here—"

"Jen, as I've said before—"

"Listen, dammit. If she can communicate with Jake and get it on tape or film, we can have a really sweet setup going on."

"You're not going to be able to make enough money to do what you want to do."

"I intend to try, and nobody's gonna stop me from—"

I blew in her left ear.

Startled, she jerked away.

"What's wrong?" Ralph asked.

"I...don't know..." She rubbed her ear. "Funny breeze out here."

"Hi, there," I whispered. "How's every little thing?"

"Oh, shit!" She jumped in her seat, pulling back and whacking Ralph's forehead with the back of her head.

Ralph was slammed backward with a harsh grunt. The car shook as he groped for the door handle. "Him again?"

"Who the hell else?" Jenna groped for the door, shoved it open and crawled outside. She scrambled toward the rear of the squad car and hunkered behind it.

I drifted over to the cop car and focused. I'd wanted to get the siren going, but the ignition started up instead.

The headlight beams also flicked on.

It wasn't exactly the siren, but I knew it would keep everyone busy for a little while.

The two cops gaped at their car. One stood there in shock, his eyes bulging, his hand gripping the handle of his Glock. His partner rushed over to Ralph and Jenna. A third cop entered the picture, jumping over hedges separating the office from the street behind it. When he was close enough to the squad car, I yelled, "Bacon, bacon, bacon!" then did an impression of a pig's grunt.

He spun around, his right hand automatically reaching for the handle of his night stick.

The first one, finally recovering from his shock, let go of his Glock and cautiously approached the squad car.

Two hundred feet behind the commotion, a flash of long sandy hair and my red tee shirt appeared behind the lawn furniture on the deck of my condo just before vanishing behind the bushes.

Chapter 19

We reached the main road in minutes.

"That was totally awesome," Sierra said breathlessly.

I wondered if she was putting me on. Her smile—as well as her confused expression—told me she was sincere. "Whaddya mean?" I asked.

"That was super cool, stirring up all that shit."

"It wasn't that difficult."

"I thought it was. So cool, I wanted to stick around."

"That wouldn't have been very bright."

"Too bad the TV dudes weren't around." She laughed. "Those cops were morons."

I snuck a quick look back toward the complex. No suspicious activity. No squad cars pulling out. We were probably safe for the moment.

Sierra stopped walking and stared in my direction. I wondered what she was looking at. I saw only passing traffic and the activity at the 7-Eleven at the corner.

She was probably trying to look at me, or trying to determine where I was.

"Gonna stay that way for a while?"

"I think I should. Especially if you want to catch another ride."

"Just don't wander off, 'kay?"

"Not a chance."

A small green S-10 pickup slowed down beside us. A white-haired man around seventy stuck his head out the window. "Who ya talkin' to, missy?"

Before I could react, Sierra said, "My buddy Jake."

The driver snickered. "He your imaginary friend?"

"He's not imaginary."

"No?"

"He's dead."

The driver scratched the back of his neck. "You and your dead friend need a ride?"

"Whaddya think?" she asked me.

"Ask him where he's going," I whispered.

"Where ya going?"

"Across the street, to the breakfast place. I'll treat you and your buddy."

"No, thanks," she said. "We have stuff to do."

The driver shrugged, then pulled out and went up to the light.

Once again she'd impressed me. "You really have a pair," I told her.

She looked down at herself. "I keep waiting for them to get bigger."

"That's not what I meant."

She smiled but didn't reply.

It was only about a block to 436. Once we made it, it would be much easier to hitch a ride. Judging by how things were going, finding someone to stop for Sierra wasn't going to be the problem. Finding someone to stop who wasn't a pervert or serial killer would be the problem.

Another difficulty I could see was which direction we should take. Once the cops discovered Sierra wasn't on the complex property, they'd contact the cops patrolling the area and provide them with Sierra's description. Then it would only be a few hours before someone found her.

Then, of course, there was Jenna. When she realized the cops might get in the way of her potential reward, she'd notify her medium contact or any news team that would listen. When she'd finished her campaign, a lot of nosy people would be stirred up and anxious to find out what happened at my place.

"Any idea where we should go?" I asked as we walked.

"South."

"How far south?"

"Back home."

"St. Cloud?"

She nodded.

"Are you sure that's wise?"

"Everyone thinks I'm here, right?"

She had a point. But she'd obviously forgotten a detail or two.

"What about Parker?"

She just shrugged.

"Don't take him lightly. He's probably been looking for you since you got away."

"Think he'll call these cops?"

"If he suspects you know where Santos' money is, he won't stop at anything to find you again."

"I still have to get back."

"What can be so important to risk your safety?"

"Got something to do."

She sounded mysterious. I could also tell she didn't want to go into it right now.

But I had to make her reconsider. Parker was dirty, greedy, and had connections—three qualities that told me he wasn't going to give up in his pursuit of her.

But her home was gone and was probably being staked out. She was intelligent enough to realize that. Even if she had something else on her mind, she shouldn't forget such important details.

I'd have to remind her.

"Sierra—"

A bright-red classic '68 Mustang pulled over directly in front of us, stopping abruptly on the shoulder of the highway. The driver was around nineteen, with a red buzz cut and a goatee that was no more than a smattering of peach fuzz. "Where to?" he asked.

"St. Cloud."

"Whereabouts?"

"One-Ninety-Two would be totally awesome."

"Live close to there?"

She nodded.

He kept staring. "Look kinda familiar," he said. "Seen ya around somewheres?"

I sighed. The trouble had already started.

She shrugged. "Play football?"

"Used to." He puffed up. "Graduated last year."

"Mighta seen ya at a game."

"Cheerleader?"

She nodded.

Good girl.

"Listen. I was only goin' far as Colonial, but—"

"Cool. Drop me off there, then."

250

"What I meant was, I could take ya to St. Cloud, ya need to get there quick."

She got in and I drifted in right behind her. "Don't wanna mess ya up and stuff."

"No worries."

"Nice ride. How fast does she go?"

He grinned. "*Fast*."

"It's…kinda old…"

"They made 'em fly back then."

She shrugged. "Never seen 'em go *that* fast."

"Baby, you ain't seen nothin' yet." We tore out of there, spinning gravel.

I wanted to laugh.

Whoever said women didn't know what they were doing had never bothered to watch them in action.

***

Despite the heavy traffic, we reached St. Cloud in twenty minutes.

Luckily, we hadn't seen any cops. Otherwise, we would have been pulled over, the driver arrested for speeding and reckless driving, Sierra identified and handed over to the St. Cloud authorities.

The driver's name was Will Johnson. He was probably an okay kid in normal circumstances. But when guys are puffing up, they tend to act like brainless imbeciles. To make matters worse, Johnson was the proud owner of a vintage muscle car and had no intention of passing up the chance to show what it could do.

If Sierra was scared during the hectic trip, she didn't let on. She sat quietly, watching the traffic as

251

Johnson swerved in and out of it, zooming through yellow and red lights in explosive bursts of speed.

Living in an abusive household either destroys or strengthens one's nerves. In Sierra's case, she'd learned to zone out and withdraw into her own quiet little world. And nothing happening outside its walls could force its way in.

When we reached St. Cloud, she asked him to take us to the small plaza on the main drag of 192 three blocks up from her place on Virginia. The mall provided a laundromat, used bookstore and seafood restaurant. The parking lot in front was nearly deserted.

Sierra got out of the Mustang. Johnson left the engine running and walked over to where she stood, about twenty feet from the restaurant entrance.

"What's goin' down?" he asked.

"My mom'll meet me here."

"Where's your mom?"

"Works. She usually leaves around two o'clock and comes here so we can grab lunch before we head home."

"Where ya live?"

Sierra pointed west. "About four blocks down there, past the tire place. We have a small house back there."

"Near the Walmart?"

"Down the road that goes behind it. We live in a subdivision."

"Maybe I'll see ya around."

"I usually hang at El Rancho, it doesn't get too late."

He blinked. "They letcha in?"

She smiled. "Doorman likes me."

"Awesome. Place is heavy-duty. They won't even let *me* in."

"I'll ask Bruno to look out for ya. He might letcha sneak in."

"Bruno?"

"Does the door. My uncle works on his car."

Damn, she was good...

"Cool." He winked. "Tonight, maybe?"

"Maybe..."

"Maybe I'll see ya, then."

"Thanks for the ride."

"No worries."

As he eased back out into traffic and headed east, I said, "You're a naughty little babe. Anyone ever tell you that?"

"Once or twice. You just figuring that out?"

"I was being—".

"I know. That gentleman number."

"So tell me...why are we here?"

"I didn't want Will to know where I live."

"He's gone now."

"Something I gotta do."

"Where?"

"My house, silly," she said, her expression solemn.

This didn't make any sense. The house was scorched and torn up. By the time the firefighters finished with it, nothing was salvageable in the living room or kitchen. The fire hadn't reached her bedroom, but I didn't see anything in there earlier, when she was hiding from Santos. Aside from her dresser and a few clothes hanging in her closet, she had very few possessions.

An insurance policy?

That didn't seem likely. If her mother had such paperwork hidden somewhere, I didn't think Sierra would know about it. Even if she did, she wouldn't be thinking of such things after what she'd just been through.

"Sierra ,I hate to remind you, but your house is pretty well gone."

"So?"

"I don't know what you intend to do, but there's probably not much left. Even if there is, going back wouldn't be bright. I'll bet someone's watching for you."

"You mean Parker?"

"Maybe one of his men. Or Miguel's cronies. Everyone's probably in on this. Parker wants the money he thinks Miguel stole from him. Miguel's friends want the money, too. And when there's big money involved, the word gets out fast."

"I have to go back anyway."

"But—"

"Got anything better to do?"

"You can be really stubborn when you want to be. "

"C'mon."

Before I could say anything else, she was dodging traffic as she ran across the street.

Chapter 20

Except for the empty drive, Sierra's house remained unchanged. The vehicles were all gone, possibly impounded by the local DEA.

Red tape surrounded the building. The blackened tatters that had once been drapes stretched across the living room windowsill like charred carcasses torn apart by predators. The couch and armchair, scorched from flame and smoke, sat in tall grass in the front yard, still smoking.

Two charcoal-gray cars rested near the curb at the end of the block. The windows were rolled down. Two men sat in the front seat of each vehicle, smoking cigarettes.

Chills immediately trickled down my spiritual form.

"Who are they?" Sierra asked as we stopped at the corner.

"Who do you think?"

"That Parker asshole?"

"As I've told you, they're not going to stop looking until they find the money they suspect Santos stole. That's why I didn't want you coming back here."

Just as we stepped down from the curb, the driver's door of the first car opened. Watching her closely, Parker got out.

"Shit." Sierra stopped walking.

Parker quickly crossed the street. The doors of the second vehicle opened. Two big men in dark suits got out and followed.

"What now?" she whispered anxiously.

I had no idea. We both knew Parker was dirty. We also knew he had full access to Police Department resources and limitless connections backing him.

He'd brought along three others. I was reasonably sure that the men with him were also crooked—which made Sierra's predicament even more dangerous.

At present, I couldn't imagine a way out of this. Sierra might be able to outrun them, but they wouldn't give up very easily. Money was a strong motivator. Big money, an even stronger motivator, caused people to turn into savages.

"I don't think you can get out of this right now," I whispered.

"What about later?"

"That's our best bet."

"Think of something, okay?"

"I'll try."

"And don't take too long...*please*?"

"I'll do my best."

The two cops from the other car and a third guy who'd gotten out of Parker's car crossed the street just ten yards behind their leader.

"Where the hell have you been, girl?" Parker asked. "We've been looking for you for two days."

She shrugged. I could tell she was forcing herself to be brave. "I've been around."

"Who were you talking to?"

"Myself."

"You talk to yourself?"

"When I'm scared."

"No need for that. We're here now."

"That's why I'm scared."

Parker blinked. "Just be glad we found you," he said. "All sorts of weirdoes out, looking for you."

***

Flanked by two men, Sierra sat in the back seat of Parker's car.

I sat on the lap of the man on Sierra's left and forced myself not to do anything silly. I wanted to blow in his ear or make the back of his thick neck tingle.

I thought the neck tingle thing would be a nice touch and might make Sierra relax. If anything, it would remind her I was right there at her side.

It just wasn't the right time for such shenanigans. Best wait and see what happened. I had to find out where we were going so I could start planning some way of getting her away from them.

Parker pulled out onto 192 and headed west. The other car kept close behind us. I strongly suspected that we weren't going back to Police Headquarters.

"Where we going?" she asked nervously.

"We're taking you to a safe place." Parker glanced at her in the mirror. "Don't worry. We won't let anyone get at you."

"Not what I'm worried about," she muttered.

"Don't sweat it, kid," said the man on her right. "You're all right with us."

"Uh-huh."

"He's right," said the guy I was sitting on.

"Uh-huh."

"You sound skeptical," Parker said.

"Just don't leave me," she said softly.

257

I knew she'd addressed that to me.

"Don't worry, kid," the guy on her right said. "We'll stay close."

"*Real* close," said the other guy, grinning.

I blew lightly on her left cheek. She smiled faintly and winked.

"How come you left my place?" Parker asked.

"Marla saw a ghost."

"A what?"

"You know. Invisible dudes? Dead? They float around and scare people. Like in *Ghostbusters*."

"Where?"

"Where what?"

"Where'd Marla see this…this ghost?"

"In the kitchen."

"What kind of ghost was it?"

"Dead."

Parker sighed. "I meant, what form was it?"

"Looked like a dude."

"A guy?"

"Yeah."

"A man?"

"Like you, only good-looking."

Both guys in the back seat grinned.

I had to force myself from cracking up.

Parker, obviously miffed, glared at her in his mirror. "You saw it, too?"

"Nope."

"Then how do you know what it looked like?"

"Marla told me."

"She said it was good-looking?"

"Yeah."

258

Parker scratched the crown of his head. "A dead guy. Marla saw a dead guy. In the kitchen."

"A good-looking dead guy," she said.

This girl was truly amazing. It made me wonder where she'd be if she'd been given the same opportunities I'd had.

"Yeah, whatever."

"That's what she said."

"Then what happened? After she saw this good-looking ghost."

"She freaked. Packed all her stuff, then ran out to get her car."

Parker lit a cigarette. "I always knew Marla was a fruitcake."

"Why were you with her, then?"

Parker glanced at the guy sitting beside him, then at his rearview. "I'd tell you if you were a year or two older," he said.

She nodded "Good lay, huh?"

The guys flanking her grinned.

Parker shook his head. "Kid, sometimes you talk like some trashy chick."

She didn't reply.

If only they knew how sly this girl was...

"Why didn't you stay put?" Parker asked. "You didn't have to leave. You didn't even see what she saw. I came back about an hour later. Everything would've been okay."

"You didn't see a ghost when you came back?"

"Like I said, Marla was a fruitcake. When she's doing her coke, she sees a lot of things that aren't there."

"She wasn't snorting while I was there."

"She sees things anyway. Hears things. Imagines all sorts of shit."

"I didn't wanna take the chance. I don't like ghosts either. Nothing personal," she whispered to me.

I wanted to laugh.

"How's that?" asked the guy I was sitting on.

"I said I don't like ghosts."

"You also said you didn't see it."

"I didn't want to stay there all alone."

"You should've. Look what happened."

"What happened?"

He blew out smoke. "You didn't hear?"

"Hear what?"

He blinked. "You really don't know what happened?"

She shrugged.

"What happened when you got to her place?"

"Some guy was there, waiting on her deck."

Parker shrugged. "Might've been the bug guy."

"Wasn't the bug guy."

"How do you know?"

"Bug guys don't shove you around when ya come home."

"That's what he did?"

"Yeah."

"What'd *you* do?"

"I ran."

Parker and the man I was sitting on exchanged wary looks in the rearview. "Did you see him? Get a good look?"

"I was on the sidewalk. Marla had already run upstairs."

260

"Why'd she run?"

"Some dude's car was parked in her spot. Pissed her off."

"Sounds like her. You didn't actually see him, then?"

"I was on the sidewalk."

"You already said that."

"Why'd you ask, then?"

He scratched the back of his neck. "You didn't go up the stairs? Maybe try to help her?"

"I was gonna but changed my mind."

"Why?"

"Her bag came back down over the balcony. Almost hit me in the head. I already have a black eye and split lip. I didn't wanna get beat up again, so I decided to haul butt."

Sierra amazed me sometimes.

"That guy follow you?"

"For a while. I found a good hiding place and stayed there. She ever tell you what happened?"

"Marla's no longer with us, kid."

Just as we'd figured...

"Where is she?"

"She just disappeared."

"No one's seen her?"

He shook his head.

"What about her car?"

"Car's gone, too. She tell you anything?"

"About what?"

"Me."

"Just that you're an asshole."

Everyone but Parker laughed.

He shook his head and puffed on his cigarette. "She say why?"

"Why what?"

"Why I'm an asshole."

"She told me a lot of stuff you do."

Parker rubbed his cheek and took a deep breath. "Just tell me what was bugging her the most—all right?"

"You shoulda told her about the ghost. She didn't want to stay in a place that was haunted. You were an asshole for not telling her."

"What happened with that guy?"

"Who?"

"The one that followed you at her place and pushed her around."

She shrugged. "I hid. When I thought it was safe, I got outa there."

"Anything else?"

"Where we going?"

"Not far."

"The Police Station?"

"Not exactly."

"You're the police, right?"

"Yeah. We're the police."

"Then why aren't we going to the Police Station?"

"See, kid, the bad guys'll expect us to take you there."

"What can they do at a Police Station? Aren't there all kinds of cops there?"

"Kid—"

"Wouldn't a bad guy wanna stay *away* from the cops?"

"You just don't understand." Parker rubbed the back of his neck. Sierra was apparently getting to him.

"Then tell me what's going on."

"We don't want anyone to know where you are, so we're going somewhere else."

"Where?"

"Safer if we just take you," the guy on her right said.

"Then what?"

"It's simple." Parker lowered the window a few inches, flicked his cigarette outside and closed the window. "We take you somewhere safe. Then we find out a few things."

"Like what?"

"Things the bad guys also want to know."

"What do the bad guys want to know?"

"For starters, where your buddy Miguel Santos stashed a million and change."

263

Chapter 21

A weathered warehouse sat half-hidden behind stacks of junk automobiles in an overgrown field one mile west of St. Cloud, down a narrow dirt path two miles south of 192. Scattered garbage littered the area. Several rows of trashed mobile homes, victims of hurricane damage, blocked the rear path leading to the woods.

Nothing else was visible down the road. It looked like civilization had ended when Parker turned off the main drag.

Sierra appeared calm as Parker pulled up to the warehouse and parked about ten feet from the door. I didn't know if it was because she knew I was with her or because she realized she couldn't get away. Or maybe she'd just zoned out again. She slid out of the car and followed them down the short sandy path to the metal door of the warehouse.

Parker unlocked the door and pushed it open. He reached inside and flicked on a light switch.

Inside the large open area, barrels and crates piled along both walls reached halfway to the ceiling. More than a dozen palettes stacked with sacks of sand and concrete covered the floor toward the back. Two piles of empty palettes sat in a far corner.

One of the detectives slammed the door behind us. It echoed loudly in the large open area. Sierra cringed at the sound. She kept her cool and followed Parker to the center of the big room, where several metal folding chairs had been set up.

"Rhodes?" Parker gestured to one of the detectives who'd been sitting in the back seat with us. "Stay right here. Harrity? Goldman? You two stick around, keep an eye out. Make sure no one else shows up out there."

Their heels scraping the concrete floor in unison, the detectives walked back toward the door.

"Siddown," Parker told Sierra.

Sierra sat uneasily in a chair.

Parker removed a cigarette from his shirt pocket and lit it. "Feeling cooperative now?"

Sierra shivered. "I think so."

"Good. Great. We all leave here in just a coupla minutes, whistling a happy tune. It'll be a good deal all around. Know why?"

Sierra didn't reply.

"This damn place gives me the creeps." Parker frowned. "It's dark and damp. Smells like oil, turpentine and dirty rags. Who knows what they used to do in here before...before a friend of mine bought the place. Just between you and me? I'd rather be anywhere else than right here. How 'bout you?"

Sierra nodded.

"Good. We're in business, then." Parker finished his smoke, dropped the cigarette onto the concrete floor and squashed it with his shoe. "Ready to talk now?"

Sierra stared at the squashed cigarette.

"Just tell us where the money is and we'll get the hell out of here. Okay? No more bullshit. Like I just said, we don't want to be here. Right, Rhodes?"

"Right," Rhodes said.

Parker turned back to Sierra. "Okay, where's the money?"

Sierra said nothing. She squirmed in her chair.

Parker took a seat facing Sierra. "Rhodes? Over here, on my right."

Rhodes walked over and stood beside Parker.

"Take out your gun."

Rhodes blinked.

"Now."

"Now?"

"Yeah. Now. As in, now. Right this second. And stop being a dickhead."

Sighing, Rhodes reached into his jacket pocket and pulled out a silver automatic pistol.

Parker pulled what looked like a Glock from the holster in his left armpit. He sat back, crossed his legs and rested the gun in his lap.

Sierra trembled.

"I can see you already understand the situation, kid."

Still shaking, Sierra bit her lower lip.

I moved closer to Parker, staying between him and Rhodes. I was ready to let my ectoplasm splatter. I just hoped I could focus and aim faster than they could.

"Isn't that right?" Parker asked.

She continued trembling.

"I said, *isn't that right*?" he repeated, the last three words resonating off the metal walls like gunshots.

Sierra nodded.

I wanted to grab the gun from Parker's lap and accidentally let a round fly into his lower gut.

"I'm only gonna ask this once more. We really don't have the time to baby-sit your ass all night. We've got other things to do. If you're a good girl, this should only take a minute and we're finished. Understand?"

Sierra nodded. Tears welled in her eyes.

"Great. Now. Where's the stash?"

Sierra began to cry.

"I'm not gonna ask again."

She buried her face in her hands.

"Rhodes, do her left kneecap for right now."

Sierra gasped.

I focused on his gun, imaging what I could do before Rhodes could aim and squeeze the trigger.

Rhodes didn't move.

Parker looked up at him. "You heard me, didn'tcha?"

"Listen, uh, Parker, I think we need to try this another—"

Parker picked up his gun and calmly shot Rhodes in the forehead.

Sierra screamed.

The deafening explosion crashed off the walls, settling seconds later into a heavy hum. The mixed smells of cordite and the sourness of Rhodes's released sphincter drifted heavily over the area. Rhodes swayed a moment before his body dropped quietly to the concrete floor. The sound of his gun clattering echoed in the large space.

Goldman and Harrity rushed over, their guns drawn. They reached Rhodes's body and stopped, staring at it, then at Parker.

"What the fuck's happening?" Goldman asked.

267

"Rhodes decided at the wrong moment to be a dickhead."

Goldman and Harrity shook their heads and went back to their post.

Parker put the Glock back in his lap. While Sierra sobbed loudly into her hands, he reached into his jacket pocket, pulled out his cigarettes and calmly lit another one. His hands did not shake at all. This told me the worst—that Parker was a psycho killer.

He flicked the match away and watched Sierra for a few tense moments. "Rhodes was a buddy of mine," he told her. "My drinking buddy. It doesn't get any better than that. We worked together the last five years. I really didn't like doing that, you know. Nope. Didn't like it one bit. I would've preferred having a drink with the boy rather than blowing his brains all over the walls. But it's like this. Loyalty's everything in this business. When I give an order, it has to be obeyed. Big money's at stake. Important people have to know where their merchandise is. Santos was skimming off the top. We figure he was into us for at least a mill, possibly two. You lived with him. Did runs, made drops. If anyone knows where his stash is, it's you. Where is it?"

Sierra continued to sob.

"Where's the fucking stash?"

Sierra trembled.

Parker stared at the girl and sighed. He was obviously trying to control himself but was running out of patience. "I'm not going to ask again. Either I leave here happy or someone who shall remain brainless stays here with Rhodes forever. Which is it to be?"

Sierra kept her face buried in her hands.

Parker puffed on his cigarette and regarded the gun in his right hand. "Let's get one thing straight. This might make your decision a little easier. I have no qualms about kneecapping a female. I don't even care if the kneecap belongs to a stupid kid."

Sierra kept sobbing.

"Know what a kneecapping is, kid? Know what it does? Let me be blunt about it. It ain't pretty, and it hurts like a bastard. It'll also give you a seriously funny walk for the rest of your life." He shrugged. "Want a demonstration?"

I figured it was the perfect time to rattle him a little.

I moved behind him and stood about three feet from his chair. "Go pound sand up your ass," I said, amping up all my stored ectoplasm.

Parker jumped up and spun around. His chair, knocked backward, slapped loudly to the concrete. His gun pointed directly where I was standing. "Who the fuck *said* that?"

"Guess," I said.

He squinted, peering into the semi-darkness. When he realized he couldn't see anyone, he squeezed off three quick rounds into the crates piled along the rear wall. Puffs of sand and concrete mix jumped wildly, sliding down the piles then settling on the floor.

Once again, Goldman and Harrity rushed over, their guns out.

"Either of you two idiots tell me to pound sand up my ass?"

The two men shook their heads.

"Ya sure?"

Goldman said, "Not me, Parker."

Harrity shrugged. "I've *wanted* to, Boss, but—"

"Someone else is here, then."

"Where?" Goldman asked.

"How the fuck should *I* know?"

Harrity scratched his brush cut. "Then how d'ya know someone's—"

"Stop being a moron. You think I'm being paranoid?"

"Well..."

"That didn't require an answer, you idiot. Just shut up and do as I say. You two go check it out over there. I'll work from the other side."

"Wait till they're closer to the crates," I whispered close to Sierra's ear. "I'm about to cause some serious pandemonium again. When you see a break, sneak over to the door."

Sierra nodded in the midst of her sobs.

The detectives split up, all three sneaking over to the huge piles topping the palettes. I moved toward the center and yelled, "Hey, dickhead! Over here!"

Parker spun to his left and got off a quick round, nailing Goldman in the right thigh. Goldman screamed and went down hard.

"That sure was stupid," I said. "You just shot one of your own men."

Parker gulped audibly.

270

I moved closer to Harrity, slipping through him. "Over here, dickhead."

Parker spun around and slammed two rounds into the pile, missing Harrity by less than a foot.

Harrity dove to the floor. "Dammit, Boss! You almost nailed my ass!"

Cursing, Parker rushed over, keeping an eye on the crates. Goldman rolled on the floor, the blood pooling beneath his big form. Parker found a handkerchief in his pants pocket and mashed it to the wound.

"Hey, Harrity," I yelled. "Are you as stupid as your boss?"

He spun around, his gun out and ready. He was about to pull the trigger when he realized his gun was pointed directly at Parker. He cringed, pulling his arm back.

"Harrity! Go find that son of a bitch! And try not to point that fucking thing at me again, okay?"

Harrity cautiously approached the pile from the rear.

I crept up behind him and blew on his neck. He jumped and spun around. When he realized his gun was pointed at Parker again, he pulled back and cursed. I blew on his neck again. He spun around and faced the pile. His gun roared. Less than five feet away, explosions of sand and dust jumped from the pile, landing in his eyes. He cursed loudly, coughing and shielding his face.

I turned toward the front.

Sierra's chair was empty.

The slightly opened doorway revealed the gleaming surfaces of the cars parked outside.

Chapter 22

I found Sierra behind the wheel of Parker's car, frantically searching for the keys.

They weren't in the ignition. Or on the seat. Or on the floor.

Or anywhere else.

"Shit. He has the keys." Her hair flew everywhere as she looked for them, yanking open the console, the glove box. "Damn..."

I appeared briefly. "You know how to drive?"

"I've seen Momma and Miguel drive a zillion times," she said, wiping her eyes.

"That doesn't mean you can drive."

"Everyone knows you don't have to be smart to drive."

"That's not the point."

"Miguel was a moron. He drove. Momma could drive while she was smoking, putting on her makeup and talking on her cell. How hard can it be?"

This girl sure was observant. "Good point."

"How many smart people have you seen driving?"

"That raises another good point."

Two quick gunshots roared inside the warehouse. Apparently Parker and his men were still entertaining themselves.

"Can you start this up—please?"

"I'll give her a try."

I focused.

Nothing.

"Please hurry." She twisted around in the seat and gawked at the warehouse doorway.

"It would help if you didn't distract me."

She went silent.

I focused again.

The lights went on.

Sierra gasped and jumped up and down in the seat.

C'mon, dammit. Focus...

The engine started up.

With a moment's hesitation she slammed it into gear and spun gravel, roaring out of there and back onto the main road.

She kept it a steady sixty on the bumpy dirt road, her head repeatedly tapping the roof. She didn't notice. She was too obsessed with getting away. When her hair slapped her face, she merely flicked it away.

After a quick glance at the busy intersection, she pulled out onto 192 and joined the eastbound traffic.

"You okay?" I materialized again.

"Why'd he do that?" She began trembling again. "Why'd he have to kill that dude?"

"Drug people." I couldn't think of a better explanation than that. "They're a lot of things. Human isn't one of their qualities."

"He killed his friend. He...he shot him right in the head!"

I shrugged.

"Right there. In the head. In front of me!"

"As I just said..."

"But a *friend*?"

"He did say he didn't like doing it, right?"

Sierra glared. "Parker's a total sicko."

"Loyalty only goes so far where big money's concerned."

"Is that a grownup thing?"

"I think it's more of a mob thing."

"But how could he even be sure I know anything? He only thinks I do, doesn't he?"

"He wants to be certain."

"And what if I don't?"

"I'm sure killing a thirteen-year-old girl wouldn't bother him much."

"Just for money?"

"That's all they live for. Where we going, by the way?"

"My place."

"You're still intent on going back there?"

"I've got something to do."

"You know he's gonna be after us very shortly, don't you?"

She glanced in the rearview. "It won't take me long at all. He can even have his stupid car back."

"I'm sure getting his stupid car back isn't his primary concern right now."

"I can't give him his stash if I don't know where it is, can I?"

"That sounds reasonable."

"Do you think Miguel would tell me if he was stashing money?"

"Seeing what little of him I got to see before they killed him, I'd say he wasn't your basic kiss-and-tell kind of guy."

274

"He wouldn't even tell Momma if he was stashing money."

"That sounds reasonable."

"But you don't think any of this matters, do you?"

"Remembering how the delightful Mr. Tibbs recently treated a fellow drinking buddy, I'd say the man has a serious problem with people who don't like playing by his rules."

***

Sierra left the car at the curb in front of her house.

Invisible again, I followed her as she trudged through the tall grass in the front yard. She then veered off to the left, squeezing past two overgrown bushes taking over the yard between the house and the chain-link fence separating the properties.

The backyard was in even more of a shambles than the first time I'd seen it. Holes had been dug all through the yard. The dirt sat in piles in more than a dozen different places. The push mower had been tossed on its side. Potted plants had been torn apart and tossed in the weeds. The metal shed lay on its back, its door wide open, the ground beneath it dug up. Three bushes lining the rear wall of the house were also dug up and tossed.

Someone was definitely searching for something.

Sierra didn't notice, didn't even pause as she made a beeline for the tree house.

"I hope you know what you're doing," I said.

Without replying, she climbed the makeshift steps. I stayed where I was at the base of the tree, keeping a lookout.

Sierra was gone only seconds. When she climbed back down, she carried her teddy bear, holding it in front of her chest.

My God. "All this for a bear?"

"It's my only friend." She said it softly. By her tone I knew it was the only explanation that mattered.

"Sierra..." I couldn't believe this. "You're thirteen..."

"So?"

"Aren't you a little old for—"

"I've been sleeping with Teddy since I was five."

"Like I said, aren't you a little—"

"Daddy gave me Teddy when I was four."

"Do you realize you've risked your life for—"

Her eyes glistened. "It's the only thing I have from my daddy..."

I didn't say anything. I couldn't. Although I no longer had a heart, she'd managed to touch whatever I still had, nonetheless.

"I want to have it with me when—if—I see him again," she said. A tear had drifted down her cheek.

"This is what you really want?"

A nod.

"Then that's what we'll do."

"You think I'm being stupid?"

"For coming back for the bear? Or for going after your father?"

A shrug. "Both?"

276

Anyone with a working brain cell would be stupid for even considering doing both. Parker would probably be here any minute. He wouldn't be as patient this time. And hauling around a filthy, beat-up teddy bear wasn't the most sensible career move I could think of.

But her glistening eyes, the way she stood and the way she gripped the bear destroyed whatever logic dictated this situation.

Logic was not the answer here. It had never been. I suspected that with Sierra, only the heart really mattered.

She'd just told me that although she'd been robbed of her childhood, she didn't mind risking her life to save the only scrap of it she had left.

"Hell, no," I said, and hoped I sounded sincere.

Because I actually meant it.

***

We crossed the main highway, back to the shopping mall where the Johnson kid had dropped us off earlier.

"Now where?" I asked.

"The seafood placc."

"You're hungry?"

"No…"

"Then what—"

"I need change." She held up a bill. It was a hundred.

"Where the hell did you get that?"

She just smiled.

I couldn't take my eyes off the bear as I followed her inside.

***

277

Half an hour later, we sat in the back seat of the cab as it took us to the train station in downtown Kissimmee.

I still couldn't take my eyes off her bear. It was filthy and wrinkled, its stitches pulled out and dangling. Some of its stuffing, yellowed with age and dampness from the elements, poked out of its ears and its paws like remnants of old memories coming back for one last viewing.

Had she really gone back for it because it was the only memento she had of her father? Or had she lied to me all along about the money Miguel had stashed?

I wanted to think she'd gone back for it because of her father. I couldn't see her doing it for any other reason. Sierra just didn't seem the type to be motivated by money.

Anyway, finding out could wait. We had more important things ahead of us.

By the time we crossed the railroad tracks and eased down the congested street leading to the crowded station area, cops wandered around everywhere in pairs.

"Somethin's goin' down." The cabby, a little bald guy in his late forties, shook his head. "Either the damn President's here for a visit or we got ourselves another batch of psycho camel jockeys wantin' to blow somethin' up." He took the bills for Sierra's fare and grinned his thanks for her ten-dollar tip.

We got out and squeezed through the small crowd blocking the ticket booth.

"You wouldn't want to ditch that bear, would you?" I whispered.

She gave me one of her frowns.

"Just checking."

Sierra joined the rear of the line. She turned in my direction and whispered, "How're we gonna do this?"

"I'll think of something."

"Think fast. A cop's coming over."

He was a big boy, probably six and a half feet tall. He checked everyone out as he walked our way. Luckily, two people got in line behind Sierra, hiding her just as he was about to pass. But when he stopped to retrace his steps, I decided that a subtle distraction might help the situation.

I drifted behind him and said, "Can I interest you in a little bribe money?"

He spun around, scanned the crowd and charged right over to the well-dressed middle-aged man walking briskly in our direction.

"What was that?" The cop stepped in front of the unsuspecting guy and rested his huge fists on his hips.

The poor guy cringed. "P-Pardon me?"

"You heard me. What'd you just say?"

He shrugged. "I said, p-pardon me."

"You some kinda wise guy?"

"I...don't know what you mean."

"You said—"

"All I said was—"

Two fellow officers rushed over.

"We got us a funny boy here," the first cop said.

"I don't know what you're talking about…"

"Got any ID, fella?"

Sierra reached the ticket booth and purchased a single berth. A one-way for Gulfport. The next one was leaving in a few minutes for Jacksonville. The ticket guy told her she could get off and get on board for the line stopping in Gulfport on its way to Houston.

A crowd had gathered in the area between us and the train. Another batch of cops showed from a different direction, blocking the path. The train was at least a hundred feet from us.

Sierra left the ticket booth and got behind another crowd a few yards from one of the gates. I could tell she was looking for me.

I drifted over. "I'm right behind you."

She must have been getting used to me. She didn't jump or even flinch. "Any ideas?" she whispered.

"Just do whatever I say."

"Then ya do have an idea?"

"I didn't exactly say that."

"Then—"

"Just listen and take my cue."

I only had a vague idea what to do. Since I had the terrific advantage of being invisible, I could come and go easily. Sierra, however, was not only highly visible, she was probably just as recognizable right now as your average Hollywood celebrity. Her face had been splashed all over the tube during the last couple of days and would be fresh in everyone's mind. And if a reward had been mentioned during the news stories, everyone's memory would be razor-sharp.

The cops would be even more difficult to deal with. They'd probably all been given a photo and knew exactly who they were looking for.

I strongly suspected Parker was around somewhere. And he'd have the backing of the uniforms to help him find her.

Hopefully, he didn't know about her bear.

I decided to make this venture as challenging as possible for everyone concerned. No one would get her—not as long as I was around. And willing to cause my own special brand of chaos.

"Try using the crowds as cover," I told her. "The more people, the better chance you'll have of slipping by. Stay close to everyone taller and bigger than you."

"Everyone's taller and bigger than me."

"Just don't make it obvious."

She slipped into the crowd passing us. A cop moved toward us, checking out everyone on his way over.

"Bend over and fix your shoe lace," I whispered.

Without a pause of protest, she bent, put the bear on the ground between her feet and did as I suggested.

The cop passed, glancing at her butt as he moved toward his peers.

Damned pervert…

When he was a safe distance away, I said, "Now get back up. And keep moving."

She scooped up the bear, straightened and hurried away.

Another cop marched straight toward her. His eyes had focused on her. He'd apparently seen her and was already making her ID.

A short, skinny guy around sixty in shorts and a stained white tee shirt appeared behind him. He suddenly reached out and nudged the cop's hat forward.

The cop immediately pulled off his hat and spun around. He stared right at the skinny guy but obviously couldn't see him.

I smiled in relief. Another dead guy to the rescue.

Two teenage boys rushed past. The cop caught one by the elbow and yanked him off his feet. The boy's companion stopped abruptly and ran back to see what was going on. The first boy straightened, brushed himself off and yelled at the cop. The cop yelled back. Two other cops came over to see what the fuss what about.

I told Sierra to veer around them.

As we passed, the guy who'd pushed the cop's hat winked at me.

"Thanks," I said.

"No problem," he said. "I love fucking with cops."

"Been here a while?"

"Since I died."

"When was that?"

He shrugged. "Five years? Ten? Who the hell's counting?"

"Well, have fun."

He chuckled. "I don't know what's goin' on, but this place has become a giant pork smorgasbord. This is heaven for me. I used to be a pickpocket. Needless to say, I hate cops." He winked again then disappeared. He reappeared about ten yards farther down, where another cop frantically searched his pockets for something. The dead guy held up his hands and wiggled his fingers. "Still have the touch," he said proudly, grinning.

Sierra was less than ten yards from the train.

More cops. The entire Kissimmee Police Force had shown up. They'd spread out and were scanning the crowd as well as the train.

I hoped my dead pocket-picking friend could keep up with the demand.

I crept up to Sierra. "Wait for more pandemonium."

"Cool."

A few yards to my right, half a dozen elderly people stood around in a small semicircle, checking their tickets. I said in a loud voice, "Someone said they saw a dark-haired guy carrying a gun!"

Two cops turned in my direction. Another cop twisted his head around.

Two of the women in the group gasped and bumped into the people behind them. One lady dropped her handbag. A scrawny teen boy stepped on it while scurrying past. The lady bent to retrieve it and was knocked down by another teen boy rushing by.

The cops frantically searched the crowd.

My dead buddy showed up and began fiddling with the loop holding the cop's revolver in its holster.

The gun quickly clattered onto the pavement.

I shouted, "Gun!"

Gasps. Screams. Another stampede. Three cell phones dropped to the pavement and were promptly stepped on.

Sierra hurried up the steps of the car and disappeared inside.

Chapter 23

Sitting in a chair in her small single berth, her teddy bear in her lap, Sierra had become the same lonely little girl I'd first seen walking along the road just a few days ago. That same depressed young soul shuffling along, head down, shoulders hunched, totally oblivious of the heavy traffic roaring by. Locked in her own little world, where the monsters couldn't reach her.

Now, exhausted and sad and just as alone as ever, she remained locked in her own little world. The monsters wanted her badly. Right now they searched the crowds on the other side of the window. Sierra didn't notice. She'd simply closed her mind to the outside world. This single berth was much like the tiny room in the oak tree she frequently escaped to, where she could take refuge in her own imagination.

Outside, the Kissimmee cops scoured the hectic crowd. Three grim-looking men in dark suits talked on cell phones and checked everyone they saw. One of them stood off to the side, carefully studying each passenger boarding the car.

I assumed Parker had been the one who'd alerted the police. He'd probably decided Sierra might choose the train station and rushed here as soon as he retrieved his car. But I knew better than voice my thoughts to Sierra. She'd come this far—I didn't want anything to jinx her journey.

I made myself visible.

"You okay?"

She smiled. "I'll make it. Thanks for getting me here without…without him finding me again."

"How soon will the train be leaving?"

"Just a few minutes. They said it's eight hours to Jacksonville, then an hour's wait for the one stopping at Gulfport on its way to Houston."

"I'll watch out for you at Jacksonville. You can sleep there if you can find a comfortable seat. I'll wake you when it's time."

"I'll probably be too nervous."

"You'll be fine."

"Thanks."

"Hey, it's what I do."

"You've done a lot."

I just shrugged.

"I couldn't…I wouldn't be here if—"

"Don't get sloppy, now."

She wiped her eyes. "How'd you…how'd you even know about me? You told me you've been with me since those jerks picked me up. You never said where you first saw me."

"I saw you walking along one-ninety-two."

"I knew I couldn't get very far. I had no money. I had to get away for a little while. I figured I'd walk around, then go back home when Miguel was asleep. But he wasn't. He was in the living room with Momma. It pissed me off, you know?"

"I saw how angry you were when you were standing near the mailbox."

She smiled. "You saw a lot."

"Felt it, too. The heat coming off you could light up the block."

"I was upset. And totally bummed out. And my lip hurt. And my eye. You saw me when I passed the cemetery, didn'tcha?"

The question caught me by surprise. I remembered when she stopped walking that night and turned in my direction. "How'd you know?"

"When I passed it, something weird happened. I didn't feel so bad. I don't know why. It just happened. You know how sometimes you're depressed and you think of something else, maybe a joke or something, and you're not depressed anymore?"

"I know what you mean."

"That's what happened. But it was weird because I was thinking of Miguel and how I wanted to do something to him, and suddenly I didn't feel so bad. I figured maybe I was feeling good because thinking of doing something to him made me feel good. But now I'm not too sure. Now I wonder...well, maybe it was because of you. Maybe...maybe I felt you, your being right there. It didn't last very long, though. Just a few seconds. Those jerks pulled over and I was depressed all over again."

"Those jerks would depress anyone."

"Why'd you follow me?"

"You reminded me of someone."

"Who?"

"Another lost little guy who needed help one Saturday afternoon a long time ago."

Her eyes searched mine. "Did he get it?"

"He managed."

She sighed and sat back. Her eyes glistened again. She hugged her bear.

"Sierra, how much cash do you have stuffed in your bear?"

She held it in front of her, examining it. More stitching had ripped open and come loose, probably when she was fighting the crowds. More strands of stuffing had also squeezed out. The bear looked like it had been run over on the highway.

I sympathized completely.

"I never kept any money in Teddy. I knew they'd rip him open if they ever came to look for anything."

"You suspected they'd come looking for money?"

She shrugged. "I guess I was always afraid something would happen. I never trusted Miguel."

"Where was the money?"

"I kept it rolled up in the floor, underneath a ledge. There was a jagged crack in the board. You couldn't see it unless you knew exactly where it was."

"Ingenious. How much is there?"

"I never counted it."

"Where'd you get it? Miguel?"

She shrugged. "He left money all over the place. He'd pull it out of his pockets and leave it crumpled all over the top of the dresser. Sometimes the bills dropped on the floor, but he didn't even care. Momma picked them up and put them back. He'd even leave a bill in the john or on the living room floor. Every once in a while, I picked one up and took it down to the tree house. He didn't even miss it."

"Why?"

"Why what?"

"Why'd you take it?"

She sniffed. A shadow passed over her fine features. "I was saving up."

"For what?"

"I didn't want us living with him anymore. I was scared all the time. So was Momma. I didn't tell her because…because she would've freaked and told me to put it back." She wiped away a tear.

"So you don't really know how much Miguel actually skimmed? Or where he kept his stash, other than in his pockets?"

"He kept it in the attic."

"You're sure?"

"He'd climb up there once in a while. I saw him take two brown paper bags with him a couple of times. It might've been the money, I don't know. If it was, it burned up in the fire."

"I'm pretty sure they checked the attic. We saw what they did to the backyard. These guys aren't stupid."

"Then they found it?"

"Most likely."

"Then why'd they take me to that warehouse?"

"Maybe they didn't find as much as they thought and figured you also had some stashed. Just making sure, I guess."

She pulled the bear close and let it rest in her lap. His ears were matted with a brown sticky substance, his belly smeared with something else. He smelled funky.

I hated to ask. "What's the brown stuff?"

"Peanut butter."

"How about the other stuff?"

"Jelly."

"He's a mess."

Sierra smiled. "He's been with me a long time. I love him."

"I'm glad they didn't tear it to shreds."

She rubbed its matted head. "I'd really hate them if they did that. It'd be like they were killing Daddy, too. Sometimes I hug Teddy at night and when I close my eyes it's almost like…like Daddy's still with me. Sound weird?"

"Not at all."

"You're not shitting me, are ya?"

"Nope. And watch your language."

Sierra smiled and hugged the bear.

"He's a lucky man," I said.

She just looked at me.

"He just doesn't know it yet."

She lay back and stared at the faded white ceiling. I could tell she was nervous. There was no reason for her not to be. She was leaving the only place she ever knew, traveling all alone to a strange place. She didn't know anyone where she was going and the one person she really wanted to see hadn't seen her since she was just a child. He was her dad, but he'd left her long ago, before she'd grown into the person she was now.

"Things will turn out," I said. I hoped I'd sounded convincing enough.

She still stared at the ceiling—as if it held all her answers. "He hasn't seen me since…well, since I was little."

"He's your dad. He'll love you. He already does."

"Then why didn't he—never mind." She sighed.

"It wasn't because of you. I hope you know that by now."

"I'm still nervous."

"He'll go crazy when he sees you. I know *I* would."

She stared at me, her eyes probing mine. She was trying to read my expression. I could tell how vulnerable and sensitive she was right now. "I wish you…I wish--"

"I know."

"You don't know what I was gonna say."

"How can I? You didn't finish."

"Then why'd you say you know?"

"I was being polite."

"Bull."

"What?"

"Bullshit."

"I meant, why'd you mean bull about my being polite? And watch your language. I don't think your father will like that."

"Why would a grownup wanna be polite around a kid? Especially when the grownup's dead?"

"The way I was brought up, I guess. I'm usually polite around everyone."

"Sometimes you're totally weird."

"Hey, I'm dead. I can be whatever way I want."

291

"You're weird, but really cool."

"Thanks. So what did you mean?"

"About what?"

"Something you were wishing."

She shook her head.

"I thought we were buds."

"We are."

"Then tell me."

"I'd...totally like us to be buds."

"Like I just said, we are."

"I mean, I want us to be buds longer. I want us to...to—"

"I know."

She groaned. "You did it again."

"I knew what you were going to say that time."

"What was I gonna say?"

"You want us to stay buds forever."

She nodded.

I didn't reply. I had no idea what to say. I no longer had a body, but something inside me melted anyway.

"Don't you want that, too?"

I nodded.

"What can we do?"

"I'm dead. My life's over. You've got your whole life ahead of you."

"Can't you just hang around? That'd be *so* cool. We could do stuff together."

"Do you really think that would work? What if someone caught you talking to me?"

She shrugged. "I talk to myself a lot. I even did it before I met you."

Someone knocked on the door.

Sierra stiffened.

"Tickets!"

She grabbed her bear and held it close. "Think he's for real?"

"I'll check." I vanished and peered through the door.

A short, stout black man in a porter's uniform stood on the other side of the door, fiddling with something in his pocket.

I drifted back in the room. "He's legit," I whispered.

Relieved, she got up, dropped Teddy on the seat and went to the door.

***

Exhausted, Sierra finally fell asleep in her berth, barely moving, her bear held against her chest. The air-conditioning made the little area a tad cool. I wanted to cover her with the blanket on the tiny shelf but didn't know how I could do it without waking her. She seemed to be all right, so I let her be.

About half an hour later, I heard something on the other side of the door.

I drifted out there to investigate.

Parker Tibbs stood out in the hall, his ear pressed against the door. After a few moments, he straightened and buried his hand in his pants pocket. Then he pulled out a silver penknife with an assortment of keys attached to it. He went through them until he found one he liked, then glanced behind him. When he was sure he was alone, he applied his lock-pick to Sierra's door.

I decided it was time to have a face-to-face talk with the man.

I materialized just a few feet behind him. "What the hell do you think you're doing?"

A gasp exploded from his throat. He jumped then spun around. Trembling, he looked me up and down. "Who're…where'd you…I didn't hear anyone behind me…"

"That's very informative—even interesting. But it doesn't really answer my question."

His hands shook. I'd obviously scared the shit out of him. That amazed me. As a detective, he was supposed to have nerves of steel.

"You're supposed to have nerves of steel," I said.

"*Wh-What*?"

"I didn't think you'd be able to wrap your brain around that one."

He didn't catch the insult. "How'd you…how'd you sneak up on me? I didn't hear anyone—"

"You just don't pay attention too much, do you?"

He kept looking me up and down. Recognition slowly registered. "That voice. We know one another?"

"Not socially, but I did visit your warehouse a few hours ago."

He flinched.

"I remember the experience well," I said. "You really are a class act, you know. Truly one of a kind. Right after you shoot your drinking buddy Rhodes in the head, you tell a thirteen-year-old girl how much it upset you to shoot your drinking buddy

294

Rhodes in the head. Then you tell her you're going to shoot her in the kneecap if she doesn't tell you what you want to know. Yeah, you're a real class act, slick."

His jaw dropped. He didn't move.

I decided to keep pounding away. This asshole needed to be shocked. "You really ought to change your methods, you know. You keep wasting your partners, you're liable to end up all by yourself in prison, bending over for Bubba." I couldn't hold back the smile. "Sounds like a catchy title, doesn't it? Bending Over for Bubba? I guess it could be a comedy, but Cable would have to produce it because of its extreme adult subject matter."

He backed up. His eyes stayed on me.

"Was it something I said?" I asked. "Has my deodorant stopped working?"

He backed up some more.

"If you don't contribute just a teensy-weensy bit to this conversation, I'll be forced to take my business elsewhere."

His eyes bulged. He backed up some more.

"Cat got your tongue?"

No reply. It was time to get serious.

"Do us both a favor, all right? Stay away from that girl. Get it? Let me put it this way: if you don't stay away from her, I'm going to hunt you down and make you do something really stupid to yourself. So stupid, in fact, that people all over will be talking about it for years to come. Want a demonstration?"

His lower lip quivered.

"I guess that means yes. Watch and learn, grasshopper."

Concentrating, I forced his hand straight up, bringing the sharp tool in his lock-picking kit toward his right eye. He struggled at first, pulling his head back and out of range. The tool kept coming. Gasping, he trembled, slamming his shoulder against the wall. His eyes filled the sockets.

It kept coming and stopped about a quarter of an inch from his eyeball.

"Get the message?"

No reply. He struggled with the lock-pick, fighting to lower his arm. I finally released my hold on him.

"Understand the situation now?"

Breathing heavily, he nodded eagerly.

"If you don't want to pull out your own eyeball and swallow it, you'll leave her alone. Understand?"

A nervous nod.

"I guess this is it, then. So long." I made myself invisible.

His lock-pick dropped to the carpet. His eyes trembled. His gulp could be heard above the steady moan of the engine. He spun around and bolted down the hall, to the door leading out to the smoking car.

I slipped back inside Sierra's room.

She was still sleeping peacefully.

I intended to make sure she stayed that way.

Chapter 24

We reached Gulfport shortly after ten the next morning.

In the lobby of the train station, several payphones covered half the tile wall straight ahead. She'd seen them, but for some reason avoided looking at them.

"I think you need to get a little closer," I whispered.

"Huh?"

"To the phones."

"Phones?"

"Those funny-looking blue metal things bolted into the wall."

She nodded but said nothing.

"Unless your eyesight is on the same level as Superman's, you can't possibly read the phone book from here."

She stared at the phones as if trying to remember why she'd need them. "I'd better get closer," she whispered as if she was talking to herself.

"Sounds like a nifty idea," I said. "I wish I'd thought of it."

Taking tiny steps, she approached the one on the far end, near the hall leading to the restrooms. She stopped two feet away and stood there a few moments, staring at the object in front of her as if she'd never actually seen anything like it before. She was obviously frightened at the thought of touching it. I suspected she wasn't afraid of the phone itself but of the prospect of using it to talk to her estranged father.

She rested Teddy on the scuffed tile floor between her feet then gazed at the phone book as if trying to decide once again what to do.

"What's the worst he can do?" I asked. "Tell you he doesn't remember you? That he's got some weird daughter phobia?"

She began to pout.

I felt as though I'd just slapped her.

"I was kidding..."

"I know."

"What's the problem?"

"I...don't *know*..."

"He'll want to come. Trust me."

Tears gathered in her eyes. "Would *you*?" She sounded like the little girl she actually was—not the tough young chick she'd been forced to be. "Would *you* want to?"

I stared into the pleading eyes and felt another strong tug where my heart once was. I realized right then that this was probably the most important moment in her life, and that she'd just asked me the most important question she would ever ask anyone.

"If I was still alive and found out you were here, I'd bust my ass to get here. I'd hop a train. Or plane. Or the closest fast-moving cloud. Or jet stream. I'd kill myself to get here if I wasn't already dead."

She smiled through her tears.

And opened the phone book.

***

298

Hiram Johns was working on his boat when her call went through. It went to his answering service, which switched it directly over to his cell. He answered right away.

I could tell by Sierra's gleaming smile—plus the way she jumped up and down and squealed—that I'd been right. Her father was extremely happy to hear from her and definitely wanted Sierra back in his life.

I moved in closer so I could hear the conversation. Johns told her he loved her and that he'd been thinking of her almost constantly in the years since he'd walked out of their lives. When Sierra told him that her mom had met a violent end, he made no comment, just said he'd be there just as fast as he could, then hung up.

"I feel so *ugly*," she said, forcing a hand through her hair.

"You're not that bad," I said. "Your hair's messy and you've been crying. Your clothes are wrinkled and smell a little, but after a bath, a change of clothes and a breath mint or two, you'll look great."

"You wouldn't lie, would you?"

"I could say you looked like you just stepped off a runway, but you wouldn't believe me."

"I have a black eye."

"I've noticed."

"And a swollen lip."

"I've been thinking about that. You know, if you turn slightly to your right and let a strand of your hair fall over your cheek, it's hardly noticeable…"

299

"Jake..."

I shrugged. "Honestly, it doesn't look as bad as it did."

She looked down at her bear. I could tell this was tough for her. She was fighting to hold herself together. It was tough for me, too. "There's a lot I never got to say…to you…"

The inner tug grew even harder. I forced myself to ignore it. This wasn't the time to get sloppy. I had to help her focus. The rest of her life was about to start in just a few minutes. She was shifting to a new phase and obviously wasn't ready. She'd have to get to know her father all over again. There would be new people in her life. She'd be moving to a different location and would have to get used to an entirely new way of life. Her father would most likely send her back to school. That in itself would be traumatic, but once she adapted, she'd finally have the chance to continue her education. She was a smart girl and deserved a chance. Her father had to understand that his daughter had just endured a lifetime of stress in a very short time.

I had to stay strong and remain a positive influence on her until she walked away. It wouldn't help her at all if I crumbled.

"Why don't you spend the next few minutes in the restroom?" I said. "It's right there behind you. You have time to fix your face."

"I totally need to, don't I?"

"Especially your nose."

She crossed her eyes trying to look at it.

"You've got a big, fat crusty growing in there—"

"Oh, ga-*ross*!"

"Hurry, okay?"

"Are you *sure* there's time?"

I didn't know how far the docks were from here but suspected her father would be here any minute. But it didn't matter. She had to wash her face and mop up the tears. If she wanted to present a positive image for her father, the time was now.

And it would be okay if he showed while she was in the bathroom. He needed to know where she was coming from, what she'd been through. What he should expect.

"Hurry, now," I told her. "I'll yell when he gets here."

She picked up her bear and rushed off.

"Make sure you pick the right room," I yelled after her.

Her laughter bounced off the tile walls.

A battered white Dodge Ram pickup pulled up to the building a couple of minutes later. A man with thinning light-brown hair got out quickly and hurried to the front door. He was tall, broad-shouldered and burly, about forty, and wore overalls and a stained white tee shirt.

I materialized just as he pushed through the glass doors. He smelled faintly of fish. As he drew closer, I saw that he had the same fine features as Sierra. He stood there, looking around at the few people milling about.

"Hiram Johns?"

"Yes?"

"Sierra's in the bathroom, making herself presentable."

301

"Who're *you*?" he asked softly.

"A friend."

He blinked. "Sierra didn't tell me—"

"She was so excited at hearing your voice, she probably forgot to tell you. She was worried you wouldn't want her back in your life."

His expression instantly softened. "How could she possibly think that? It was her mother—"

"I know. She told me."

He tilted his head and stared at me. "Who'd you say you were?"

"A friend."

He scratched his thick tanned neck. "And you came all the way here with my daughter?"

"Let's just say some very bad people wanted to make sure Sierra didn't leave Orlando."

He stared harder at me, trying to determine my role in this. I concentrated on maintaining my image while my energy slowly drained. I didn't know if it was the stress or the excitement. Or perhaps the disheartening realization that in just a few minutes, I wouldn't see Sierra again. Whatever it was, it had weakened my concentration, draining my reserves at a steady clip.

"Bad people?" he asked softly.

"Drug people. Your ex-wife—"

"You don't have to say anymore. Flo...well, she was weak. Cigarettes, booze, painkillers." He shook his head. "I...stuck it out as long as I could, but..."

"So did Sierra."

"Those people you mentioned. They didn't...I mean, how bad was it?"

302

"Bad."

"Did they…do anything to her?"

"The man living with them…he hit them. Both of them. A lot."

Her father's face tightened. So did the fists at his sides. "Any way I can find him and—"

"He's dead. And no, I don't think anyone can find the body."

He sighed and looked down at the floor.

"Sierra's been traumatized. Right now she's carrying around a black eye and a swollen lip that asshole gave her. She's really self-conscious about it. I hope you'll be subtle about it and don't mention it right off."

He shrugged and held out his hands. "I just want her back."

"Well, very shortly you'll have your wish."

His small green eyes filled. "I've wanted her back with me ever since, but Flo made it impossible."

"I've been there."

"You have a daughter?"

"Worse. Two ex-wives."

He nearly smiled. I could tell he was a good guy. I could also tell Sierra would be okay from now on. My job was nearly finished.

"Daddy?"

She'd come out of the ladies' room and stood beside the phones, staring at both of us. When her gaze locked in on him, it stayed there and her eyes immediately filled. I knew I could vanish and neither of them would even notice.

303

She ran to him. He wrapped his arms around her and the bear and held them tight, both of them sobbing.

While Sierra smothered his face with kisses, I turned and went back outside.

The train sat there, its passengers already boarding for Houston.

What could I do? Who did I know in Houston?

Should I just wait here and take the next train back to Orlando?

What awaited me there?

The cemetery offered no interest. Wandering around a graveyard with other dead guys didn't exactly do it for me. Wandering around Walmart would be even worse.

I didn't have many options waiting for me. Even so, I had to do something...

But at least I no longer had to worry about anything. Not train tickets, alimony, mortgage payments or even ex-wives. When you're dead, you can move around pretty much as you please. You might not have much to do, but you didn't have to worry about much, either.

"Jake?"

Her voice jarred me out of my thoughts.

Sierra approached me. Behind her, her father stood beside his pickup, watching us, his eyes glistening in the morning sun.

She was happy—happier than I'd ever seen her. She'd washed her face, but the tears kept coming. They'd made her eyes red, but the sparkle emanating from her overshadowed everything. I was happy for her. And also very sad, because I knew I'd never see her again.

"Thanks, Jake."

"No problem, kid. I just happened to be in the neighborhood anyway…"

"I wish I could hug you."

"Some things definitely suck when you're dead."

She nodded.

"You're going to be just fine."

She smiled. "Daddy said I already have a room at his place. He also owns a small tree farm, and—"

"Maybe he'll build you another tree house."

She sniffed. "I'm a little too old for that."

"Sorry. Forgot. Sometimes you seem younger than you actually are."

"You're fading."

I looked down. Sure enough, my energy was making me slightly transparent. "I guess I'd better be going before I end up freaking out a bunch of people."

"I'll never forget you."

"Me, too, kid."

"We're buds, remember?"

"Through and through."

"You never did say why you did all this for me."

"All what?"

She shrugged. "Helping me. Bringing me here."

I couldn't tell her why—it would take too long. Besides, she probably wouldn't understand that all this had happened because of the little guy forced off the playing field because he had no glove. That

305

same little guy who grew up in a good home with two parents who loved one another just as much as they loved their three sons. The same little guy who went to school and had friends and toys and a place to play. A child with a mom and a dad who stood behind him and protected him. Two people who loved one another and stayed together until they both died of heart ailments just months apart.

The same two people who'd made it possible for their youngest son to see what could happen when a child wasn't given the same chances he was.

"Let's just say I did it because of a little boy I once knew a long time ago," I said. "A little guy who was brought up just like you except for one thing that made all the difference."

"What was that?"

"His daddy never left home."

She didn't reply but I could tell by her sad expression that she understood what I'd just told her.

"Sierra!" her father yelled.

"Daddy's remarried," she said softly.

"He didn't tell me."

"He said Patty'll love me. And I'll love her."

"You're going to forget all about Florida. You may not know that yet, but you soon will."

"Not all of it," she said, her eyes filling again.

"You'd better do something about those blood-shot eyes," I said. "Someone'll think you're a lush."

She sniffed and wiped her eyes. "I love you, Jake."

"Me, too," I said. This time, the tug threatened to pull what was left of me apart.

306

"I'll never forget you. Never *ever*."

"'Bye, kid. Stay happy."

She remained staring at me long after I'd disappeared in the passing crowd.

***

I decided to return to Florida. Hell, I could go wherever I wanted. Why shouldn't I do exactly what instinct told me to do?

I might even go after the morons who'd given me a rough time when I was alive. In my case, it would be brain-dead idiots in tricked-out pickup trucks. Or arrogant megalomaniacs running software companies. Or well-dressed crooks manipulating the stock market. Or sleazy divorce lawyers. Or ball-busting ex-wives.

I might even hitch a ride back to Winter Park to see what Jenna was doing. If she'd brought in a medium. Or found someone from one of the TV stations to listen to her. I could make a brief appearance, just for laughs, and cause some serious chaos for her, the medium, or the TV people.

Or all three, if I felt like it.

If other spirits were having fun haunting Walmart and train stations, why couldn't I spend my time picking on whoever I damned well pleased?

I stepped through two elderly women picking up their luggage and a small group of middle-aged men and women arguing about which casino they wanted to try first.

The train was only a few feet away.

What should I do? Go back to Orlando? Harass Jenna? The TV people she might contact? I'd never

307

really liked TV people or reporters in general. They all seemed more concerned about advancing their own careers than reporting the truth.

A slender white-haired man in baggy shorts and a sloppy Hawaiian shirt stood in front of the porter, grinning at me. He had a thick handlebar mustache. His hair was combed straight back and reached well below his stooped shoulders. His light-blue eyes twinkled in the sunlight.

Despite his bright grin and sparkling eyes, he was obviously dead.

I could tell where this one was headed. A dead tourist haunting porters. Or maybe train stations in general.

"Let me guess," I said. "You died trying to cross the tracks at the wrong time and now you want to spend eternity tormenting train people."

He pointed directly past me. "I may be wrong, but it looks to me like someone else could use a helping hand."

About fifty feet behind me, a small boy about ten years old shuffled away from the parking lot, head down, shoulders slumped. He wore a green baseball cap, a loose-fitting red jersey, faded jeans and tennis shoes. No one noticed him as he headed for the main street.

"He does look sorry, doesn't he?" I said, mostly to myself.

No answer.

I turned back around.

The dead guy had already vanished.

Strange...

Who *was* that old man?

And why did he tell *me* about the boy when there were probably plenty of other dead people wandering about? How did he know that I'd even give a damn about the boy in the first place?

Was I wearing some sort of sign?

Curious, I glanced up at the sky.

Nothing but clouds and sun.

What did I expect? Harp music? An instruction manual dropping quietly to the ground?

The boy ambled away. I wondered where he'd come from. Where his home was. If he even had a home...

If he was running away.

Whatever the answer, he certainly pitiful.

Oh well. So much for going back to Orlando. Let Jenna and her TV news team do whatever turned them on. I'd accomplish much more right here.

As I followed the boy, I couldn't help thinking once again about the lonely little girl walking along the road just a few days ago, beaten and scared and desperate. All by herself in a big scary world, hoping that someone would drop by and chase away the monsters. And hear her cries for help.

Totally unaware that someone would actually hear those cries.

THE END

ALSO BY DAVID BERARDELLI

THE APPRENTICE
THE WAGON DRIVER
DEMON CHASER
DEMON CHASER II
ESCAPE CLAUSE
FATAL INNOCENCE
THE FUNNY DETECTIVE
JUST A SIMPLE ERRAND
COLORS
WORKING FOR A MOB BOSS
AND DARKNESS FELL
AFTER DARKNESS FELL
DEMON CHASER III
IN ANOTHER REALM
BEYOND RECOGNITION
THE NIGHTMARE COLLECTOR
HIDDEN
DEMON CHASER IV
DEMON CHASER V
LOOKING FOR A DEAD GUY
ENLIGHTENMENT
REDEMPTION
BEYOND GUILT
A RIPPLE IN TIME
YESTERDAY'S JOURNEY